The
FIRST LOVE

Books by Beverly Lewis

The First Love • *The Road Home*
The Proving • *The Ebb Tide*
The Wish • *The Atonement*
The Photograph • *The Love Letters*
The River

HOME TO HICKORY HOLLOW

The Fiddler • *The Bridesmaid*
The Guardian • *The Secret Keeper*
The Last Bride

THE ROSE TRILOGY

The Thorn • *The Judgment*
The Mercy

ABRAM'S DAUGHTERS

The Covenant • *The Betrayal*
The Sacrifice • *The Prodigal*
The Revelation

THE HERITAGE
OF LANCASTER COUNTY

The Shunning • *The Confession*
The Reckoning

ANNIE'S PEOPLE

The Preacher's Daughter
The Englisher • *The Brethren*

THE COURTSHIP
OF NELLIE FISHER

The Parting • *The Forbidden*
The Longing

SEASONS OF GRACE

The Secret • *The Missing*
The Telling

The Postcard • *The Crossroad*

The Redemption of Sarah Cain
Sanctuary (with David Lewis)
Child of Mine (with David Lewis)
The Sunroom • *October Song*
*Beverly Lewis Amish Romance
Collection*

Amish Prayers
*The Beverly Lewis Amish Heritage
Cookbook*
*The Beverly Lewis Amish Coloring
Book*

www.beverlylewis.com

The FIRST LOVE

BEVERLY LEWIS

BETHANYHOUSE

a division of Baker Publishing Group
Minneapolis, Minnesota

© 2018 by Beverly M. Lewis, Inc.

Published by Bethany House Publishers
11400 Hampshire Avenue South
Bloomington, Minnesota 55438
www.bethanyhouse.com

Bethany House Publishers is a division of
Baker Publishing Group, Grand Rapids, Michigan

Printed in the United States of America

Library of Congress Cataloging-in-Publication Data
Names: Lewis, Beverly, author.
Title: The first love / Beverly Lewis.
Description: Minneapolis, Minnesota : Bethany House Publishers, a division of
    Baker Publishing Group, [2018]
Identifiers: LCCN 2018020577 | ISBN 9780764219689 (trade paper) | ISBN
    9780764219948 (cloth) | ISBN 9780764219955 (large print) | ISBN
    9781493416011 (e-book)
Subjects: LCSH: Amish—Fiction. | GSAFD: Christian fiction. | LCGFT:
    Religious fiction. | Domestic fiction.
Classification: LCC PS3562.E9383 F57 2018 | DDC 813/.6—dc23
LC record available at https://lccn.loc.gov/2018020577

Scripture quotations are from the King James Version of the Bible.

This story is a work of fiction. Names, characters, incidents, and dialogues are products of the author's imagination and are not to be construed as real. Any resemblance to any person, living or dead, is purely coincidental.

Cover design by Dan Thornberg, Design Source Creative Services
Art direction by Paul Higdon

18 19 20 21 22 23 24   7 6 5 4 3 2 1

To
John and Cynthia Bachman,
my delightfully
encouraging cousins

A sheltered life can be a daring life as well. For all serious daring starts from within.

—Eudora Welty

Prologue

Summer 1998

Sometime in the wee hours, I was awakened by laughter against a background of trotting horses and clattering carriages—certainly Amish courting couples. The air was so still that the merriment seemed to waft in through the open upstairs window . . . straight into my foggy head.

Slowly, I raised myself in bed, and in my drowsiness, the room seemed to turn. I listened carefully, and except for the squeak of the bedsprings and a lone cricket outside, all was quiet now.

Just a dream, I thought. Yet it seemed so real.

I lay awake for a while, pondering the meaning as my thoughts sailed back to my own courting-age years, when life should have been filled with zest . . . and hope. Instead, I had been consumed with disappointment, grieving the loss of one I'd held so dear, and secretly fond of a young man who deserved someone who was whole.

The strength of my emotions caught me by surprise, and

the rush of feelings was so unsettling, it was a long time before I could calm down enough to sleep.

My mind was still fixed on the past when the morning sunlight prodded me from the bed. Honestly, I couldn't say just what had gotten into me. Could it be that my coming birthday had prompted a dream . . . and the memories?

It wasn't that I was dreading this birthday, but it was nevertheless a milestone, one that firmly clinched my status as a senior citizen. Growing older wasn't for cowards. Yet without God's grace and goodness, where would any of us be?

I brushed aside thoughts of my frail and agonizing youth and sat down at the kitchen table near an open window. There, in the golden light of early summer, with a chorus of mockingbirds sounding like angelic flutes, I pushed the latch on my well-worn recipe box and thumbed through the handwritten recipes passed down by dearest *Mamm* so long ago.

Which favorite shall I cook today?

Birthdays were a gift from God above, my mother used to say, taking care to point out to my younger siblings and me the importance of gratitude in all things. *"Gratitude for sickness?"* I had once whispered to her when the others left to do barn chores and *Dat* headed off to work at the nearby gristmill. Mamm had looked at me so sweetly, my heart nearly broke in two.

"Ach, Maggie-bird," she said as she opened her arms, and I limped into her embrace, letting her hold me while I cried.

"Will I ever be well again?" I whimpered.

Beginning when I was eleven, I struggled with what one doctor had called severe growing pains. In my teens, another doctor diagnosed the pain as something far worse—juvenile rheumatoid arthritis. Whatever the cause, I wanted the pain to stop. I wanted to walk without a cane. I wanted to scrub floors and weed gardens, and I wanted to be the kind of bride any Amishman would have been pleased to marry.

Dat often talked about God's sovereignty, insisting that we not question His will. I tried to pay attention, I truly did. And although his words were intended for our entire family, my father emphasized this so frequently, I sensed it was particularly meant for me.

Being the eldest, I wished I might contribute more to my family . . . and to the community of the People. It was one of the deepest longings of my heart.

Presently, my eyes fell on a recipe for my favorite childhood meal, Amish meatloaf, made with cracker crumbs, onions, and catsup. It was one Mamm had first concocted back before I was born. *Dear Mamm* . . . I missed her clear to this day.

Sighing, I glanced up at the wooden wall plaque I'd helped make in the midst of the most trying time of my young life. A summer of questioning, to be sure.

I stared at the words my father had etched into the wood, words taken from First Timothy, chapter six, verse six: *But godliness with contentment is great gain.*

A devout and compassionate man, Dat had been mighty concerned over my seeking nature and how it might alter my plan to be baptized into the Amish church.

Jah, that was undeniably a difficult time, one that opened my eyes in countless ways. And my heart, most of all. It was a season of sorrow and searching, of questions and answers.

It was the summer of my first love.

CHAPTER

1

The morning was warm and oppressive that seventh day of June. Occasional breezes rippled over Joseph Esh's field and up the gentle rise through a narrow swath of woodland to the sprawling house, which stood like a beacon over the farm on Olde Mill Road in Lancaster County, Pennsylvania.

In the past decade, a *Dawdi Haus* had been built onto the home's east side, and in that smaller residence lived Joseph's widowed aunt Nellie. Beyond the main house, below the rise, stood a modest white barn, as well as a woodshed and a rather run-down six-stall stable. Across the road and up a ways stood the gristmill where Joseph had worked all of his adult life.

His daughters, seventeen-year-old Maggie and her sister Grace, sixteen, sat on the wraparound porch, both hulling strawberries. Right after breakfast, Grace had gone to pick the day's ripe yield, and since then, she and Maggie had been working together there in the sunshine. But as was often the case, Maggie's fingers were beginning to feel cramped, and they already ached terribly.

Peering at Maggie just now, Grace asked, "Need a little break?" Grace's light brown hair was pulled back into a tight bun pinned low at the back of her slender neck, a dark blue bandanna tied beneath her chin.

"Maybe so." Maggie felt not just achy but weary. And to think the day was only getting started.

"I'll help ya into the house." Grace offered a smile. "*Kumme.*" Ever kind and understanding, Grace's usual caring nature had become nearly motherly the past year since Mamm had suffered heart failure.

"No need waitin' till your hands are numb, *Schweschder.*" Grace reached to remove the stainless-steel bowl from Maggie's lap. "I daresay you'd work your fingers to the bone if I didn't speak up . . . sufferin' in silence."

Maggie realized that her sister was only trying to remind her to go easy when the pain became too great. It had been so hard to bear after Mamm's funeral, and things had only worsened when Dat had decided to marry a young woman just seven short months later.

"*Jah,* I'd best be stoppin' for a while." Maggie rose slowly. She struggled to live with the near-constant discomfort, despite the aspirin she sometimes took when it felt nearly intolerable.

"It'd make *gut* sense for Rachel to offer to finish up for ya, if you ask me." Grace glanced toward the window. Then, offering a hand to Maggie, she added in a softer voice, "Ain't like she's busy with any little ones."

Maggie almost said it was a good thing their siblings were all old enough to look after themselves, at least for the most part. "Well, she's keepin' the house tidy and making the noon meal," she said, going around to the side door with Grace.

"That's her responsibility, *jah?*" Grace was grinning now.

"Not just hers," Maggie said, gently correcting her sister. It wasn't right to put all of that on their stepmother. Even when Mamm was alive, they had always worked together—cooking, cleaning, canning, sewing, and mending. They made at least two quilts every winter, too. *Mamm had Grace and me sit on a bench near her to practice piecing together quilt squares,* she recalled.

But Rachel was part of their family now, having caught their widower father's eye. There wasn't anything that Maggie or Grace could have said or done to change Dat's mind— remarriage was expected of an Amishman with children, after all. And their father liked to say that Rachel was "a peach." The thing that baffled Maggie was that Rachel had still been single at the age of thirty-two. *Why was she passed over for so long, pretty as she is?*

Grace had voiced this question a few weeks after their father and Rachel's wedding, when the two sisters were alone for a walk. And Grace had admitted wanting to ask Rachel this very thing, but Maggie had intervened, insisting it was not at all proper. Who knew what had kept an attractive woman like Rachel Glick from marriage till now?

Maggie followed Grace into the kitchen, with its tan-and-white linoleum and green shades rolled up high at the window tops. "We did fairly well this mornin'," Grace announced to Rachel as they entered, not saying they'd quit working because of Maggie's pain.

Something delicious was baking in the black cookstove, and the aroma invited Maggie's attention. For a moment, she felt overcome by the sight of Rachel at the counter, a reminder that someone else had taken over their Mamm's kitchen, along with all the cooking utensils and pots and pans and nearly everything else in the house. Maggie was conscious of a sudden lump in her throat. It was hard to ignore the memory of spending so much time alongside her mother here in this room. How she missed Mamm's cooking know-how and sympathetic ways! *Mamm understood me like no other,* Maggie thought, missing her terribly for that reason alone.

Rachel, dressed in a brown choring dress and long black apron, turned from opening a quart jar of chow chow and glanced at the two of them. "Yous worked a full hour on the berries," she said. *"Des gut, jah?"*

Maggie slumped onto the wooden bench at the table. *Just an hour?*

Rachel's frown came quickly, and she walked over to touch Maggie's shoulder. "Too much sun, maybe?" She looked out toward the porch where they'd sat earlier.

"Nee, not that," Grace was quick to say, barely concealing her annoyance. "Sun has nothin' to do with it." Grace looked at Maggie and tilted her head, a tender expression on her face.

Maggie's eyes met Grace's. *Be kind.*

Grace raised her eyebrows and nodded.

"Ach, you seemed all right yesterday, Maggie." Rachel stepped back and looked a bit flustered. "'Least for a while, weren't ya?" she added, blinking her bright blue eyes.

Maggie didn't remind Rachel that she never knew how she'd feel each morning when her bare feet touched the floor. "Yesterday was a better day" was all she felt like saying.

"I see," Rachel said, returning to the counter and dumping the jar of chow chow into a large bowl.

She's put out with me. Maggie felt worse.

"Maggie runs a temperature when her pain's real bad," Grace spoke up, still wearing the concerned expression Maggie had come to notice so frequently these days.

Wishing to change the subject, Maggie leaned against the table covered with Mamm's faded red-and-white-checked oilcloth. "I need to rest here a while longer."

Meanwhile, Grace hurried to the sink and washed her hands, then offered to help Rachel set the table. Maggie realized anew that if Rachel had grown up around here, she surely would have understood Maggie's difficulties. She would have known, too, how close and caring Mamm had been to all of her children through the years, and to Maggie especially. But Rachel had moved here from Myerstown in Lebanon County and, after being courted by Dat for just two short months, had permanently joined their family five months ago.

Pondering this for what must have been the hundredth time, Maggie wondered, *How could Dat marry someone who was practically a stranger . . . and so soon after Mamm's passing?* Maggie hadn't forgotten how her fourteen-year-old brother, Leroy, had first reacted to the surprising news. Dat had talked with all of them one evening several weeks before the planned private wedding, sitting around this very table after dessert. Twelve-year-old Andy and ten-year-old Stephen had seemed to take it more in their stride than Leroy, who had shaken his head in anger when Maggie looked his way.

Leroy's still mad about it, she thought.

———

Rachel felt rushed to get the noon meal on the table and asked Grace to go and sound the dinner bell. Within minutes, Joseph, her tall, fair-haired husband, came across the lawn

toward the hand pump; he always came home from the mill
for dinner. Andy and Stephen poked playfully at each other,
then waved to her as they quickly followed behind their father
and Leroy, who kept his gaze down.

Through the window, Rachel watched them take turns
washing their hands, talking in *Deitsch* while Joseph glanced
toward the house. Seeing her there, he grinned, and her stomach fluttered. *How'd I end up so blessed?* She hoped Joseph
would enjoy the hearty pork pie she'd made with him in mind.
Leroy might just enjoy it, too, if he'll let himself. She was beginning to wonder if Joseph's eldest son would ever warm up to
her. Joseph, bless his heart, was concerned enough that he'd
mentioned the possibility of confronting him about the obvious standoff, but Rachel wanted none of that. *"Isn't it better if
he comes around on his own?"* she'd suggested gently.

Yet Joseph had been adamant that he would not have any
of his children rejecting his new bride, and she felt all the
more cherished for it, though a bit concerned that forcing
Leroy wasn't going to win him over. Even Maggie and Grace
were still hesitant around her, often holding her at arm's
length, though neither would likely admit it. At least they
were helpful. Even so, wanting to be compliant and not make
waves, Rachel would let Joseph have the last word when it
came to his children. Thus far, he hadn't taken the step of
confronting Leroy, but she couldn't help noticing that her
husband appeared irritated when Leroy failed to respectfully
address her.

Once Joseph and all six children were seated at the table,
Joseph folded his hands, bowed his head, and asked the silent
blessing. Rachel, still getting used to having a husband and
a ready-made family, thanked the Lord God for her many

blessings, including the food on the table. She also offered her gratitude for the opportunity to be loved by such a thoughtful man as Joseph.

After a few moments, her husband cleared his throat and lifted his head, glancing at Rachel as she reached for his plate and dished up a generous portion of the baked dish of ground pork and sweet potatoes.

"Smells *wunnerbaar-gut*," he said with a wink.

Rachel smiled, her heart full to overflowing despite her concern over Leroy. From the very start of their marriage, Joseph had complimented her on her good cooking. As for the children, the youngest, eight-year-old Miriam, was the most expressive about her appreciation for Rachel's carefully planned meals. Cheerful Miriam would also ask to help bake bread—and cookies. The older girls, however, were not nearly as talkative, and there were times when Rachel caught Grace or Maggie studying her . . . nearly scrutinizing. Really, though, should it surprise her if any of the children were comparing her to Joseph's deceased wife, beloved Sadie Ann?

I mustn't expect too much, she thought, noticing Maggie struggling to get her slice of pie onto her plate. "You all right?" she asked.

Maggie blushed and nodded quickly. "*Denki.*"

Sighing, Rachel kicked herself for trying too hard, but it was difficult to know just how to respond to ailing Maggie. *Poor girl.*

Rachel served herself last, picked up her fork, and took a bite. *Delicious,* she thought, pleased that she'd added just the right amount of fresh milk and cinnamon sugar to the baked dish. She was still learning to double the recipes she'd made for herself and her grandparents back when she lived with them in their *Dawdi Haus* in Myerstown. Cooking for three was quite different than cooking for eight, she had swiftly come to realize.

"I saw Cousin Tom Witmer's eldest, Luke, at the mill early this mornin'," Joseph said just then. "He had a big talk on, let me tell ya."

"What's Luke up to?" Leroy asked, his oily blond bangs stuck to his forehead.

Joseph finished chewing before replying. "Well, he's been helpin' wire floodlights at the big tent in town."

"The revival tent?" Leroy asked, his hazel eyes suddenly wide.

Reaching for his water glass, Joseph nodded. "It's the oddest thing, really."

"Luke helpin' out . . . or the tent comin' to Lancaster?" Leroy asked.

"Both, I s'pose." Joseph looked at Rachel and grimaced. "Luke said he's also on the set-up crew for the public-address system."

"That's real neat," Leroy said, sounding a little too enthusiastic. "He must've learned all that at his Mennonite college."

Joseph gave his son an appraising look. "Now, son, remember . . . education that counts in the eyes of the Lord God is all we Amish desire. College ain't for you."

Leroy dipped his head immediately and resumed eating, not making eye contact with Rachel during the meal even when she passed him the apple butter. Once, however, Rachel noticed him looking Maggie's way. He seemed to be comforted by her, even though Rachel knew it was Grace who had taken on the role of surrogate mother after Sadie Ann died.

The talk of the tent meetings ceased. According to one of the *Englischers* at market last week, the meetings were to last

18

for six straight weeks, wrapping up near the end of July. The young woman in cuffed blue jeans, bobby socks, and dark brown loafers had been rather bubbly about the news, saying the local paper had interviewed the evangelist, who declared he believed God had called him to bring a "strong gospel message" and that he was "hoping to convert many sinners."

Rachel had wondered about it at the time, but she'd given it no further thought till now. And by the tone in Joseph's voice—and the look on Leroy's face—she knew not to show a speck of curiosity about it.

CHAPTER

2

Maggie was sitting at the kitchen table six days later, helping Grace with the Wednesday mending. Mamm's day clock on the shelf near the sink struck twice, and Maggie remembered the day Dat brought it home—a replacement for the old one that had continued to lose time. She shook off the memory, just as she'd tried to do with so many since Rachel married Dat.

"Look, we've got company," Grace said, glancing out the window.

"Who?" Maggie turned to see Tom Witmer's two-toned green sedan coming up the lane. "*Wunnerbaar!* I hope Lila came along."

Grace leaned closer to the window, squinting now, her sewing needle poised. "*Jah,* looks like Tom brought the youngest boys, and there's Lila, too."

I've missed her, Maggie thought, pleased as pudding to have a visit from her close-in-age cousin. Lila Witmer was her favorite of their Mennonite relatives.

Soon, brown-eyed Lila was calling through the side screen door, and Maggie and Grace waved her inside as her father and brothers headed toward the barn.

Lila, wearing a dark blue dress with a tiny yellow-and-white floral pattern, its hem falling to midcalf, burst into a smile as she greeted them. "I thought I'd ride along and come see yous. "

Grace nodded, and Maggie invited her to sit with them. "Would ya like something cold to drink, maybe?"

"Sounds real *gut*," Lila said, her face pink and her usually tidy hair bun windblown from the warm car ride.

Maggie placed on the table the shirt she had been mending and poked her needle into the collar for safekeeping. Then, pushing her weight onto her arms and hands, she managed to get up from her chair.

"Aw, you're hurtin' real bad," Lila observed, insisting that she get something from the fridge and spare her the bother.

"*Nee* . . . I need to move around some." Maggie limped to the counter and stood there for a brief moment. "*Ach*, I left my cane," she whispered and then wished she hadn't said it, because Lila hurried to the table to retrieve it. *I'm not an invalid yet*, Maggie thought, increasingly frustrated with her condition as each week passed. High humidity like today's made her limbs ache more than usual. "*Denki*, Lila," she said, accepting the cane.

Grace stood. "How about I get all of us something to sip on, to cool us off."

Maggie relented, a little embarrassed as she shuffled back to her chair. Lila took a seat beside her and fanned herself with a hankie, eyes on Maggie. She didn't say anything, but from her expression, Maggie suspected her cousin had noticed her declining health. *I'm weaker every time she visits*, Maggie thought.

Hoping to get Lila's mind off whatever it was she was thinking, Maggie said, "Glad to see ya again."

"It's been some time, *jah?*" Lila glanced about the kitchen and craned her neck toward the next room. "Is your *Schtiefmudder* around?"

Grace was the one to reply as she carried a large wooden tray with glasses filled with ice-cold lemonade. She set the tray down near the oval bowl of bananas and apples at the center of the table. "Rachel's out hoeing the vegetable garden with Miriam." Grace bobbed her head in that direction. "It's a real busy time round here . . . like most Junes."

"I s'pose you're getting used to things little by little?" Lila pressed, her fingers tapping the table. She reached for her lemonade glass.

"We are, but it'll take some time," Grace said, giving Maggie a look.

No one expected Dat to remarry so soon, Maggie thought suddenly.

Lila sighed. "Must still seem strange to yous." Then she went on to say how hard it must be, too, for Rachel to step into their Mamm's shoes.

"It'll all work out," Grace said as she finally sat down across from them. "'Least Dat's happy again."

Maggie nodded. "Seems so."

Maggie had not forgotten how very sad their father had been after Mamm's death. He rarely spoke for the weeks immediately following, but she had overheard him quietly telling his aunt Nellie next door that he felt disoriented without his

Sadie Ann around. *"How can everything just keep goin' on as if nothin's different?"* he'd said, his voice breaking.

Maggie had held her breath, hearing her father in such distress. And she had prayed daily for him, as well as for all of them.

Just then, petite Miriam burst in the back door, her chubby cheeks bright red and perspiration dripping from her chin. Miriam dashed to the sink and turned on the faucet, then splashed cold water onto her face and the golden-blond hair tightly bound in a knot at the back of her head. *Silkiest hair ever,* thought Maggie.

"Somebody else is overheated, too," Lila said, observing the youngest Esh with a grin.

"Hullo, Cousin Lila," Miriam said, drying her face with a blue hand towel. *"Wie geht's?"*

"Oh, we're makin' hay at our house. Well, my older brothers are," Lila said, going on to tell about the oodles of berries she'd sold at her father's roadside stand, too. "They're comin' on real fast now. Every single day we're out pickin' those—and peas."

Miriam looked fondly at Lila and wandered over to the table, her cheeks still the color of berries. "Mamm used to put up more jam for us to eat than to sell."

"Well, there's more of yous to feed than at our house, for sure." Lila smiled at Grace. "You're the fastest berry picker, *jah?*"

"Not just me," Grace said. "Some days it's actually hard to keep up with Miriam in the berry patch."

Smiling at that, Miriam sat there for a while longer, then glanced at the day clock and began to fidget. "Wish I could stay longer, but Mamma Rachel's gonna wonder what's happened to me," she said. "Oh, and I almost forgot. She asked if you'd come help for a while, too, Gracie."

Mamma Rachel, thought Maggie, still jarred by Miriam's apparent ease in addressing Rachel that way.

"Why didn't ya say so?" Grace hopped out of her chair to hurry out the back door with Miriam, leaving Maggie there with Lila.

"Honestly, I'm kinda glad it's just us now," Lila said, taking a sip of her lemonade before setting it down. Suddenly, Lila's eyes sparkled, and she clapped her hands.

Maggie stifled a laugh. This was the cousin she knew and loved. And there was always something up her sleeve. "What's on your mind?" Maggie asked.

"Well, I went with my family to the first revival meeting last evening, and, my goodness, I've never seen such a huge tent! It's like a Billy Graham crusade, Mamma says!" Lila lifted her hands to demonstrate the size. "And I've never heard such singing, either. Just beautiful, like we'd all died and gone to heaven!" In that moment, her eyebrows rose high, and she looked absolutely horrified. She sputtered, "*Ach,* I didn't mean to say . . ."

Maggie felt sorry for her. "'Tis all right. You didn't mean anything by it. Just that the singin' was joyful, ain't so?"

"No better word to describe it, truly," Lila said, her face all the pinker now with obvious embarrassment. "But what I really wanted to tell ya is that I'd love for you to go, Maggie." She had lowered her voice to nearly a whisper.

Why me? Maggie felt uncomfortable. It was one thing for Dat's cousins to belong to a completely different Anabaptist group, but to hear Lila suggest that Maggie come along to attend revival services like this . . . well, Maggie didn't know what to say. She glanced out the window and saw Cousin Tom's car parked there, big and bold as you please. And she remembered Dat's reaction to Leroy's enthusiasm for the revival tent coming to town, too, and assumed that their father would be none too happy to hear that any of his children had been in attendance.

"We could pick ya up, Maggie . . . maybe even get you a wheelchair if that'd help." Lila looked at her so pleadingly, Maggie felt awful about turning her down.

"I have work to do here," she replied. "And it takes me so long, there's no time for much else."

"But the meetings are at night," Lila argued. "You wouldn't be missin' out on anything at home. Won't ya consider goin'?"

Once more Maggie was struck by Lila's excitement. She'd never seen her like this before, let alone about a church service. Maggie's curiosity was sparked.

All the same, she was about to say she could not think of going, when Lila softly touched the back of her hand. "With everything you've been through, cousin, I think you'd find some comfort in it. Might be exactly what you need."

Overcome by Lila's gentle understanding, Maggie blinked back tears.

"Aw . . . I didn't mean to make ya cry." Lila moved closer.

The truth was, sometimes Maggie hurt so much it was hard to think about anything but the fiery pain. At night, while lying in bed, she often resisted the urge to sleep curled up on her side, for fear her tensed muscles might throb all the more.

"I'm sorry your life's so hard right now," Lila said, the corners of her eyes glinting as she took Maggie's hand. "Just come with me one time, cousin."

Feeling torn between her own hesitation and Lila's seeming passion, Maggie turned to look toward the gristmill up the road, though she couldn't see the building from this distance.

"Remember, I'm taking baptismal classes . . . started at the end of May. . . . I'll have to talk it over with Dat."

Lila slumped down a bit on her elbows on the table, as if she knew that would put the nix on the whole thing.

"But don't hold out hope for this week, even if he gives me the okay." Maggie needed time to think this through, never having been impulsive nor drawn toward church-related events outside the Amish community. She wasn't about to change that now.

Maggie switched the subject and eventually got around to sharing that Grace had been after her to attend the upcoming Sunday Singing at the deacon's house, not far from there. "She thinks someone might just ask me to go riding again," Maggie said, wondering what Lila would say to that.

"And just who might that someone be?"

Maggie felt her face redden.

"Is it that good-lookin' Jimmy Beiler?"

Maggie nodded, her heart lifting at the thought of the brown-haired boy she'd secretly liked since she was sixteen and going to the youth activities. "He's real nice, for certain, but I can't help but wonder."

"What? If he's sweet on ya?"

Bowing her head, Maggie felt sure she knew the real truth behind Jimmy's motives, kind as he seemed.

Lila peered at her. "You clammin' up on me?"

Maggie sighed. "Jimmy only asked me that one time 'cause he felt sorry for me."

"How do ya know?"

"Isn't it obvious?" Maggie shrugged. "I was all alone, and he was nice enough to notice."

"Aw . . . I think you should go with him if he ever seeks you out again."

"I doubt he will," Maggie said. "A fella doesn't like to be rejected twice. Besides, I don't want his sympathy, Lila. I couldn't bear it."

With a frown, Maggie slowly rose from the table and went to stand at the back door. Looking out, she felt misunderstood and alone, in spite of Lila's presence.

CHAPTER 3

That night, while lying in bed, Maggie recalled how her mother had often come into her former room upstairs and sat on the edge of the bed, quietly singing "Jesus Loves Me" before reciting the Lord's Prayer. These days, because the stairs were often too difficult for her to manage, Maggie slept in the downstairs spare room around the corner from the large front room, where they hosted Preaching service once a year.

Maggie let her thoughts return to the days before she felt so poorly. Days when she'd run across the road and up to the old stone gristmill, standing just outside the dark brown door where her father appeared at four-thirty sharp every weekday afternoon. His eyes always brightened when he spotted her there, and even though she rarely missed, he always welcomed her affectionately with a surprised and happy look on his face. Sometimes they would skip home for fun, and other times Dat would whistle a made-up tune.

Maggie rolled over gingerly and stared into the darkness, a

tear coursing down her cheek. Remembrances of those light-hearted, healthy days continued to plague her. Was it possible Cousin Lila was right? Would attending a revival service bring some type of comfort?

Slowly, Maggie pressed her hand beneath the feather pillow and drew a long breath. She'd taken two aspirin with milk and an oatmeal cookie before coming to bed, hoping for a better night of sleep than the past few. And, while offering her silent prayers, she added a new request to the Lord God. *If it be Thy will, may Dat permit me to attend the tent meeting with Cousin Lila. I pray this in the name of Thy Son, Jesus.*

She assumed it wouldn't be long before she had her answer, and she pondered now how best to present her request to Dat tomorrow. She had little doubt how he'd respond. *Whatever befalls us is God's will,* she thought as she stared at the moonlight peeping beneath the dark green window shade.

Denki, Leroy," said Rachel the next morning, still believing that if she was consistently courteous, Joseph's son might come to realize how much she wanted him to accept her as family. "This is very helpful . . . and I appreciate it."

"No trouble to gather a few eggs," Leroy said. "It's normally Miriam's chore." Then he quickly made his way out the back door with the empty wire egg basket to store it in the coop. Rachel remained at the kitchen window to watch him as he crossed the expanse of newly mown lawn. She wished she could get through to him somehow. How long would it take?

"He doesn't dislike me, I don't think." Reluctantly, she moved from the window to put the fresh eggs in the refrigerator. *Am I misreading him?* she wondered. She'd had no previous experience living with a teenage boy, having grown up in Myerstown with four sisters, all of whom were now married with children of their own.

She went to the broom closet, still pondering her surprising place here in Joseph Esh's family. And while sweeping the kitchen floor, she thought of a number of recipes that might appeal to Leroy in particular. Either fried chicken or hearty beef patties and thick gravy would be ideal for the noon meal today. Oh, it was such a challenge to keep this family well fed and the house as neat as a pin, day in and day out!

She quickened her pace, planning to pick cherries that afternoon at a nearby orchard with Grace and Miriam and several neighbors, thankful for these few moments to herself to think how best to fit in here. *Dear Lord, help me do just that!*

It was a relief for Maggie to drift out of the heat and attend the Sunday night Singing at the home of Deacon Mast, a distant cousin to Mamm. Getting out of the buggy, she and Grace waved happily to Leroy, grateful to be dropped off. As Maggie and Grace entered through the back door, the deacon's wife greeted them and explained that since it was so warm and muggy, the youth would be gathering in the basement, where it was cooler.

Downstairs, Maggie noticed the usual arrangement of long tables and benches—young women on one side and the young men on the opposite, so each side could look at the other while they sang. It was the time-honored way of pairing up.

Despite the heavy dew on the grass before Preaching service that morning, Maggie felt better than usual today, so much so that she'd left her cane at home. Whatever the reason her pain faded on some days, Maggie was thankful for this unexpected reprieve—one of the truest of blessings.

Almost immediately after she sat down with Grace, Maggie spotted blue-eyed Jimmy Beiler at the end of the table with several other young men in their early twenties, including two of Jimmy's cousins. Smiling, Jimmy nodded discreetly, as he'd done at every gathering since the baptismal candidates started their nine sessions of instruction that fell during the first forty minutes of Preaching service.

Maggie tried not to smile back too broadly, even though seeing him made her heart melt a little, as it did each time he greeted her politely. She remembered what Cousin Lila had said, and despite her own determination to avoid others' pity, Maggie couldn't help wondering how she might respond if Jimmy offered her a ride home yet again.

While waiting for the rest of the youth to arrive, Maggie quietly looked around to see if there were any new faces. She spotted one, a young man whose red hair peeked from beneath his straw hat. Glancing her way, he offered her a big smile in return.

"Goodness, who is he?" Maggie whispered without thinking.

"Who's *who*?" Grace asked, seemingly distracted by tonight's crowd, her eyes wide as she scanned the basement room.

Maggie ignored the question and straightened a little, raising her hand to wave at one of their cousins as he came down the stairs and joined the unfamiliar young man.

Grace frowned. "Are you ignoring me, sister?"

Maggie shrugged and turned a smile on her. Gracie could be as sweet as honey, yet at times she was a little too determined for answers. "Do you have your eye out for anyone special, Gracie?" she asked, changing the subject.

Grace raised an eyebrow at her. "I might, but whether he has his eye out for me is another matter."

Maggie shifted in her seat, thankful to be free of her cane this night. *Try to enjoy the evening,* she thought.

Rachel loved the sounds of Joseph's small farm, especially the cheery birdsong. She was sitting with her husband on the back porch, enjoying a fresh batch of homemade vanilla ice cream drizzled with rich chocolate syrup. As a relative newlywed, she valued these quiet moments alone with Joseph, few and far between though they were. Rachel felt she gained more knowledge of him when they were together like this. When the children were around, which was most of the time, she felt like a bride in need of a honeymoon, but she'd never shared this with him and never would, not wanting to seem to complain. *Is it natural to want Joseph all to myself sometimes?* she wondered.

"Maggie must be feelin' better tonight," Joseph said, his straw hat perched on the porch rail.

She agreed. "It seems so."

Joseph gave her an endearing smile. "I'm real thankful, since we just never know how she's gonna feel. I remember how she used to scamper and play like all healthy children—even climbed the tallest trees in this yard." He gestured toward the old oak trees. "She certainly didn't come into the world sickly." He went on to say that his aunt Nellie believed Maggie was inclined toward arthritis because of the prevalence of the disease in the family's previous generation.

Rachel spooned up another bite of ice cream, listening.

"Various relatives in the family suffer with it."

Rachel considered that. "Grace says Maggie got a diagnosis some time ago—ain't that right?" She didn't mention that Grace sometimes seemed to pamper Maggie, which seemed odd when Grace was younger by more than a year.

"Well, it took trips to several doctors—one an osteopathic physician. It was confusing to Sadie Ann and me that each doctor had a different opinion."

"Were tests done?" Rachel asked.

"Most definitely. The sedimentation rate—or sed rate—in her blood was elevated when Maggie suffered with severe pain." Joseph paused for a moment, then placed his empty bowl on the porch floor. "But since she was in her early teens, it was considered to be juvenile rheumatoid arthritis, something she might possibly outgrow. Of course, we were also told it could become worse."

Poor, dear girl . . .

"One doctor even said she could be crippled by her thirtieth birthday . . . suggested that a drier climate might be something to consider." Joseph shook his head and looked at Rachel. "'Tween you and me, it's a blessing that all the other children are so fit."

Not having heard any of this before, Rachel's curiosity rose, and she decided to seek out Nellie's opinions about Maggie's health . . . find out how it varied from day to day. *If it can vary, maybe it can go away for good,* she thought hopefully, wondering how she might help.

CHAPTER

4

During the evening table games, Maggie thought she felt Jimmy's eyes on her, but it would never do to look his way, not even a glance.

After an hour or so of games, Hannah Mast, the deacon's wife, suggested they sing the birthday song for all those celebrating a June birthday. They did, everyone looking at Maggie and another fellow born that month. The minute that song was finished, one of the more confident fellows led out in a thank-you song to the deacon and his wife for hosting this Singing, and all joined in.

As they sang, Maggie recalled the first time Jimmy Beiler had sought her out . . . before a rug-braiding frolic right here at the deacon's house, more than a year ago. Jimmy had driven his mother and two sisters over and dropped them off, while Maggie had ridden over in the pony cart, since the walk was too far for her. Lo and behold, Jimmy had abruptly halted his horse on the road just to strike up a conversation, his brown bangs ruffling in the breeze. Maggie remembered it as though it had happened last week, the recollection warm and ever so special. *"Was nice seein' ya at Singing last Sunday, Maggie,"* he'd said, sporting a contagious smile. *"Real nice."*

That grin still captured her attention every time she ran into him—at Saturday market, Sunday Singings, and especially before baptismal class. *Too often to simply chalk it up to chance. . . .* And he never failed to take a moment to say hello and visit for a bit.

What if he asks me riding tonight . . . for the second time? she wondered, having mixed feelings about what it might mean if he did. Secretly, she wished she could somehow know if he had been sincere in his initial invitation months ago. On the other hand, she feared the thought of his interest in her—what a burden it would be to him if they ended up together!

Truly, it was best for all if Grace might include her in the ride home with whoever invited her sister out this night, because Maggie did not want to end up alone.

The singing of hymns and gospel songs lasted an hour and a half, and then Deacon Mast and his wife served homemade root beer floats and cookies as the youth lingered for another hour or so of fellowship.

Maggie spent the time chatting with three of her girl cousins while Bishop Lantz's youngest grandson, Martin, led Grace over to one of the corners to talk. Maggie was also conscious of Jimmy's proximity, though for now he remained with other fellows his age, including the unfamiliar red-haired fellow, who had reappeared and was again sending glances Maggie's way— so frequently that Maggie felt certain even Jimmy had noticed.

Nee, she thought, wishing she could crawl into the woodwork.

A few minutes passed, and the tall redhead walked to her table. He was certainly from another church district, because his hair was cut slightly shorter, though still in the bowl cut her father and brothers wore.

Just then, Jimmy made his way over to visit with one of Maggie's second cousins, Deborah Esh, a year older than Maggie. Goodness, Maggie felt uneasy at seeing the two of them together; it took everything in her to focus solely on the smiling young man sitting down across from her. She needed to be polite.

I should've stayed home, she thought.

"Hullo," the redhead said as he folded his hands on the table. "Someone told me your name is Maggie."

She nodded; the basement was abuzz with conversation. "And what's yours?"

"Timothy Blank," he said, "from Leola."

"Near the big turkey farm there?" She paused for a moment, hoping someone else might catch his eye, but his attention only seemed to increase. Finally, she said, "My Dawdi Mast lives in Leola. Do ya know of a Reuben Mast?"

Elbows on the table, Timothy frowned and rubbed his chin. "Not sure. There are a number of them. Where's your Dawdi live?"

She strained to hear him. "I'm sorry . . . it's so noisy here."

Seemingly frustrated, Timothy motioned for them to leave the table and go to a quieter area to talk.

She hesitated. *Is this wise?*

Then, thinking of Jimmy and Deborah just across the room, she decided to give it a try. After all, today had been one of her better days.

Maggie rose slowly to join Timothy, stepping gingerly at

first, but on the way, she began to limp forward and almost stumbled. She stopped suddenly, fighting for balance, and he turned back, confusion etched on his face.

"*Ach,* sorry . . . I'm ever so *dabbich!*" She tripped over her tongue, too, trying to explain.

Timothy's look of disappointment, or shock, one of the two, made her cringe inside. "Do ya need help?"

She shook her head. "*Nee,* I can manage."

And with that, he nodded awkwardly and excused himself.

"What was I thinkin'?" she murmured, wishing she'd just stayed put at the table. *Where it's safer,* she thought, not blaming Timothy Blank for abandoning her, upsetting as his reaction was. *What young man would want a sickly sweetheart, after all?*

Cautiously, she made her way back to the table again. Preoccupied with what had just happened and the notion that Jimmy might be pursuing Cousin Deborah, Maggie forced herself to turn her attention to the girls there, who were talking about watching some chicks hatch yesterday, and how they'd enjoyed the glee in their younger siblings' eyes as the wee birds began to peck their way out of the shells. She remembered the first time she'd witnessed this remarkable happening. *Mamm held my hand as we watched in awe until the tired little chicks finally emerged from their broken shells,* she recalled, missing her mother all the more. *She was so whole and energetic then.*

When it was time to disband, Grace came over and mentioned that Martin Lantz had offered to drop Maggie off at home before he and Grace went riding for a while in his courting carriage. As they prepared to leave, Maggie purposely avoided looking toward Jimmy and Cousin Deborah, but she couldn't help hearing Jimmy's hearty chuckle as she headed outside with Martin and Grace. It made her heart pound with sorrow. *He's found someone better for him*, Maggie decided, guessing Jimmy had seen her earlier with Timothy.

I did the right thing, turning Jimmy down that time, she reminded herself, relieved and yet crushed all at once. *I would never be able to cope with the needs of a husband and children of my own.*

Two days later, Maggie was sitting in the kitchen, lightly sprinkling the clean clothes from yesterday's wash before rolling up each dampened garment for Grace to iron. An hour prior, Rachel had left with the family carriage to take some homemade ice cream to a neighbor.

Now that they were alone, Maggie wondered what Grace might say about her first date with good-looking Martin Lantz. Thus far, Grace had been mum about it, and Maggie was hesitant to probe.

They worked without saying a word until Maggie finally broke the silence. "I've decided not to go to Singings anymore," she said flatly.

"Wha-at?" Grace looked shocked. "You don't mean it."

"There's no reason to go . . . never was."

Grace frowned. "Are ya feelin' worse again?"

Maggie nodded. "And let's be honest: Why would any fella our age want to court me?"

"I'm sorry, Maggie-bird." Mamm's nickname for Maggie had slipped from Grace's lips. "*Ach*, I mean . . ." Grace was red-faced as she set down the iron.

"It's all right. It's nice to hear it again," Maggie said.

Grace walked to the sink and turned on the faucet. While the water ran, she took down a tumbler from the cupboard and filled it with water. She was obviously upset, and when she turned around to face Maggie, she said, "It's still so hard without Mamm."

Maggie nodded, but she couldn't talk about their mother right now without getting emotional, so she quickly changed the subject to exactly what she hadn't planned to voice. "I'm guessin' you had a nice time with Martin Lantz after Singing."

Grace's face flushed all the more, and now her eyes sparkled. "I didn't realize how much I would like him."

"Well, you can't really know a fella till ya spend time with him," Maggie replied. "Isn't that what Great-aunt Nellie always says?" she said of Dat's elderly aunt, who lived with her blue-gray cat in the attached *Dawdi Haus*. A short hallway connected the gregarious woman's dwelling to the front room of the main house, and sometimes the cat wandered over against Dat's wishes.

Grace continued to smile as she picked up the iron again and began to press Dat's white dress shirt.

She's already smitten. Maggie was glad for her sister, who'd only been attending Singings for a short time.

After a supper of fried chicken and mashed potatoes with rich, creamy gravy, Maggie followed Dat out toward the stable with her cane. He slowed his pace to accommodate her, and she was touched by his kindness as he talked about his workday at the gristmill.

The early evening sun beat on the old stable, its long wooden slats gray and tattered. *"Nearly a relic,"* Dat had described to his father-in-law last summer during a picnic, when they were discussing the possibility of tearing it down and rebuilding.

Although not trying to eavesdrop, Maggie had overheard them while sitting on a lawn chair not far from young Miriam, who was playing with paper dolls on an old blanket after they'd all eaten rhubarb pie and ice cream.

Inside the stable were stalls and feeding troughs, as well as an area used for storing harnesses and driving lines and gear. But because extra money was hard to come by, no such demolition had yet taken place.

Waiting for the right moment to say what was on her mind, Maggie took down one of the grooming brushes from the pegboard and made her way into the first stall. There, she talked softly to Buster, one of their road horses, as she shuffled to his side. She could hear her father getting the water buckets and heading out to the hand pump.

Gently, she began to brush the horse, still murmuring and enjoying Buster's company as she got up the nerve to ask her father about going to the tent revival meeting with Cousin Lila tomorrow night.

Rachel was so grateful that evening for Grace's earlier help with all the ironing. Grace had even hung everything up in the respective bedrooms during the space of time Rachel had gone with ice cream to visit Ruth Zook, who was suffering with a badly sprained ankle.

Ruth, my very own matchmaker, she thought of Joseph's longtime neighbor. Truth be known, Ruth had met Rachel's older sister Sarah on one of the occasions when Sarah had come to town to sell her homemade relish at market. There, Sarah and Ruth struck up a friendship, and one thing led to another. Soon they were concocting a plan for Ruth and her husband to invite Joseph for dinner on the same evening they invited Rachel. Sarah had set the whole thing in motion, even paid for the driver to bring Rachel to Lancaster County for the meal and take her home. The idea of a blind date, so to speak, had been a real challenge for Rachel, but she had trusted her sister's judgment from the start. After all, Sarah's own marriage was wonderful, and Rachel hadn't dated since her late teens.

Rachel smiled as she recalled meeting Joseph for the first time—and the flutter of nerves she'd endured prior to that day.

None of it would have been possible without Ruth, she thought fondly, hoping the ice cream she'd taken today had perked Ruth up.

Rachel had gone at the request of Hannah Mast, who'd called for a card shower for Ruth during a work frolic at the deacon's house last week. Soft-spoken Hannah had urged the womenfolk present to either go and visit Ruth or to send her a pretty card.

I wish there were more I could do for her, thought Rachel, knowing her own responsibilities kept her mighty busy.

Just then, Rachel spotted her husband out at the pump, filling buckets of water, the sun still relatively high in the sky. *How quickly he won me over!* She remembered how attentive Joseph had been at that blind date supper at the Zooks', sitting across the table from her—the way he asked questions that put her at ease. Things like *"What sort of flowers do ya plant in your garden back home?"* and *"Do ya have a favorite meal to cook?"* The latter had made her smile inwardly . . . it was obvious that Joseph was interested in having a cook of his own.

Watching him now, Rachel wanted to drop everything and help him, but Miriam came rushing down the stairs and into the kitchen, her blue bandanna slipping back, revealing her middle part. The darling girl wrapped her slender arms around her. "Can I help ya with the dishes, Mamma Rachel?"

It warmed Rachel's heart to hear Miriam already use *Mamma* so freely; the girl seemed the sincerest of the children in her affection. To think Rachel might never have had a family apart from marrying Joseph. "I'll wash, and you dry. How's that?" Rachel proposed.

A cheery smile appeared, and Miriam hurried across the kitchen to the apron drawer, where she pulled one out and promptly tied it around her tiny waist. Then she removed a fresh tea towel from the next drawer up. "Can we make bread tomorrow mornin'?" she asked, leaning against the counter, looking up at Rachel.

Rachel nodded and smiled as she finished heating water to add to the water she'd run in the sink.

"Mamm always said I talked a lot . . . sometimes got on her nerves, Dat would say."

"I'm sure your Mamm enjoyed hearin' what you had to say, just as I do."

"Well . . . I've never said *this* before," Miriam said matter-of-factly, her tea towel poised. "I'm real glad Dat married ya." Her little eyes blinked fast.

Rachel's heart was filled with tenderness for her stepdaughter, and she struggled to hold back her tears of joy. Mothering this one, and spending time with her, was truly a delight.

While her father lugged in one of the buckets and filled the water trough in Buster's stall, Maggie finally asked, "What would ya think if I went to the tent meeting tomorrow night?"

"You want to go to the revival?" Dat replied, his nose twitching a bit.

Maggie nodded, her throat turning dry.

Her father was still for what seemed like a long moment. Then, drawing a breath, he said, "What's your interest?"

"Cousin Lila was talking a lot 'bout it."

Dat frowned hard. "And she wants you to tag along, is that it?"

Maggie felt as if her words were locked up in her throat somewhere.

Removing his straw hat, Dat swatted at a fly. "I don't see how goin' to an outsiders' meeting is a *gut* idea, daughter."

She quietly considered that, feeling nervous as Dat studied her and surprised by how much she wanted to go. When she'd told Lila that she would ask Dat about going, she had fully expected him to refuse outright, which she was sure he was about to do. But oh, she longed to see why Lila had been so enthralled. "I'm not baptized just yet, Dat," she said quietly, wondering if that was the right thing to say.

"And that's another worry," he said with a tug on his auburn beard.

"No need to fret," she said. "I'm planning to join church come September. Honest, I am."

"Why go to the tent meeting, then?" Dat peered at her, his blue-gray eyes somber. "Curiosity?"

"*Jah*," she said. "Only that."

Her father cleared his throat. "Always remember that contentment with the life the Lord has given us is the godly path—not chasing the notions of the English," he said.

"Don't ya want me to go, Dat?"

He frowned again. "Just think long and hard 'bout what

I just said." With that, he turned to carry the empty water bucket out of Buster's stall.

Silently, Maggie accepted his final remark, very surprised he had not forbidden her to go to a religious gathering that was anything but Amish.

CHAPTER

5

Early before breakfast the next morning, Rachel let sweet little Miriam gather the dry ingredients for bread making. Meanwhile, Rachel dissolved the yeast and sugar in water warmed on the cookstove, then reached in the cupboard to take down their largest bowl.

When they'd added the flour to the yeast mixture and blended it thoroughly, they gradually mixed it until it was ready to knead. Once done, Rachel set the dough aside to rise while she turned her attention to cooking breakfast with Maggie and Grace's help—Maggie stirred the eggs and milk for scrambling as Grace pricked the sausage links with a fork before transferring them to the black skillet for frying. All the while, Grace hummed the melody to "What a Friend We Have in Jesus," a hymn Rachel assumed she'd sung at the recent Singing.

As Maggie was cooking the big batch of eggs, Rachel glanced over at her and noticed how flushed she looked. Was she running a fever again? Her beautiful face was ever so pained; she seemed to be worse off than she had been lately.

Then and there, Rachel decided that this was a good day to go over and visit with Joseph's aunt Nellie. The woman might have useful insight on how others in the family had dealt with this confounding disease. Maggie seemed to be almost well one day and then awful sickly for days on end. Had it been like that for other relatives, too? Rachel wished she could depend on Joseph's eldest daughter to help more consistently, but the erratic nature of Maggie's condition made that hard. And Rachel didn't want to cause friction between them by expecting too much from her.

She found it almost shocking that Joseph hadn't told Maggie that she couldn't go to the tent meeting, as he had shared with Rachel last night in the privacy of their bedroom. More of the People were beginning to talk about the meetings, including Ruth Zook yesterday morning. Folk from all walks of life were literally packing the tent, many going to the altar at the end of each service to proclaim their faith. Rachel had to admit that she shared Maggie's apparent interest in attending a service. Of course, she wouldn't think of asking to go, as well, but she would like to hear Maggie's account of it, if she actually ended up going tonight. *Frail as she seems today.*

"Knock, knock," Rachel said as she tapped on the screen door of Nellie's *Dawdi Haus* instead of going through the shared interior hallway.

She waited, but there was no answer.

Rachel wondered if Nellie was out walking, perhaps, as she sometimes did after an early breakfast.

She rapped again, and it dawned on her that Nellie might be sitting on the front porch. So she made her way around the side of the house and, coming upon her, called, "Hullo, a real perty mornin', ain't?"

Nellie grinned. "Well now, I *thought* I heard someone at the other door." Nellie's cheeks were rosy as she motioned for Rachel to join her in the spare rocking chair. "A body can see so much goin' on from right here," Nellie said, waving toward the road. "Why, I just saw Leroy take the pony cart and go somewhere mighty fast."

"He's headed down to Witmers'," Rachel explained, "to let them know to pick up Maggie this evening."

"Where are they takin' her?"

"To the tent meetin' so many are talking 'bout," Rachel replied.

"Ah, that's somethin'." Nellie didn't frown, but she looked surprised.

Rachel changed the subject. "It's gonna be warmer today than yesterday, and the bumblebees are already flyin' every which way. I do love summertime round here."

"Where else have ya spent summers?" Nellie asked, a sparkle in her light brown eyes.

Rachel smiled. Nellie was a good one; you never knew what she might say. "Oh, back home, ya know. Ain't been out travelin' anywhere else."

Nellie nodded and rocked harder. "What brings ya over?"

Rachel dove right in. "Joseph and I were discussin' Maggie's health . . . that arthritis runs in the family."

Nellie's face turned serious. "*Jah*, Joseph's grandmother suffered so from her thirties on till she passed away in her mid-fifties. Same thing struck two of his great-aunts and a cousin, all gone to Glory now."

Rachel was saddened to hear this.

"Thankfully, so far Maggie is the only one in the youngest generation to get it." Pausing a moment, Nellie glanced at Rachel. "Of course, most of the other grandchildren are still young, so it's hard to know just yet." She placed her hand on her chest and shook her head. "I hope an' pray that none of the rest of them come down with it. Such an awful disease 'tis."

"Might there be something I could do to help Maggie?" asked Rachel. "Home remedies, maybe?"

"That's real kind of ya, but Maggie's quite aware of the most useful of them," explained Nellie. "Most of all, Maggie needs to rest when she can, 'specially when she's running a temperature. The pain takes so much out of her."

A silence ensued, other than the gentle sound of the rockers and bees buzzing in a nearby flowering shrub.

Then Nellie asked, "Might ya be worried your own children with Joseph will be afflicted with it?"

A jolt hit Rachel. Goodness, she hadn't even considered such a thing! And she certainly wanted babies with Joseph. "*Nee*," she was quick to say. "Never crossed my mind. But should I be worried?"

"Oh now, I wouldn't fret over it. Even if a wee one comes along with health problems, we can count on the Lord above to supply patience and wisdom when needed." Nellie reached to clasp Rachel's hand.

Rachel appreciated the woman's kindheartedness. And she caught herself pondering what Nellie had shared. So, while there was no easing up on chores, Rachel considered how best to show more understanding to Maggie, poor thing, while they shelled peas that afternoon.

The evening's breezes were warm, and it was still quite sunny when Maggie's cousins Luke and Lila Witmer picked her up in Luke's automobile—a black-and-white Buick with white sidewall tires. In the car, Lila explained that, since Luke needed to be there early, their parents and the rest of the children would meet them at the tent.

The car's interior smelled of new upholstery, and sitting in the back with Lila on the cushy seat, Maggie smiled when Lila teased her brother about being their private chauffeur. Luke merely bobbed his head and chuckled up there in the driver's seat. Maggie, however, clutched the armrest, not having ridden so fast in a long time, far more accustomed to the trotting of driving horses!

She stared out the window as they went, eventually noticing a billboard featuring Maxwell House Coffee . . . *Millions of tiny Flavor Buds.* For a split second, she wondered if Dat would ever succumb to the quick way some of their English neighbors made coffee. Nee, *Dat wants a rich, dark brew,* she decided, *the way Mamm always made it.* In his opinion, nothing was better than coffee percolated atop the cookstove.

When they arrived at the tent's site in Lancaster, Maggie was surprised at the size of it and the vast field it was pitched in, as well as the hundreds of automobiles, nearly a sea of them. "Never saw so many in my life," Maggie whispered as she reached for her cane before Luke came around and opened the car door for her. Lila got out on the opposite side of the four-door sedan.

Maggie thanked Luke for driving. "It was a much smoother ride than Dat's buggy," she said, taking solemn note of the distance between their parking spot and the tent. She told Lila she'd have to take it slow.

"Of course! We're so glad you've come along," Lila said and offered her arm.

Luke excused himself, needing to go on ahead.

"Luke's gotten acquainted with the evangelist and his family," Lila commented now, looking nice in her long floral print dress and its matching cape as they picked their way between the many vehicles. "They're really somethin'."

After a couple minutes of walking, Maggie stopped to rest, there in the midst of the great number of automobiles. Many people were streaming across the parking lot toward the tent. Now that they were nearer, the height of the temporary structure dwarfed her with its magnitude, and she felt terribly out of place.

Though all of the side tent flaps were rolled and tied up, Maggie could easily imagine how hot it must be inside. "Let's sit toward the back, where there's more fresh air," she suggested, still questioning her decision to come.

"My parents like to sit up front, but we can sit wherever you'd like," Lila said, staying right beside her.

Slowly, they made their way inside, where Maggie chose a spot on the far left, ten or more rows from the back and away from the heat of the sun. She removed the cardboard fan from the folding chair, a flower garden printed on one side and the name and address of a Lancaster insurance company on the back, very glad for it.

The lights inside the tent were quite glaring, and she wondered why they had to be this bright at six-thirty on a summer evening.

A group of older women came and sat in the chairs in front

of them, two wearing cup-shaped Mennonite head coverings and black dresses with capes over the bodice. Once they were seated, one of the women began to fan herself with short, erratic motions while she looked around nervously, as if this might be her first time at such a meeting, too.

A tall young woman wearing a brightly striped cotton vest over a short-sleeved white blouse took the end seat on the middle aisle as two younger girls in their early teens wandered in with tan pants rolled up to just below the knee. Although Maggie didn't want to be critical, she wondered what the Good Lord thought of such casual attire for church. She also noticed that families were sitting together, not men on one side and women and children on the other, like at Amish services. The whole atmosphere was disorienting, and Maggie felt uncomfortable.

Steadily the seats filled up, and right at seven o'clock, a stout, middle-aged man clad in black trousers and a long-sleeved white shirt walked out onto the front platform and began to pray into a hand-held microphone. He invited the Holy Spirit to rest upon the meeting and on all who were seeking the truth of God's Word.

Maggie couldn't help but take notice of the way the man prayed so loudly, far different from what she was used to.

Soon after, a song leader began to lead them in hymns and gospel songs, some of which Maggie had never heard. She listened, amazed by the blending of so many voices at once—in four-part harmony—just as Lila had described. *Unison singing is what's expected at Preaching,* she thought. Maggie found the music to be lovely, and after a while, she shyly joined in the melody, looking around at the faces of others as they sang.

But it was the evangelist who really commanded Maggie's

attention. The gathering fell quiet as Lloyd Brubaker stepped up to the wooden pulpit, attired in a plain suit with a standing collar and no lapels. He began his sermon by asking the crowd, "Do you believe that God has ordained this tent crusade? Yes or no?"

A resounding "Yes!" came from the gathering.

"Is your heart open to hearing the Word of the Lord?"

"Yes!"

Maggie was startled by the back-and-forth interaction between the dramatic preacher and the enthusiastic crowd, never having witnessed such a thing. Lloyd Brubaker spoke boldly, certainly seeming to believe he was God's messenger, "appointed for this hour," as he stated.

Preacher Brubaker opened his large black Bible. "In the book of Acts, chapter two and verse twenty-one, we read: 'And it shall come to pass, that whosoever shall call on the name of the Lord shall be saved.'"

Maggie sat straighter, paying close attention. She had believed in the Lord as her Savior since she was a little child hearing Dat read the Bible aloud. But to declare that one was saved was something different, wasn't it? The People certainly didn't talk like this. The Amish bishop had even once stated at a Preaching service, *"If you are so haughty and high-minded as to say that you're saved, you certainly are not!"*

Yet, according to this preacher reading from his open Bible, there it was, written right there in the New Testament.

Suddenly wanting to see it for herself, Maggie made a mental note to look up the verse at home—in fact, the entire chapter. The words of the Scripture continued to ring out in her mind as the minister preached.

"Whosoever shall call on the name of the Lord . . ."

After the hour-long sermon, which to Maggie seemed anything but lengthy, thanks to Lloyd Brubaker's earnest and compelling approach, the evangelist called for the listeners to bow their heads. He prayed for the lost to repent, then raised his eyes to look again at the crowd. "Each person who hears my voice, here in this tent or outside, come to the Lord . . . receive your Savior and make Him Lord of your life." He also urged those who had gone astray to return to the fold. "Do not delay—there may not be another opportunity. Come back to your heavenly Father, Who created you and is calling you now, this moment, to live all the days of your life for Him."

The song leader returned to the pulpit, and everyone began to sing in that glorious four-part harmony again. In a few minutes, the preacher took the microphone and spoke over the song. "Salvation is the Lord's work and not man's. I urge you not to wait another day . . . another moment."

Maggie had heard of an altar call, but she hadn't pictured the dozens of people that now got up from their seats to walk down the sawdust-covered aisle toward the platform. She was awestruck by the number, some with tears trailing down their cheeks, some with serious expressions, and others with little ones in their arms. The sight touched her deeply.

Yet, in spite of how inspiring it all was, there was much that still seemed foreign. She began to feel feverish again—and very tired. "I ought to get home," she whispered to Lila.

"Maybe you can come with me another time," Lila said as she reached for Maggie's cane and handed it to her.

"We'll see," Maggie murmured. "Right now, I just need to rest."

"I'll drive ya home, then come back later for Luke," Lila

said, grabbing her small purse from beneath her seat. "First, though, I need to let Luke know. . . . I'll try to find the evangelist's son. Glenn Brubaker will know where Luke is. You can just wait here."

"All right," Maggie agreed.

Lila gave Maggie's shoulder a gentle squeeze, then headed forward along the outside aisle.

Maggie sat there waiting, observing the people still flocking toward the front, her heart so tender she thought she might cry.

CHAPTER

6

Maggie was relieved when Cousin Lila returned after a few minutes.

But Lila was not alone. She was accompanied by a wavy-haired blond man who introduced himself simply as Glenn. "I'm glad you came to the crusade," he said, offering to shake her hand. "What's your name?" He smiled broadly, his broad, sharp shoulders evident beneath his crisp navy suit coat.

Maggie suddenly felt shy as the good-looking young man took the chair next to her, where Lila had been sitting. "I'm Maggie Esh," she replied.

"It's wonderful to meet you, Maggie." He paused. "I hope you'll come again."

She thanked him quietly.

"Is this your first time at one of these meetings?" His green eyes twinkled.

She admitted it was as Cousin Lila lowered herself onto the chair opposite Glenn, not looking Maggie's way. Instead, she folded her hands in her lap.

Glenn smiled, his gaze not wavering from Maggie. "Well, I'll be happy to talk with you anytime, if you have questions," he said, his smooth hand resting on his brown leather Bible.

"I appreciate that," Maggie said to be polite. After all, the preacher's own son was here seeking her out, and yet, if Glenn hadn't been so convincingly sincere—and strikingly handsome—she might have said that wasn't necessary. She was that ready to return to the comfort and security of her father's house.

The sun was close to setting when Rachel looked at the day clock high on the kitchen shelf. She had already written a circle letter that would be read by her older sisters in Myerstown. She had also read from the King James Bible that Joseph used for his personal devotions. Her own Mamm preferred the English Bible, as well, and Rachel remembered being read to from its version of Genesis, back when she was just seven years old and learning to speak English in the public schools. *Mamm was determined for me and my sisters to be able to read both German and English,* she thought with a smile.

At times, Rachel felt downright homesick for Myerstown, and with the house so quiet, this evening was one of those. Grace and Miriam were outdoors catching lightning bugs. While helping them poke holes in the lids of two Mason jars earlier, Rachel had recalled chasing the twinkling bugs all over her father's meadow with her own sisters. Those days were long past, but flickers of happy remembrances like that had a tendency to catch her off guard. It wasn't like she could just go on foot to visit her parents and sisters, like most married Amishwomen. Being this far away from home had its drawbacks, but it was worth it to be with Joseph, the answer to her many heartfelt prayers.

Glancing at the clock again, she realized that she'd looked at it quite often in the past couple of hours, wondering about Maggie.

At that moment, Rachel heard the screen door open. And even before she saw Joseph's aunt Nellie appear with her cat, Siegfried, in her arms, Rachel wondered if she might be coming to visit.

"*Kumme* in, Nellie!"

"I thought you might be over here twiddlin' your thumbs, so here I be," Nellie said, smiling as she came in and sat down at the table, keeping Siegfried low on her lap. Her cheeks were rosier than usual.

"Nice to see ya," Rachel said. "Joseph and the children cut through the knee-high field grass to go an' see some of Joseph's Esh cousins. They should be back before too long."

One hand still on Siggy, Nellie seemed to study Rachel. Her pure white hair was pulled tightly into a bun, her white organdy *Kapp* over the top. "And you stayed behind?"

"Thought someone oughta be home when Maggie returns."

"Well now, are ya frettin'?"

Rachel shrugged. She wasn't worried as much as she was curious and hoping to talk privately with Maggie upon her arrival.

As she was known to do, Nellie kept the conversation moving. Settled onto the wooden bench, she brought up the fact that she'd gone to visit Ruth Zook this afternoon. "Ruth was eager to tell me 'bout her cousin who went to a tent meeting last week."

Now Nellie really had Rachel's attention. "Is that right?"

Nellie was nodding her head. "I guess the cousin was a bit nervous about possibly being spotted in a crowd of all those *Englischers* an' all."

"Why'd she go, then?"

Nellie's features came alive. "She went with her husband to see what all the hoopla was about."

Rachel traced her finger along the edge of the closed Bible still in front of her, remembering her own encounter with revival meetings as a teenager. "So, do ya think many Amish folk are goin'?"

Nellie shook her head. "It's mostly Mennonites—two Mennonite churches are sponsoring the meetings. More than a thousand people are expected tonight, Ruth said."

"Joseph says baptized Amish have no business goin'." Rachel sighed and thought that Maggie ought to be home fairly soon.

"Ya don't sound so sure."

This was the thing about Joseph's widowed aunt—she sensed things, even when a body tried to conceal them. "Oh, you don't have to wonder, Nellie. I was real surprised Joseph didn't keep Maggie from goin' tonight, even though she hasn't joined church just yet . . . still in *Rumschpringe*, ya know."

Nellie glanced toward the window. "Well, she'll be eighteen soon, but even so, an unmarried woman oughtn't go against her father's wishes while she's still under his roof."

"Well, Maggie *did* ask his permission," Rachel reminded her, "but he'd rather it didn't get around that Maggie went, all the same."

Nellie nodded her head. "I'll keep it mum."

Rachel smiled. "I know ya will." She glanced at the cookie jar on the counter. "By the way, I have some sweets, if you're interested."

Nellie smiled a toothy grin. "You know me, I'm always ready for goodies. But let *me* get them; looks like you're all in."

Rachel had to keep from laughing. Here was Nellie, five decades older, wanting *her* to take it easy! "For goodness' sake, you just sit there with Siggy."

But Nellie put her cat down and rose to walk to the side door to stare out, talking to herself.

She's restless till Maggie's home, too, thought Rachel, going to get the cookies and some meadow tea.

CHAPTER

7

"I'm real curious what ya told the evangelist's son," Maggie said as she and Lila rode together in the sedan. They'd left Luke behind; he planned to get a ride home with his parents and other siblings.

"Only that you're my cousin and it was your first time ever to such a meeting," Lila said, keeping her eyes on the road as she gripped the steering wheel.

"Well, it was nice of him to take time for me." Maggie paused a moment. "Is he planning to be a minister, too?"

"He'll be a senior at Eastern Mennonite College this fall, pursuing biblical studies."

Maggie listened, curious. This was wholly unlike the Amish way of drawing lots for ordination for ministry. To think that a young fellow like Glenn could be *taught* to be a preacher! It was mind-boggling. *He does have a winning way about him,* Maggie thought.

When they turned into Dat's treed lane and parked up near the house, Maggie thanked Lila for bringing her home.

Lila asked, "Would ya like to go again tomorrow? Luke has to go anyway."

"Are *you* goin'?"

"I definitely can," Lila said. "If you want to."

"Not sure I oughta." Maggie remembered how uncomfortable she'd felt in the heat and the hubbub. And she couldn't dismiss Dat's reluctance about her attending, either. "Guess I'd better get goin'."

"I hope you aren't too worn out," said Lila, looking at her kindly. "Here, I'll help ya."

Reaching to open the car door, Maggie nodded. "*Denki*, cousin."

"Your Dat will be glad to see you're home safely," Lila said as she assisted Maggie out of the car and walked with her around to the back door.

"*Jah*, and I 'spect Rachel will be, too."

"Well, if you decide to go, let me know, all right?"

"I'll see if Leroy can ride over to tell ya, if I choose to."

Maggie was glad to have time to let things settle in her mind, even though she secretly wanted to know more about Scripture—especially the verses Lloyd Brubaker had read tonight. And the man's words continued to spin in her head. *Ever so much to think about.*

Several minutes after Lila backed the car out to the road, leaving Maggie in the kitchen with Rachel, her stepmother mentioned that she'd just missed seeing Nellie. Then Rachel began asking questions about the meeting. It was peculiar, her being so curious, and something within Maggie made her feel hesitant. *Why does she want my opinion?* she wondered, though she did her best to describe the magnitude of the tent, the enormous crowd, the many vehicles—too many to count—the soul-stirring music, and the spirited evangelist. She left out the part about the altar call and meeting Preacher Brubaker's handsome and very friendly son.

"Are ya glad you went?" Rachel asked, eyes wide.

"Honestly, I'm a bit overwhelmed," Maggie admitted, hoping Rachel would not press her further. She wasn't at ease talking to her stepmother about something so personal . . . something that Rachel might later pass on to Dat.

"Did it make you want to go again?" Rachel asked, her hands cupped around her tumbler.

"I can't decide." Maggie looked out the window and saw her father and Grace, Miriam, and the youngest boys ambling across the shadowy yard, talking as they came this way. Leroy, however, was lagging behind.

Rachel must have heard them coming, too. "Well, it's been nice talking 'bout this with ya, Maggie."

"You an' Dat could go and see for yourself sometime, maybe," Maggie suggested, not knowing what else to say.

"Oh, ain't something he's interested in, and I wouldn't go without him."

"*Jah* . . . and only a few Old Order Amish were there," Maggie said.

Rachel's eyebrows rose slightly.

"Mostly older teens—courting couples—lookin' in from the edge of the tent."

"Interesting," Rachel said, and she rose quickly as Dat and the others came inside.

Maggie headed to her room, glad to be alone at last. She took down her long dark hair, putting the many hairpins in a tiny pin box on the dresser one by one, then began to brush the whole length of it, down past her waist. She had to brush slowly, lest her arm play out, painful as it was. *I certainly overdid it.*

Still, she pondered all she'd heard and seen, including Glenn Brubaker's surprising welcome. And the minute she was dressed for bed, she pulled back the sheet and Mamm's pretty summer quilt and slipped under them, making herself comfortable with several pillows to cushion her back and arms. Then she began to read the passage from Acts, wondering if it would affect her the same way it had earlier.

At the breakfast table the next morning, Rachel asked who wanted to go along with her to the fabric store, and before Maggie could offer, Miriam had raised her hand, like she was in school, which made Dat and the younger boys chuckle. Quickly, Stephen raised his own hand, mimicking Miriam and rolling his eyes. Nearly just as fast, though, Andy reached up and pulled it down, whispering to his brother to behave.

Leroy, however, ate his cornmeal mush and sausage as fast as he'd ever eaten. The entire time, he was slumped over, head close to the table, something he'd never done when Mamm was living—surely she would have taken notice and said something. Only once did he lift his eyes to look over at Maggie.

He's struggling terribly, she thought, reaching for her chamomile tea, which Mamm had urged her to sip every morning, hot weather or not.

"Maybe Maggie would like to go, too," Miriam was saying about the trip to the fabric store, looking expectantly at her. "I'll be happy to share Mamma Rachel."

Dat grinned at that, and Leroy scoffed audibly.

"Son?"

Leroy looked at Dat, his face grim. *"Jah?"*

Andy and Stephen exchanged startled looks, and Maggie held her breath. Leroy had never behaved so.

"Are ya finished eating?" Dat asked in a tone that suggested her brother would have been wiser to keep quiet.

Leroy didn't bother to answer. Swiftly, he pushed back the chair, its legs scraping against the floor. "I'll take my plate to the sink and get out to the stable."

"You do that," Dat said flatly, not raising his voice, but his ears were turning pink.

Leroy set his plate in the sink with a loud clatter, and Rachel flinched. Maggie almost expected her to reach for Dat, but Rachel was wringing her hands in her lap.

"I'll be glad to go with yous to get dress material," Maggie said right then, looking over at Miriam, who clapped her little hands.

"Do *you* wanna go, too, Gracie?" Miriam asked right quick.

After what had just taken place, Grace appeared quite flustered, and she merely nodded her head.

For pity's sake, thought Maggie, wondering if Dat would head out and give Leroy a good scolding.

Surprisingly, though, Dat rose to go to the next room and get the King James Bible. He returned with it and sat back down at the head of the table, appearing calm and unshaken as he began to read a psalm.

CHAPTER

8

The gray family carriage moved steadily along the paved road that snaked between the ditch on one side and the cornfield on the other. Banks of blossoming honeysuckle vines lent a lovely fragrance to the drive, and Maggie enjoyed seeing the occasional wild lilies growing along the roadside, too.

Miriam sat up front next to Rachel, at the reins, and Maggie and Grace sat in the second bench seat, watching the familiar countryside go by. Within earshot of others, they couldn't really talk about the last Singing or anything more about Grace's first date with Martin Lantz. And Maggie felt sure the tent meeting was off limits, as well.

She couldn't help but remember all the times Mamm had held the driving lines, taking her three girls off to a work frolic or canning bee or whatnot. It was still a bit hard to see the back of Rachel and realize it wasn't Mamm up there anymore.

Their stepmother was the first to speak. "I'm glad yous came with me." She glanced over her shoulder at Maggie and Grace. "Your father gave me extra money for sweets on the way home."

"Ice cream, maybe?" Miriam looked up at Rachel, her expression hopeful.

"You guessed it."

"Goody!" Miriam looked back at Maggie and Grace, a big smile on her cute face.

Rachel laughed, looking at Miriam with obvious affection. "The stop at the fabric store shouldn't take long, since I know what dress material and sewing notions I'm lookin' for."

"My dresses are getting too short," Miriam announced. "Or maybe I'm just inchin' up."

Grace spoke then. "I'll let down the hems for ya when we get home. How's that?"

"*Denki*," said Rachel over her shoulder. "We need to try an' make her dresses last through the summer if possible."

Maggie felt like an observer as she noticed how well the three of them seemed to be getting along. As reticent as she felt toward Rachel, she wished Leroy might at least give their stepmother a chance. "I'll help make the noon meal," Maggie offered, "since Grace'll be adjustin' hems and you'll be cutting out a dress pattern, Rachel."

"Are ya up to it?" Rachel asked, her eyes still on the road.

"So far." Just then, Maggie thought of Lila's invitation to go to the tent meeting again tonight. To her surprise, a sense of excitement coursed through her. *Maybe if I rest some this afternoon, I'll feel like going.*

The quaint little fabric shop was busier than usual with customers, which pleased Rachel no end. It was, after all, owned by an Amish widow, and Rachel preferred to spend money where it could go to help others of like faith.

Rachel went right to the many bolts of dress material while the girls wandered about the store.

"Hullo there, Rachel."

She turned to see Ruth Zook's married daughter Lavina carrying a thick bolt of black dress fabric. "Nice to see ya." Rachel eyed the fabric. "Looks like you've got some sewin' to do, too."

"Goin' to a funeral for an old friend," Lavina said. "And my for-*gut* black dress has seen better days."

"I understand." Rachel wondered how Ruth was feeling. "I sure hope your Mamm's on the mend."

"Oh, she is. An' she says up and down that your ice cream hit the spot—some of the best she's tasted." Lavina smiled radiantly, then waved and hurried to the cash register with the bolt of fabric.

Glad she enjoyed it, thought Rachel, finding the royal blue fabric she was looking for. As she turned toward the spools of thread, she noticed Maggie and Grace talking to Lillian Beiler over in the corner. If she wasn't mistaken, it looked to her like Maggie had gone pink. *Is she feverish again?*

Goodness, thought Maggie, *but Lillian Beiler has a talk on.* And it was all about Jimmy!

"My son wants to be an apprentice," Lillian said as she looked directly at Maggie. "Already workin' with the smithy."

Maggie wondered if anyone could tell how warm her face was. The way Lillian, bless her heart, just kept sharing things about Jimmy, moving on now to mention the new straw hat he'd finally purchased, as well as some new black shoes, too, over at the Amish shoe store on Belmont Road.

Why's she going on so? Maggie glanced at Grace, who was having a hard time keeping a straight face.

Eventually, Maggie mentioned to Lillian how pretty the soft pink fabric was that she had in her hand. And, thank goodness, Lillian commented right then on her youngest daughter's growth spurt.

"Like me?" Miriam said with a grin as she sidled up to Grace. "But we're just letting down my hems for now."

Lillian nodded. "That's *schmaert*. Seems children grow extra fast durin' the summers."

It was then that Maggie noticed Rachel moving toward the front of the store, coming this way. "Well, it was nice to see ya, Lillian," Maggie said cordially, ready to bring the awkward conversation to an end.

"You too." Lillian singled her out with her gaze.

Grace and Miriam said good-bye, as well, and, gripping her cane, Maggie smiled through the flashes of pain as she headed toward the door.

Later, on the way home, Maggie wondered what Lillian—and Jimmy, too—might think if they knew she was planning to slip away to meet her Mennonite cousins that night to attend the tent meeting again. *Maybe I can step out without attracting Dat's or Rachel's attention. . . .*

"When did ya see Maggie last?" Rachel asked Grace after the supper dishes were washed and dried.

"She was in her room for a while, but then, far as I know, she went out for a walk," Grace said.

"A walk?" Rachel felt surprised. "She must be feelin' much better."

"Well, she was movin' real slow when I saw her leave by way of the front door. She's usin' her cane again."

"How long ago was this?" Rachel wondered if someone should go and look for her. What if Maggie fell and wasn't able to get help?

"Oh, I'm sure she's fine," Grace said. "She knows not to take on more than she can handle. And it's still light for another couple of hours."

For a moment, the thought crossed Rachel's mind that Grace might know more than she was saying. But then Grace offered to go and find her, if Rachel really thought it necessary.

"*Nee*, I won't worry. But if Maggie's not back before dark . . ."

"Then I'll see what's up." Grace looked thoughtful. "What if she met up with a fella and doesn't want anyone to know?"

Rachel laughed. "'Tis possible."

Grace smiled and went to wipe down the oilcloth on the table.

Rachel knew something of the courting rituals in Lancaster County, but it had been a long time since her own dating years. In fact, till Joseph courted her, she hadn't dated again after being jilted in her teens. To be sure, she scarcely thought about such things anymore. But considering that she was now a stepmother to two dating-age girls, she figured she had better start paying attention.

CHAPTER

9

The song service was even more soul stirring to Maggie than last night's gathering, and there was an air of almost tangible expectancy. When it came time for people to give testimonies, she listened closely. The first person, an older man, shared somewhat timidly that he had wandered far from the straight and narrow. "Until I came to these meetings, I was convinced God could never forgive me," he told the vast crowd, breaking down and wiping away tears. "And now I've surrendered my life to the Lord and Savior."

There was a thunderous amen when he finished. Even Maggie found herself wanting to join in, but she wasn't accustomed to making such a public response.

The next man described himself as a Mennonite farmer who felt convicted about his tobacco crop—so much so that, after attending his first meeting, he'd gone home and plowed it all up the very next day.

Maggie was shocked that this man would give up his livelihood "for the Good News," as he put it. She was also amazed by the number in attendance, even more than last night. Lila had mentioned during the ride that word of mouth was spreading the news like a brush fire. Luke, who'd once again driven them, described it as a "phenomenon."

Whatever it was, something powerful was taking place, and Maggie realized that she, too, was caught up in the fervor. The draw was like that of a magnet, one she could not resist.

Tonight, Maggie had chosen to sit midway between the back and the front of the tent with Cousin Lila and a young neighbor woman Lila had invited, Nanette Oberholtzer. Having brought her Bible this time, Maggie followed along with the evangelist as the sermon moved forward. She used her homemade bookmarks to mark passages she wanted to read again at home, fascinated by the idea of surrendering fully to the lordship of Christ.

When the crowd was beginning to disperse a while after the altar call, Maggie noticed Glenn Brubaker across the tent, evidently coming this way. He waved when he spotted her and entered the row where she and Lila and Nanette were sitting, stopping to shake hands with various people, some still sitting and reading their Bibles.

As Glenn approached, he smiled broadly. "Hello again, Maggie." He also greeted Lila, who introduced him to Nanette.

To Maggie's surprise, Glenn sat next to her. "It's good to see you here again." He flashed his wonderful smile. "I take it you didn't care much for the back rows."

"It's harder to see from there," she admitted, unable to help smiling in return. "And I guess I just wanted to be closer to the front."

"Good choice," Glenn said with a glance toward the altar area, where people were still lingering and praying. "God's

76

Spirit is working in many hearts . . . people are being touched for eternity."

"You seem excited," she said softly, glad Lila was still talking with Nanette, pointing out a Scripture verse in the Bible they had open between them.

"Yes. It's been a humbling privilege to work alongside my father."

Maggie wasn't sure what to say, or if she should reveal the questions filling up her heart.

"Is there anything you'd like to talk about concerning tonight's sermon, or anything else?" he asked, his brown leather Bible balanced on his knee.

It seemed strange that Glenn would ask, as if he'd sensed what she was feeling. Dare she tell him? She started to open her mouth but felt hesitant to talk so openly with an *Englischer.*

"Maggie, I realize we don't know each other well, but I'm here to help." The way he spoke to her, singling her out, made her think he could be trusted.

She took a slow breath. "Last night I was reading in my New Testament," she said, going out on a limb. "Starting in Acts, chapter two."

"Yes?" His expression encouraged her to go on.

"But I didn't stop there. I just couldn't. I kept reading into chapter three, where Peter and John healed the lame man at the gate of the temple." Suddenly, she felt as if she might choke up and looked down at her hands in her lap. "If I understood verse sixteen right, the lame man was healed by faith in Jesus' name."

"Exactly," Glenn said, nodding his head emphatically. "And while you might find it hard to believe, seeing me now, I also experienced a healing like that." He glanced at Maggie's cane. "Are you seeking healing, too?"

She didn't want to talk about herself; she wanted to hear more about what had happened to Glenn. He was quite right—she couldn't imagine such a strapping young man in need of physical healing. She was about to ask to hear more, but Lila touched her arm, and when Maggie glanced over, she saw Luke standing at the far end of the row, ready to head home.

"*Ach*, I'm sorry, Glenn. It looks like I have to get goin'," she said as Luke waved to Glenn just then.

"Will I see you again?" There was a sudden rise of energy in his voice. "If you're really interested, I'd like to tell you what happened."

She was taken aback by his request. "I don't know," she said softly. "To tell ya the truth, I'm pushin' the boundaries, coming to these meetings," she confided. "My father wouldn't want me to make a habit of it."

He nodded. "I understand. But please know this: The Lord sees our hearts, not our traditions or how we're brought up. He sees the *person*, the person He alone created."

She'd never thought of that.

"God loves the whole world—every last one of us. That's why His Son left heaven to come to earth and give up His life, so we could be saved." Glenn paused. "Christ doesn't show favoritism—He came to redeem us all. He took the punishment we deserved for our sin and made it possible for us to be made whole—spiritually *and* physically."

Maggie picked up her Bible and reached for her cane, smiling her gratitude for his words, because she was too emotional to speak. *Oh, to have a healthy, whole body!*

"Whether you come again or not, I hope you'll read chapter five in the Gospel of Mark, the story of Jairus's daughter,"

Glenn said. "It will build up your faith. It certainly did mine." He stood with her as she got out of her seat with the help of her cane.

Maggie thanked him, feeling too rushed and wishing they could talk further. But she fell in line with Lila and Nanette as Luke led the way toward the parking lot.

Feeling hesitant, Rachel showed Joseph the note Maggie had left on Rachel's dresser. "Did you suspect she might do this?" She hated to break it to her husband.

Joseph, already in his pajamas, shook his head. "It really wonders me," he said quietly. "Did Maggie think I'd forbid her to go a second time?"

"Would you have?" Rachel asked as she went over and slipped into bed beside him.

Sitting against the headboard with a pillow behind him, Joseph fell silent. His chest rose and fell slowly, and with a sigh, he reached for her.

"I hope this isn't hurtful to you—Maggie slippin' out like that," she said.

"Well, I feel the same about Leroy's bad attitude toward you, love." Joseph kissed her temple.

"That's different, though—quite different." Rachel snuggled next to him, her head on his chest, where she could hear the steady pump of his heart.

"I'm afraid Maggie is getting caught up in the enthusiasm the papers are reporting," Joseph said, stroking Rachel's long blond hair.

"You've read some of the accounts, then?"

"One headline was *Tent Revival Like a Meteorite Across the*

Mennonite Church of America." Joseph was quiet for a time. "Think of it—a meteorite. Sounds mighty destructive."

Rachel nodded. "It does when you put it thataway. Yet crowds of people are goin'. And more than just Mennonite folk."

"True. It's captured the attention of people from all over Lancaster County and beyond. One fella at the gristmill today said they expect seven thousand at the meeting Sunday night. Can you imagine?"

She could not, but oh, she was curious.

Joseph moved closer. "I hope you won't lose sleep waitin' for Maggie to come home."

"I won't worry, if you don't."

"Just rest easy, dear. Her cousins will bring her home." He kissed her on the lips now, and then again.

"Oh, how I love ya, Joseph," she whispered, returning his fervent kisses.

Later, when Rachel said her silent rote prayers, she remembered the first time Joseph had kissed her—on their wedding day. She had wished he might do so sooner, but Joseph was determined to wait for the day they united before God and the bishop.

Rachel had been so pleased that her parents and both sets of grandparents had traveled to Lancaster County for the private wedding at Bishop Lantz's place, coming down nearly thirty miles from Myerstown in a passenger van. She recalled the precious mother-daughter time beforehand in one of the bedrooms upstairs in the big farmhouse. *"Your Dat and I prayed for this blessed day since you were a tiny girl,"* Mamm had whispered, eyes shining. She had held Rachel extra long that moment before she was to head downstairs with her side sitters, Marnie and Martha. Because all of Rachel's sisters were already married, her cousins were her two wedding attendants.

Earlier that wedding morning, Joseph had gone out of his way to greet her family, just as he had the few times before when they'd gone back home to visit.

Sighing now, Rachel rolled over and placed her hand gently on Joseph's feather pillow, near his dear head, and thanked God for this precious man.

Moonlight on the walkway guided Maggie as she and Lila moved together toward the back porch. The sweetness of honeysuckle blossoms was thick in the air, and the sound of chirping crickets, too.

"I'm so glad ya came along, dear cousin," Lila said, walking close, as if to make sure that Maggie made it all right.

"*Denki.* I'm glad ya invited me."

Lila hugged her quickly and returned the Bible that she'd carried for Maggie, then headed back to the car, where Luke and Nanette were waiting.

Maggie inched up the porch steps, struggling with her Bible and cane.

"You prob'ly hoped no one would catch ya, *ain't?*" came Leroy's voice, and then she saw him there in the shadows, sitting near the screen door.

Startled though Maggie was, she tried not to let on. "*Ach,* no need to think thataway," she told him, leaning hard on her cane. "I left Rachel a note, tellin' where I was."

"Well, even Gracie was worried." Leroy got up from the rocking chair and began to pace. "The tent meetings must really be somethin' for you to—"

"I just told ya, Rachel should have known from my note where I was," she interrupted. "I figured she'd tell Dat."

"But *you* didn't tell him, did ya?"

She'd never known Leroy to confront her. "You're right; I should have." She headed slowly for the side door. "I'm awful tired."

"*Jah*, everyone's in bed, 'cept us," Leroy said, stopping his pacing to rest against the porch rail.

She didn't reply; he seemed too set on arguing. This wasn't like him at all.

"Are the meetings everything that folks are sayin'?" he asked now.

She reached for the screen door. "What folk?"

"Oh, the handful I've run into, here and there."

Maggie drew a breath. "The singin', the sermons . . . all of it makes ya want to keep goin' back. I can't say why, though."

"Like wantin' a piece of candy . . . and then another?"

"Not exactly, but many people are goin' forward during the altar call. Some can hardly get there fast enough to make things right with God."

Leroy didn't say anything to that.

"Well, I'm on my last legs," Maggie said. "I'll see ya in the mornin', *Bruder*." She headed indoors, where Rachel had left a single lit lantern on the counter. Maggie set down her Bible. She caught her breath and wished to goodness Mamm were sitting there at the table waiting for her, so they could talk . . . the way she used to wait up for her the few times Maggie had gone to Singings or other youth activities. Before rheumatic heart disease had flared up, taking Mamm early. *All because of the bad case of scarlet fever she had when she was young.*

Leroy remained outside, Maggie noticed as she took two

aspirin with a half glass of milk. And even though her brother had waited up to challenge her like that, Maggie's thoughts were on Glenn's encouragement to read from the Gospel of Mark. She could hardly wait to open her Bible to do just that.

Mamm used to read the Good Book late at night, too.

As Maggie was getting ready to leave the kitchen, she heard sniffling out on the porch and crept over to the screen door. Leroy still stood there, facing away from her.

"What is it?" she whispered, opening the door to step out. She went over and stood next to him, letting him cry.

He murmured, "I'm a big baby, that's what."

"We all are sometimes." She meant it. "I hope it's not somethin' I said."

"I don't think ya wanna know, Maggie. You won't understand."

"Well, how can I if you don't explain?"

He rubbed his eyes like a child and shook his head. Then, straightening, he said, "I can't accept Rachel as our *Schtiefmudder.* It's like I'd be forgetting Mamm . . . bein' disloyal to her."

Maggie looked at him. "Wouldn't Mamm want us to welcome Rachel? Have ya considered that?" She struggled to keep her own composure, because some days she, too, felt like Leroy did just now.

"But we can't know that for sure," Leroy replied, his voice faltering. "Besides, I think Mamm would be upset that Dat pushed all his memories of her aside to marry Rachel so quick."

Maggie could see his point, but she also understood why their father had remarried. "Is there somethin' more, Leroy? Seems like somethin's a-brewin' inside of you, 'cause I've never known ya to be this way."

He huffed. "Didn't ya listen to what I just said?"

"*Ach*, you're in such turmoil. The *Bruder* I know would never talk like this."

He groaned but didn't say more, and she stood there with him for a while longer, until he calmed down.

At last, Leroy pulled out his kerchief and blew his nose. Then he thanked her for caring about him. "Like Mamm always did."

"I love ya, *Bruder*," Maggie said. "Never forget that."

They went inside together, Maggie somewhat heartened that she'd had this sisterly time with poor, miserable Leroy. She also sensed something more gnawing away at him. *But what?*

CHAPTER

10

Exhausted as she was and despite her concern for Leroy, Maggie welcomed the peace that followed to her room on the main level of the house. The house creaked and cooled off from the day's heat; the cushion of nighttime was her solace now.

First day of summer, she thought, setting her Bible on the small table near the only chair in the room. She looked at the calendar hanging near the settee against the far wall—a free calendar from Betsy Lapp's Bakery and Craft Shop up the road. Each page advertised Betsy's delectable pastries, goodies, and homemade craft items.

The next Singing is July first, she thought, a bit sad at the thought of not going. But there was no backing down. The pitying look of surprise on Timothy Blank's face still nagged at her. And, as fond as she was of Jimmy Beiler, she wouldn't let his seeming interest in Cousin Deborah break her heart, either. *I'll keep Miriam company here at home,* she decided.

Maggie slipped on her long cotton nightgown and took

down her thick bun to brush her hair. She put the clothes she'd worn into the wicker hamper and closed the lid, then moved to sit near the open window, scooting up close, glad for this room, which was certainly cooler than upstairs on such a night. She reached for her Bible.

What was it about the meeting tonight that made her want to read every Scripture verse the evangelist had referenced? And what about Glenn?—so kind and earnest, like a close friend. Maggie wondered all of these things and more as her thoughts raced. *I can't have a crush on an Englischer. . . .*

A sudden gust blew in through the window, catching her off guard. *All the better,* she thought, shaking herself. *I must keep my focus on the Lord alone,* she thought as she turned the pages to the Gospel of Mark to locate the story Glenn had suggested.

The next morning, Maggie, tired from staying up late, chose to remain at home with Grace while Rachel took Miriam to visit neighbor Ruth Zook, who was still hobbling about on crutches with her sprained ankle. Dat and the boys had gone down the road to help the neighbors chase pigs and load them into the hauling pens to put on a truck for market.

While Maggie missed having their talkative and bubbly younger sister around, she welcomed the opportunity to help Grace bake apple pie for supper that evening. One for Aunt Nellie, too. Sitting at the table to conserve her energy, Maggie found that working alongside Grace reminded her of doing the same with Mamm, and the feeling brought her a sense of peace in the midst of shared grief.

Maggie and Grace each wore one of Mamm's old work

aprons as they made pie dough and smoothed it out with rolling pins. Maggie never had to think about the next step or wonder if Grace would match her own movements—they were partners in the kitchen, to be sure. *Mamm taught us well.*

"Where'd ya go last evening, or is it too nosy to ask?" Grace asked while she placed the pie dough into the glass baking dish.

"Well, it wasn't with Jimmy Beiler," Maggie said, making herself smile. "Is that what you're hopin'?"

"Another fella, then?" Grace's eyebrows rose.

"*Nee.*"

Grace looked at her askance. "None of my business, right?"

Maggie shrugged. "I just went with Lila and Luke to the tent meeting."

This news appeared to astonish Grace. "You went *again?*"

"I did."

Smoothing out the dough, Grace leaned on the rolling pin, her face pinched up. Even so, she didn't ask another question.

Maggie felt like a fish flapping on dry ground. She disliked being made to feel guilty of wrongdoing, and no one in this house seemed to understand her interest in the meetings. But she couldn't blame them; unless they experienced the gatherings for themselves, how could they possibly know?

"Well, I hope you've changed your mind about goin' to the next Singing," Grace said softly. "'Cause otherwise, I'll really miss ya."

"I'll miss bein' there with you, too," Maggie said. "It's really not what I want," she told her. *How could it be?* she thought. "If I was normal, like the other girls—like you—I wouldn't frighten the fellas away."

"Aw . . . Maggie." Grace squinted her eyes. "I prob'ly shouldn't say it, but you're prettier than any girl round here. That's the honest truth. And you're ever so wonderful on the inside, too."

Maggie dipped her head, embarrassed. After a pause, she said, "You an' I both know that fellas want able-bodied young women to court and marry. And nothin' less." The image of the redheaded fellow backing away from her crossed Maggie's mind, and she flinched anew.

Grace didn't refute it. She poured the home-canned apples over the pressed dough in the pie dishes.

She knows it's true, Maggie thought.

Once the pies were ready to bake, she and Grace would go out to the henhouse to feed and water the chickens in Miriam's stead, then gather eggs. Anticipating that chore and all the standing it required, Maggie let the story of Jairus's daughter's healing, which she'd read last night, play over in her mind.

I'll read it again later, she thought, hungry for more.

On Sunday afternoon, Maggie went to Leola with her family to visit Dawdi Reuben, who lived next door to *Aendi* Barbieann and her husband, *Onkel* Zeke, and their five children still living at home. The trip took about an hour by horse and spring wagon. The People did not ride in automobiles on the Lord's Day, so the family had gone in the open wagon, since the whole family was along. They looked forward to spending time with Mamm's widowed father, something they did as often as possible. *He cherishes our visits,* Maggie thought, recalling how seeing their mother enter the house would always bring a hearty smile to the dear man's wrinkled face.

While the wagon bumped along, Maggie glanced at Grace

sitting next to her on the second seat, staring at the landscape in an apparent daydream. *If only I could somehow communicate what I've experienced at the revival meetings—the growing closeness I feel toward the Lord. How can I explain?*

Their brothers were sitting in the back, talking quietly in *Deitsch.* Now and then, Stephen would raise his voice a bit, but for the most part, they were behaving themselves, lest Dat ask them to quiet down. She listened for a moment as Andy mentioned the possibility of playing softball real soon. Stephen was quick to agree, and Leroy said they should get some of their boy cousins to join them.

Dat and Rachel were talking softly in the front seat, and Miriam turned to look back at Maggie every few minutes, grinning, her expression filled with mischief. Maggie smiled back at her.

"Do ya wish you were in back with the boys?" Maggie asked her.

Miriam was quick to shake her head. "They'd just pester me."

"Or maybe the other way around?" Maggie smiled.

To that, Miriam said nothing, but there was that impish twinkle in her eyes again.

"Want a Life Saver?" Maggie asked, opening her pocketbook and taking out a fresh roll with the five classic flavors, her favorite.

"Sure." Miriam reached back and grabbed the whole thing, giggling as she opened it and offered one each to Dat and Rachel up front.

Goodness, thought Maggie, having to laugh at her sly sister.

When Miriam returned what was left of the prettily wrapped roll, she apologized.

"That's okay," Maggie said. *I was a playful sort once, too.*

Returning the Life Savers to her purse, it crossed Maggie's mind how lively and happy Cousin Lila had seemed lately—not mischievous like Miriam—each time they were together. Was it because she was so enjoying the tent services, or did she have a beau, just maybe? Pondering the latter, Maggie realized that most every young woman her age, and even some younger, had a steady beau. And it struck her that she would likely be living on her own someday—like Great-aunt Nellie did.

Early that evening, following a light supper of ham and cheese sandwiches and a bowl of fruit cup, Rachel was pleased when Joseph asked her to go for a walk, leaving the girls to redd up the kitchen.

"How long's it been since we walked, just the two of us?" Joseph asked, reaching for her hand the minute they were far enough away from the house.

"Too long?" she asked, flirting back.

"I agree, and I've been lookin' forward to some time alone with ya, love."

She nodded happily, still aware of how her heart fluttered when he said sweet things like that. "To be honest, I'm real thankful for Sunday afternoons and evenings."

"'Tis a slower time, *jah*." He paused to kiss her cheek. "Remember how we'd sneak away from Sam Zook's place to go walkin'? It was worth braving even the chilliest weather."

She laughed softly, the breeze warm against her face. "You were quite romantic then, Joseph."

"*Then?*" Joseph said, his face humorously pained.

She laughed. "You still are."

Chuckling, he squeezed her hand.

This deserted dirt path, used by the mules to get from field to field during the week, was the very one she and Joseph had strolled along as a new courting couple. *While I stayed those two months with Sam and Ruth Zook*, she thought, glancing back across the wide meadow toward the couple's farmhouse.

"I haven't forgotten the way you looked at me across the table at Sam Zook's that first night," she said.

"I'll never forget, either. You laughed at all my jokes." He stopped walking and slipped his arms around her. "The surest way to a man's heart."

She loved the feel of him next to her and nuzzled in closer, lifting her face to his to initiate another kiss. "I'm so thankful for Sam and Ruth's invitation."

"I believe the Good Lord allowed them to bring us together." He glanced toward heaven as they began to walk again. "I did think you were a bit leery of me," Joseph surprised her by saying.

"Well, if I was, it only lasted a few moments." She remembered how Joseph had stuck his hand out to shake hers, his eyes soft and adoring almost immediately.

"I couldn't blame ya, really, considering you were younger and single . . . without a houseful of children."

She laughed. "Once you started talkin' about your happy life with your family, my heart went out to ya, Joseph . . . knowin' what ya'd lost." She paused a moment, conscious of his arm brushing against hers as they ambled along. "That's not to say that I felt sorry for ya."

"Well, ya must've, poor, lonely man that I was." He reached for her hand again. "But it was far more than that. I think I must've fallen in love with ya at Ruth Zook's kitchen table that very night . . . could hardly take my eyes off ya." Joseph smiled and glanced at her. "Such a perty girl—I couldn't believe the Good Lord kept ya just for me. Still can't when I wake up next to ya, dear."

Joseph was the man of her every daydream. The kind of man Rachel had always hoped to meet and marry, even as far back as when she was in her teens and attending the weddings of her sisters and cousins.

But she brushed off the lurking memory of those days, not letting herself think about any of that, not on this relaxing evening walk.

Rachel came by her love of the outdoors naturally—from her Mamm, who relished taking long romps through the meadows and up to the woods, too, when Rachel and her sisters were children. She was thrilled to be married to a man who took time to comment about the many flower gardens she was tending. And she smiled, recalling his first question to her, about what flowers she enjoyed growing.

All around her she noticed beauty—the wild flowers, the pebbles along the path, and the birds singing their joyous songs. There were occasional large rocks in the field, and clumps of purple wild thistle, but this stretch of land belonging to Joseph signified honesty and hard work. This patch of God's green earth represented His promise of blessing.

As she and Joseph picked up their pace at the end of this lovely Lord's Day, she wondered if they might end up at the big pond where Joseph had taken her several times to ice-skate during their wintry courtship. In fact, one of the times, she'd thought for sure he was going to ask her to marry him. But he'd talked instead about how she'd feel about helping him raise his children. *"I have a ready-made family,"* he'd said with an apprehensive frown.

Rachel had thought it sweet of him to bring that up, but she hadn't realized what a task it would be to win Leroy over, especially. She'd known she loved Joseph that day at the frozen pond, but she also knew that if she married him, she'd be marrying into his family, too. *"Might it be wise for me to spend some time with them?"* she had asked Joseph, starting her journey toward stepmotherhood.

"What are ya thinking 'bout?" Joseph asked now as they rounded the bend, following the path through the underbrush, toward the familiar pond.

She told him.

"Well, it sure seems like Andy and Stephen and Miriam have taken to ya, love," Joseph replied, leading the way to the water. "And aren't Maggie and Grace makin' an effort?"

"The older girls just need a sounding board or an encourager, I think."

"*Jah,* 'specially Maggie."

"I'm tryin' to be sympathetic toward her," she told Joseph, knowing she was no match for Sadie Ann's mother heart. *They're her flesh-and-blood children,* Rachel thought wistfully.

CHAPTER

11

On the afternoon of Maggie's eighteenth birthday, June twenty-sixth, Leroy asked her to ride with him to pick up some cheese from an Amish neighbor three miles away. "Would ya want to?"

"Sure, I'll go." But first she needed to finish dusting her bedroom, having already taken the braided rugs outside to beat on the clothesline before dry mopping the floor. And unfortunately, everything took longer for her.

"I'll wait for ya outdoors, then," Leroy said.

Looking forward to getting out of the house, Maggie took the dust rag out to the front porch and shook it hard, thinking that perhaps Leroy needed to blow off more steam.

As Maggie rode along with her brother, she savored the sights of neighboring farmers in the fields with their mule teams, some with their school-age children out helping, as well.

Leroy broke the peace in the carriage. "There's a spare room at Dawdi Reuben's, ain't?"

"*Jah*, why?"

"I keep wishin' I was old enough to move . . . either there or even farther away."

"Dat would never hear of it." She didn't need to remind him that he was only fourteen and years away from adulthood. "Besides, how would that make Dat feel?"

Leroy shook his head quickly. "He sure didn't consider how his *children* would feel, did he, marrying that woman!"

"Her name is *Rachel*," Maggie said softly, surprised that her brother's anger had escalated to this. "She's our father's wife, *Bruder*."

Leroy's face turned red, but he fell absolutely silent, and Maggie decided it was wisest to say nothing more. It was clear that he was still sorting through the emotions from Mamm's sudden death. And the recent late-night talk hadn't altered his anger one iota.

They passed one large dairy farm after another, and Maggie wondered why they were going so far out of their way just to purchase cheese. Not wanting to ask, lest Leroy erupt again, she tried to relax in the seat as Buster pulled them along, slowly and peacefully, the way she liked it. She hadn't forgotten how tense she'd felt riding in Cousin Luke's shiny new car.

When they arrived, she noticed a homemade sign out front advertising cheese from the Riehl farm. "I'll wait for ya in the carriage," she told him.

"It won't be long." Leroy jumped out of the driver's side, tied the horse to the nearby hitching post, and hurried to the back of the house, out of sight.

He seems mighty eager, Maggie thought.

Sitting there, she thought again of the tent meetings and how they had stirred up such an interest in reading the Scripture, more than ever before. She was glad she'd gone for several reasons—one, very secretly, was the way Glenn Brubaker had treated her. He hadn't shown pity, for one thing. Of course, she would never think of telling Cousin Lila or Grace about *that*. The truth of it was that Glenn seemed genuinely interested in welcoming her and hopeful that she might come back. *A pastoral student must be trained to seek people out,* she thought, remembering what Lila had said.

"Ach, I must be *ferhoodled*," she said aloud, and just in that moment, she glanced up and saw Leroy putting his billfold back into his pants pocket. He was talking to a blond girl, his face animated with a boyish liveliness she hadn't noticed lately. The girl's mother stood nearby. *What on earth?* Maggie leaned forward, squinting into the sunlight. Then she recalled having seen this very girl at market, where she helped her Mamm sell cheese.

Maggie knew not to inquire about the girl, considering Leroy's mood on the way here. And she assumed he wouldn't just come out and volunteer anything, either.

Leroy turned back toward the buggy, moving so fast Maggie almost expected him to break into a run. And just as she'd expected, he was mum as he picked up the driving lines and headed out of the driveway and onto the road again.

Maggie stared out the window, amused by the trek clear over here for two big blocks of cheese. *Puppy love's a-brewin',* she thought, not looking Leroy's way, lest she let out a snicker.

It was a good long time before Leroy made a peep. "Just curious, Maggie. . . . Do ya believe in love at first sight?"

"I've heard of it."

"*Nee*, I'm serious . . . do ya?"

She smiled. "Well, remember what Dat said when he brought Rachel to meet all of us?"

"Honestly, I've tried to forget it." Leroy suddenly looked glum.

Maggie nodded. "'Tween you and me, I felt the same way. It wasn't something I'd ever imagined hearing from Dat. And we were all still grieving so hard, too."

Leroy clammed up again.

"So, love at first sight?" Maggie said. "What do you think 'bout it?"

He turned to her and nodded. "I prob'ly shouldn't say, but that girl ya saw me with back there . . . well, she's the one I'm gonna court someday."

"I feel like I've seen her before," she said. "But remember, you'll meet lots of perty girls in the next few years."

"None as sweet, though . . . not like Joanne Riehl."

Maggie didn't argue; after all, Jimmy Beiler had caught her attention when she, too, was fairly young. "How do ya know her?"

"Oh, from when I've been out and around, runnin' errands for Dat and whatnot. The first time I saw Joanne at the bakery up yonder, I knew she was the girl for me. I just did."

Maggie wasn't so amused now as thoughtful. Leroy was a boy of many talents and as hardworking as the winter was long. And to think he thought he knew his future already at just fourteen. Well, it was unfathomable. "I 'spect you're a prophet, then."

"Go ahead, make fun." Leroy stared at the road. "You'll see."

She let him have the last word.

The closer they came to home, the more Maggie wondered

what it would take for Leroy to accept Dat's new wife. Or would his anger continue to fester until it caused a rift and hurt their father? And Rachel, too?

Leroy surprised her by pulling into the parking lot for the Amish bakery not far from home. "I'll help ya down," he said, then went to tie Buster to the hitching post. "Come, Maggie, it's a surprise treat from me to you."

Pleased at this turn of events, Maggie got out without much trouble. "You definitely are full of tricks."

"Happy eighteenth birthday," Leroy said as he walked with her toward the bakeshop, where two signs were posted: *No Sunday Sales* and *No Photographs Please.*

"I'll keep quiet what ya told me," she said as he reached to open the door for her.

A flash of concern crossed Leroy's face. "About Joanne, or about me wantin' to move away?"

"Both," she answered with what she hoped was a reassuring smile.

CHAPTER

12

A good many of the family were present for Maggie's birthday supper late that afternoon, including Rachel's parents, Gideon and Mary Mae Glick from Myerstown, and Great-aunt Nellie from right next door, minus furry Siggy. Mamm's elderly father, Dawdi Reuben, was too frail to ride over in a carriage from Leola.

Sitting there while everyone looked so jubilant, Maggie had a sneaking suspicion that Dat might have put Leroy up to getting her out of the house so that Rachel, Grace, and Miriam could prepare this out-and-out feast. She noticed the endearing way Dat smiled right at her just now before bowing his head to ask the silent blessing. *A father-daughter moment!* There was roast beef, creamy mashed potatoes, thick gravy, buttered asparagus spears, and Maggie's favorite side dish: lima beans swimming in butter. Chow chow and a large dish of homemade dill pickles completed the mouthwatering offerings. Rachel had used Mamm's nicest dishes for this occasion.

Maggie wondered how Rachel must feel, using Mamm's things—furniture and most everything else in the house. Even the garden trappings included reminders, like the special stepping-stone nestled in the soil, a surprise from Dat to Mamm so long ago. A treasured gift indeed.

Rachel's given up far more than any of us have acknowledged, Maggie realized. *Her own hope chest is up in the attic, collecting dust, while she keeps Mamm's memory at the forefront of our daily lives, using Mamm's things instead of her own.*

Maggie suddenly felt sad, trying to put herself in Rachel's situation, with a family that for the most part only marginally accepted her. On this particular birthday, Maggie wanted to be sure to show her gratitude to Rachel and everyone else present at the table.

The table talk was entertaining, though a little embarrassing. Her great-aunt Nellie shared about the first time she'd laid eyes on newborn Maggie, whom the midwife had declared as "pink and perty" as one could hope for.

Maggie's brothers and sisters were silent, as they usually were with extended family at the table. Adults were expected to conduct the conversation, and Maggie suddenly realized that she, too, was now considered one of them. This knowledge made her smile a little; then she glanced at Grace across the table, knowing she wasn't too far away from this birthday herself. *Less than a year and a half, and we'll be celebrating her eighteenth,* thought Maggie, wishing Mamm could have lived to see them grow into adulthood.

Maggie poured gravy over her meat and mashed potatoes, the way she'd always done since she was little, thinking how sometimes she'd like to go back and relive her childhood, if it were possible. Maggie truly cherished her growing-up years in this farmhouse, especially because of her mother's thoughtful and gentle ways.

"Maggie, tell us your favorite kind of cake," Rachel's mother, Mary Mae, was saying, her eyes dancing mischievously.

"White chocolate with dark chocolate icing," Maggie replied.

"See? Just what I told ya," Aunt Nellie said, grinning at Mary Mae and nodding her head.

Grace exchanged looks with petite Miriam, whose big blue eyes shone. *Definitely in cahoots*, Maggie thought with a smile.

"We did our best to keep the cake a secret," Rachel said with a look at Maggie, then at Grace and Miriam.

"And a *wunnerbaar-gut* secret it is!" Dat said, rubbing his hands together and looking around for the special dessert.

When Rachel carried it to the table on Mamm's beautiful glass cake stand, Rachel asked, "Would ya like to cut the first piece, Maggie?"

It startled her a little, because Mamm had always done it like this. One of Maggie's sisters must have filled Rachel in on that.

Maggie's eyes strayed toward Leroy, whose head was lowered. *He might think Rachel's stealing Mamm's tradition*, she thought, her heart going out to him.

Nevertheless, Maggie agreed to do Rachel's bidding and cut the first piece, and it crossed her mind to offer it to her peeved brother. But knowing that might embarrass him, she offered it to Great-aunt Nellie instead. *Rachel's just trying to be a thoughtful Schtiefmudder. But Leroy's too angry to see it.*

After supper, Cousins Tom and Sally Witmer arrived with their children, bringing three kinds of cookies and a home-made birthday card that Lila had created. They had worn their Sunday clothes to honor Maggie on this landmark birthday.

At this hour, all of them were seated across the back porch, the children perched on the steps, talking and laughing. One of the older Witmer boys, Benny, mentioned that they'd seen an encyclopedia salesman going door to door during the ride over. Maggie pricked up her ears, wondering what Dat would say if such a salesman came by the house.

It wasn't long until Dat and his cousin Tom and all the boys headed out to the stable, and Tom's wife, Sally, along with Rachel, her mother, and Miriam, went for a walk with Sally's youngest girls. Aunt Nellie presented Maggie with a delicate white hankie with pale pink tatting around the edges before going home for the evening, tuckered out. Maggie was so honored and grateful. Meanwhile, the young women stayed behind on the porch, talking about whatever they pleased.

Quickly, the conversation moved to how Lila had run into Jimmy Beiler and his sisters at BB's Grocery Outlet in Quarryville. "We went to stock up on dented canned goods, and they were there, too," Lila said.

Maggie exchanged a glance with Grace. *What's Lila fishing for?*

"So can ya guess the first thing out of Jimmy's mouth?" Lila asked, tilting her head in Maggie's direction.

This was so awkward that Maggie merely shook her head.

"He asked if I'd seen ya lately." Lila grinned. "And, not only that, he wanted to know if I'd be seein' you on your birthday."

He remembered? Not wanting to reply, Maggie only shrugged.

"Jimmy's such a nice fella," Grace said, adding her two cents.

"I agree!" Lila's eyes twinkled.

"Goodness' sake!" Maggie said.

Sighing, Lila looked at Grace, and now it was her turn to shrug.

Lila thinks I'm unreasonable, Maggie thought, but there wasn't anything she would do differently.

Never one to shy away from controversial topics, Grace asked right out, "Will you be goin' to the tent meetings again, Lila?"

Lila gave an eager nod. "My parents can't seem to get enough." Here Lila turned toward Grace. "Just ask Maggie how it sounds when thousands of people lift their voices in worship, all at the same time."

Maggie found herself nodding in agreement. "Lila's right . . . never heard anything like it."

Grace looked at her. "Are *you* thinkin' of going again, Maggie?"

"Not sure," she said, remembering how vulnerable she'd felt sitting with Glenn at the end of the service. It was puzzling, really, her little crush on Glenn.

But Maggie wouldn't let her heart lead her astray; she wasn't a schoolgirl anymore. Besides, Glenn obviously wasn't interested in her that way.

Rachel loved that her parents had come for Maggie's birthday supper. It was a real benefit to visit with Mamm again, to have the chance to walk with her just now behind Miriam and Sally Witmer and her girls, enjoying the early evening breezes.

It was the ideal time of day to walk like this in a group, since the People, for the most part, were having their evening meal.

"You seem real settled, dear," Rachel's mother said as they strolled along barefoot.

"Well, Joseph has certainly paved the way . . . a big help. And the three youngest children have, too."

Slowing her pace, Mamm regarded her. "Are the older girls—"

"We'll talk 'bout that another time," Rachel said, wanting to keep things on a lighter note, since her cherished visits with Mamm were few and far between. "All right?"

Mamm nodded. "You look so radiant. Still a blushin' bride."

"Well, I love Joseph dearly," Rachel replied.

"Quite obvious." Mamm smiled at her and reached for her hand.

They walked that way for the longest time, before they all turned around and headed back to the house.

Once Rachel and her mother returned from walking with Sally and the others, Maggie knew she must change her position and get up from the porch rocker. Walking stiffly, she picked up her portable seat cushion and headed indoors with Grace while Cousin Lila stayed on the porch with her mother and sisters and Miriam. Maggie could hear them talking and the younger girls giggling through the kitchen window where she stood for a while, just staring at the sky.

She couldn't help but wonder about Jimmy, considering what Lila had said about Maggie's birthday. That, and seeking her out prior to baptismal instruction, made Maggie think of asking Grace if Jimmy was seeing Cousin Deborah or not.

CHAPTER

13

After the Witmers and Rachel's parents said their good-byes, Dat approached Maggie about going to visit Dawdi Reuben in a few minutes. "I've already planned for a driver," he said, still wearing what he'd worn for the birthday supper—his best black trousers and white shirt and black vest, like he was going to Preaching.

"Will you be goin', too?" Maggie asked, glad for this opportunity.

"Oh *jah*."

Maggie wondered if any of her siblings would also be joining them, but she didn't ask, thinking Dat might want to talk with her alone. And she was right, because not long after the driver turned out of the long lane onto Olde Mill Road to head toward Leola, her father began to mention in *Deitsch* the note she'd left for Rachel last Thursday evening.

"Well, I didn't want to just sneak out," Maggie told him as they sat in the second row of the passenger van.

"Did ya think I'd disapprove?" Her father frowned.

She shrugged. "I wasn't sure."

He was quiet for a moment, then asked, "What's so compelling, daughter, 'bout these meetings?"

"Have ya heard anything from others who've attended?" she asked.

"Some. It's all over the papers now, too. But it wondered me what's caught *your* fancy."

Maggie tried to put into words the fervor she'd felt, the intense draw to return. And that she'd fallen in love with the Lord Jesus. "You simply must see for yourself." Maggie paused, not sure she should ask. "Have ya thought of it?"

"Going to a Mennonite meeting?" Dat chuckled and shook his head. "Do ya feel pressured by Luke and Lila to go?" he asked unexpectedly.

"*Nee*, I went the first time 'cause of Lila's enthusiasm, but now it's about my own yearning. The singing, the preachin' . . . it's given me such hope, Dat."

He listened, nodding his head as they rode. Maggie was glad that it was just the two of them; it was unusual that there were no other passengers to pick up.

"But you don't have to worry," she said. "I doubt I'll be goin' back." No sooner had she uttered the words than she experienced a sinking feeling. *Do I really want to quit going?*

"Well, if ya go again, let me know before you take off . . . no disappearing next time. Keep in mind, Rachel didn't discover the note till hours later, so I know she was fretting."

"It was the wrong way to handle things, and I'm sorry."

Her father was quiet from then on until they arrived at their destination and were greeted by a happily surprised grandfather. Dawdi Reuben opened the door of his little *Dawdi Haus* and welcomed them inside.

Because Dawdi Reuben was her mother's father, Maggie wondered if this visit would dredge up the pain of this first of her birthdays without Mamm.

"Mighty nice to see ya, Maggie-bird," Dawdi said, tears glistening in his pale gray eyes. He glanced at her cane, surely noticing how she struggled to get around, but to her relief, he said nothing. "How's your birthday been so far?"

She nodded, delighted to sit down with him in the front room, her father taking a place on the settee and letting Maggie have the chair next to Dawdi Reuben's old worn-out one. "Seein' you is the topping on the cake," she said, glad Rachel had sent over a generous leftover piece, wrapped in tinfoil. "Here's a nice sample for ya." She handed it to him, and his thick eyebrows flew up.

"Well now, ain't that somethin'." His hand trembled slightly as he accepted it, looking down at the large slice. "How's the family doin'?" he asked, lifting his eyes to hers.

She recited off all of her siblings and what each had been keeping busy with—all the individual chores around the house and farm. Things Dawdi Reuben knew from other visits, of course, but she repeated them anyway, because he seemed to enjoy it. She did not mention going to the tent meetings, however, nor Leroy's insolent behavior.

"And Rachel?" he asked. "Is she settling in with all of yous? I prob'ly ask this every time I see yous . . . sorry."

Dat was quick to say that Rachel was doing very well, indeed.

"Rachel surprised me with the nicest birthday supper," Maggie shared, having profusely thanked Rachel when everyone left. "And we'll be makin' strawberry jam tomorrow with Aunt Nellie," she added.

"Ah, I can just imagine the smell," Dawdi said, bobbing

his head slowly, as if remembering the days when *Mammi* was alive and they lived in the big house next door. "Will Nellie's cat be around?"

"Oh, she'll leave Siggy at home."

"Seems odd to have a cat inside, *ain't?*" Dawdi laughed right out loud. "I don't see how Nellie manages with cat hair in her food."

Now Dat was laughing, too. "'Tis a real mystery for a woman who is so, what shall I say . . ."

"Neat as a pin?" Maggie offered.

Dat snapped his fingers. "That's it!"

Maggie grinned. "Aunt Nellie's never a bother about that, though. She's so easy to be around. Did ya know that she has a daily life goal?"

Both men seemed more attentive. "Do I know 'bout this?" Dawdi asked, leaning forward slightly.

"I think we all do, if we stop and think about it. Her goal is to make one person smile every single day."

"Ambitious, for certain," Dat said approvingly.

Dawdi Reuben shook his head. "I should've guessed."

"Speaking of goals." Dat then began to share something he'd recently read in *The Budget*. "An Amish scribe from Mercer County wrote that he tries to remember each day that God won't guide his footsteps unless he's willin' to move his feet."

"Ah, now that's real *gut!*" Dawdi said, looking down at his own bare feet. "And the older I get, the more I oughta remember that."

Dat continued. "I also read this from a scribe in Kalona, Iowa: 'If you want to make both ends meet, you have to take some out of the middle,'" he said. "That's sage advice, if you ask me."

Dawdi's fluffy white beard moved along with his laughter. "*Ach*, if only my eyes were stronger. I can't see *gut* enough to read no more—sure do miss readin' *The Budget*."

Dat kept the laughter aloft by telling how Andy and Stephen had worked together the other day to try and catch pigs for auction. "It was a learnin' experience for them. After a rough start, Andy decided he'd do his part by using the barn broom, swatting 'em into the truck chute."

"Well, s'pose that's one way to do it," Dawdi said, shaking his head, clearly enjoying the free-flowing chatter.

Maggie reached for the slice of cake on Dawdi's lap. "Would ya like this on a plate, maybe?"

"Oh, I'll just use my fingers."

Maggie grinned, half expecting his response. And by the time he was finished, his white beard was speckled with cake crumbs and dark icing. "Should've given ya some ice cream with it," she said suddenly. "Do ya have any?"

"I ate what was left yesterday," Dawdi admitted, looking comically sad.

"We'll bring some more for ya next time we come," Dat assured him.

"*Denki*, I'll look forward to it," Dawdi said, scrunching up his face to inspect his beard and proceeding to pick out the crumbs . . . popping them into his mouth. Then, turning to Maggie, he again wished her a happy birthday. "You made this ol' man right pleased, hope ya know."

"Always nice to see ya, Dawdi." She reached over to pat his wrinkled hand.

Before the driver returned, Onkel Zeke, Aendi Barbieann, and the cousins who still lived at home—two girls and three boys—came over to say hullo. Barbieann kissed Maggie's cheek, and the girls—Nancy and Linda, sixteen and fourteen—offered cheerful birthday greetings, as well, and asked Maggie how she was doing. They also inquired about Grace.

Maggie didn't divulge that Grace had a beau, but she did talk about how much fun it was to be in *Rumschpringe* with her close-in-age sister.

"We'll see Gracie and your whole family durin' apple-pickin' time," Nancy said, her blue eyes shining as they brought kitchen chairs into the sitting area to make a semicircle. "We'll get to visit ya then, for sure."

"And we'll all go to the orchard not far from your house," Linda added, clasping her hands together.

"It'll certainly be fun." Maggie meant it, though she could only hope she might feel up to participating. Even if not, she would eagerly anticipate their visit. "Yous don't get over to our neck of the woods very often anymore."

"I know," Nancy replied with a grimace. "Maybe as time passes, ya know, we will again."

Maggie understood and was grateful for Nancy's sensitivity in not spelling out what she was likely thinking—that since Maggie's father had remarried so quickly, it would take some time yet. *Aendi Barbieann and Mamm were so close,* she thought. *Not in age, but in heart.*

They talked about many things, including the mosquito spray their father, Zeke, had concocted. "He sprays it all over himself and our brothers before goin' to the fields," Linda said, her voice low so as not to interrupt her father talking with Maggie's Dat and Dawdi Reuben. "It must work, 'cause he's not gettin' all bit up like before."

Maggie had to laugh. "Maybe he should make a big batch of it to sell."

Nancy nodded. "Oh, he's threatened that, all right."

They laughed together now, and Maggie's boy cousins—Zeke Jr., Josiah, and Curly Thomas—nodded their heads, grinning.

How Maggie loved seeing her cousins on her mother's side! There was something so special about sitting with these family members who had been such a big part of her life before Dat married Rachel. But lest she think on that too much, she quietly brought up the tent meetings. "Have ya heard of them?"

"Oh *jah*, and our oldest brother, Mel, even went one time, just to see what it was all about," Linda said, her voice nearly a whisper now.

"What did he think?"

"Well, you'd have to ask him," Linda said with a glance at her father to be sure this conversation wasn't being overheard. "He did say there were lots of people there."

Maggie nodded. "For sure," she whispered, revealing that she'd gone and couldn't stop thinking about the sermons.

"You were allowed?" Nancy asked, eyes wide.

Maggie put her finger to her lips. "That's a long story."

Both Nancy and Linda caught on and changed the subject to what vegetables they had been canning this week.

Later, before saying good-bye, Nancy and Linda promised to write, and Maggie was tickled to hear it. "I'd love that . . . so would Gracie."

"It's a *gut* plan, then," Nancy said, smiling and walking with Maggie to the door.

On the way home, Maggie couldn't help but be thankful that Dawdi Reuben lived right next door to Barbieann and family; otherwise, he would be very lonely indeed.

Back home, Maggie settled into a chair in the front room as her father began the evening Bible reading, later than normal. Andy and Stephen sat side by side on the floor like peanut butter and jelly, and Leroy perched over near where the breeze came through the screen door. Miriam, meanwhile, leaned in next to Rachel, and Grace rested on the settee on the far side of the room, paying close attention to Dat in his rocking chair. Looking around at her dear ones, Maggie was glad to be home. Not out shoulder to shoulder with so many at the tent revival, where she'd had to be extra careful not to lose her balance while using her cane.

She thought of Glenn's eagerness to share the account of his healing with her, and a sigh rose up. *I'm content right here,* she told herself.

Bedtime arrived with the sense that Rachel had done everything in her power to make Maggie's birthday special. She'd even asked Joseph beforehand if she'd overlooked anything that might bring Maggie joy. All the same, it had surprised her somewhat to hear Maggie practically gush her gratitude after the guests had gone their way. Was it a reflection of the way Joseph and Sadie Ann had raised her?

Thinking of it now, she did not want to question Maggie's motives. Surely her appreciation had been genuine, even if her thanks had been different from the way a daughter would typically thank her mother.

As Rachel brushed her hair in front of the dresser, she could see Joseph's reflection in the mirror. He was sitting in his favorite chair, *The Budget* open in his lap.

Seeing him so relaxed made her happy. She was glad Joseph

could smile again after suffering the loss of his first bride. Rachel hadn't forgotten Joseph's confiding in her after their third date how surprised he was to be falling for someone so soon after Sadie Ann's passing.

Mamm said I seemed so happy during our walk earlier, thought Rachel while dressing for bed.

Thinking of that lovely stroll and the chance to visit with her mother again made Rachel feel as content as dear Joseph looked. Her homesickness had subsided, at least for now.

My life is here, she thought, *with my husband and his children.*

But something in her yearned for her own babies with Joseph.

CHAPTER
14

Strawberry picking began immediately after an early break-fast the next morning. The sun was still low in the sky and the leaves dewy, but Rachel insisted Maggie not help with the harvesting. Instead, she asked the boys to join them in the mounded rows. And after a time, Aunt Nellie wandered outside, as well, wearing a blue bandanna to keep the sun off her neck.

Leroy kept to himself, Rachel noticed, though he did occasionally speak to his brothers. For the most part, though, he was a silent worker—and quick.

When all the ripe berries were picked, Grace and Miriam took them inside to wash in cold water on one side of the double sink while Maggie hulled the cleaned ones at the table with Nellie. Rachel got the large kettle ready to layer the prepared berries, then sugar, followed by another layer of strawberries and sugar, until they were all used up.

When it was time to make the noon meal, they set aside the strawberries to wait for the sugar to dissolve, then cooked them slowly on low heat for twenty minutes. Finally, Rachel poured the large quantity of sugary strawberries into an enormous bowl to sit until tomorrow morning, when the work of filling and sealing jars would begin.

After they'd eaten, Rachel served cold meadow tea to the girls and Nellie, who'd stayed around for the meal. *And for the fellowship, too,* Rachel thought. The five of them were sipping the cold tea when they all heard a loud crash come from outside, like the sound of shattering glass.

"*Was is letz?*" Nellie said, going to the back screen door and looking out.

There was a series of loud meows, and Rachel got up quickly to look out the door, the girls close behind her, Maggie moving more slowly than her sisters.

"Well, lookee there . . . Siggy's got himself a glass collar," Nellie remarked, pointing.

"He must've put his head in the Mason jar Miriam was carryin' around earlier," Rachel said, peering out at the strange sight. She recalled Miriam had been feeding corn kernels to the birds, and the girl must have left the jar out with a few kernels inside. "Poor Siggy prob'ly couldn't breathe. Good thing he broke the jar and got free."

Nellie led the way out the door, shaking her head. "*Puh!* That cat!"

When they got to Siggy, he was still meowing and jerking about, trying to get the rim of the jar off his neck. Rachel noticed a few corn kernels in the largest piece of the broken jar, on the ground nearby. "He was after the corn," she observed.

"Such a silly cat," Nellie said. "I just hope Siggy doesn't cut himself on the jagged glass. He's lucky he's still okay."

By now, Andy and Stephen had come running to see about

the commotion. Andy's eyes looked like they might pop when he saw Siggy's predicament. "Go an' get Leroy," Andy told his brother. "Tell him to bring Dat's hammer right quick."

Stephen dashed back to the barn, and pretty soon Leroy arrived, walking briskly.

"What's going on?" he asked.

Rachel was quick to explain, but Leroy did not respond. Rather, he removed his blue paisley kerchief from his pocket and carefully slipped it between the sharp glass and the cat's neck. "You'll be all right. Just hold real still," Leroy told Siggy quietly as he raised the hammer.

With a single tap, the glass broke, and Siggy zipped away across the yard.

Andy and Stephen laughed and jabbered in *Deitsch* about what they'd just seen; Rachel suspected it was a story they'd share many times with their friends.

"*Denki*, Leroy, for savin' a cat with more than nine lives." Nellie clasped her hands against her bosom. "Such a helpful young man."

Leroy smiled amiably and bobbed his head, then took his hammer and returned to the barn.

Rachel wished that one day Leroy might smile at her like that.

Sighing, she thought, *What more can I do, Lord?*

The nesting robin Maggie had recently seen began to sing at four o'clock the next morning. Beautiful as the sound was, Maggie groaned and rolled slowly onto her back, listening in the predawn darkness of her room. *So close to my window*, she thought with a yawn, still exhausted. Most days, she woke up feeling downright tired, and it took an hour or more for her to fully wake.

Still, the robin's vibrant call kept her from falling back to sleep. And imagining all the pretty little eggs beneath the jovial robin reminded Maggie of how much happiness must surely come from bringing life into the world. *Something I'll never know.*

Even so, she prayed for God's will to be done this day in all of their lives. And she prayed for those who would be flocking to the tent meetings each night for the duration of the revival, seeking forgiveness from sin and a new life in Christ Jesus. She recalled Preacher Brubaker passionately stating that nothing was more critical in the eyes of the Lord than a lost soul being found, like that one lost sheep. The memory of the yearning on so many faces was just beneath the surface of Maggie's thoughts. And even though she was already a follower of Christ, she wondered how those people had felt as they made their way to the altar to proclaim their faith in their Savior and make Him the Lord of their life. The thought gave her pause. Had she completely surrendered her own life and will to Him? What might that mean for her, with her Old Order life and beliefs?

Along with all of that, she had been pondering Glenn's declaration that he had been healed, still wishing she knew how it had come about. He seemed so healthy.

Will I be healed, too . . . someday? she wondered.

Lately, these questions had kept her awake nearly every night.

By midmorning her stepmother had stocked the cookstove with firewood and was ready to get the water boiling for the jam-filled canning jars. Aunt Nellie had been feeling a bit tired, so they missed having her fun-loving presence around to finish up the jam-making process.

I'll go an' check on her later, Maggie decided, wanting to ask about one of Mamm's oldest quilts, one she'd recently found at the bottom of the oak chest in her room. *Aunt Nellie might know when it was made and by who.*

Maggie also wanted to ask Nellie some questions about things she'd read in the New Testament. Mamm had sometimes spoken with Nellie about certain verses, too, though not because Nellie was more knowledgeable than anyone else amongst the People. She was just someone who could be trusted to listen without questioning . . . or judging.

After the noon meal, while the dishes were being washed, Rachel urged Maggie to go and rest for a while. Thankful for this, Maggie left for her bedroom and sat on the bed, the rag rug coarse and bumpy beneath her bare feet. She sighed. *If only that robin's song hadn't been quite so early,* she thought as she lowered herself onto the summer quilt.

Within less than a minute, Aunt Nellie's fluffy cat crept into the room. Siggy rarely wandered through the connecting hallway into the main house, but here he was, and meowing, too, as if to announce himself.

Maggie had to smile as she looked down at the cat. "Are ya lost, little boy?" she whispered. But she was too worn out to get up and carry him back to Aunt Nellie's, so when Siggy stretched and yawned, then settled onto the rag rug, purring loudly, Maggie let him stay. Soon he was asleep, his tiny nose frequently twitching.

He'll be fine for now, she thought, smiling. And before long, she gave in to drowsiness, too.

In the kitchen, Rachel asked young Miriam to double-check the number of pint jars cooling on the counter before Rachel left with a batch of homemade ice cream for Nellie. *The ice cream helped to cheer up Ruth*, she thought, glad to do this for Nellie, as well.

At Nellie's back door, she knocked and waited. Noticing through the screen door that no one was in sight, she pushed open the door and slipped inside without a word, in case Nellie was resting. There, she placed the container in the icebox, then left quietly.

On her way back to the main house, Rachel noticed Aunt Nellie peering under the large juniper bush. "What are ya lookin' for?" she asked, going across the yard to her, surprised.

"Well, Siggy. He's never disappeared like this before." Nellie looked worried and pale.

"I'll help ya search." Rachel wondered if he'd somehow gotten trapped inside the closed potting shed, but she checked and saw nothing of Siggy amongst the clay pots and trowels.

Just then, Andy came out to get water at the well for the hen house. "Are ya lookin' for somethin'?" he asked Rachel.

"My Siggy's missin'," Aunt Nellie informed him right quick. "Have ya seen him?"

With a frown, Andy shook his head. "*Ach*, he's round here somewhere."

Nellie nodded and wiped her face with a handkerchief she'd pulled from her pocket. "Will ya help us look?"

"Soon as I water the chickens," Andy said. "I'll tell Stephen to come, too."

"For goodness' sake!" Nellie said, fanning her face with the hem of her long apron. "It's not like Siegfried to do such a thing." She sat down on the wooden bench near the big shade tree in the backyard. "I think I need to catch my breath . . . maybe ask *Gott* for help."

"You go right ahead." Rachel hurried over and looked under the latticework beneath the back porch, calling for the missing cat. "Where are ya, Siggy boy?"

Hearing a voice outside her window, calling for Siggy, Maggie awoke with a start. She turned to look on the floor where the cat had been sleeping, but he was gone. Sitting up in bed, she murmured, "*Ach*, where'd he go?"

Maggie reached for her cane and made her way to the kitchen. When she stepped out the side door, she saw Rachel and Aunt Nellie in the backyard in a huddle with Andy and Stephen.

"Lookin' for Siggy?" she asked.

"Have ya seen him?" Aunt Nellie asked, moving this way, her face pinched into a frown.

Maggie admitted that Siggy had wandered into her room and slept on the rug. "But when I woke up, he wasn't there."

Aunt Nellie's face broke into a grin. "Well then, he's prob'ly wandered back home."

Andy and Stephen raced each other to the *Dawdi Haus*, and before Nellie and Rachel could even get across the yard, the boys came back outside, grinning. "We found him!" Andy hollered.

"Thank the dear Lord," Aunt Nellie said right out.

Maggie took her time walking across the yard to Nellie's, but when she stepped inside the small home, she apologized.

"If only I'd gotten up and brought Siggy back the minute he came to my room, I could've spared ya." She looked at poor Nellie's overheated face.

"Now, don't fret, Maggie-bird," Aunt Nellie said, shaking her head. "Siggy must love ya a lot to seek you out like that. To tell the truth, it's kinda sweet."

"They even had a nap together!" Stephen declared with a big smile. "*Jah*, a cat nap."

All of them had a good, hearty laugh. But when Maggie glanced outside, she could see Leroy peering out the barn door, looking mighty curious . . . and perhaps a little sad.

Like he feels left out. . . .

CHAPTER

15

When Rachel and the boys left, Maggie stayed around to talk with Aunt Nellie in her cozy kitchen, replete with pale blue and yellow accents and more knickknacks than Mamm had ever owned. Decorative plates were on display inside the corner cupboard behind the small table, and dish towels in blues and yellows, too. With similar colors, the quilted placemats on the table added to the cheerfulness.

"I think Siggy must've sensed you weren't feelin' so well today," Aunt Nellie said, looking at Maggie affectionately from across the small kitchen table, near the open windows. "Pets seem to know when comfort's needed."

"Hadn't thought of that," Maggie said. "Somehow he found his way to my room."

"Like I said . . ." Nellie smiled.

"I love Siggy, but he's not much for cuddlin'." Maggie wished the cat would sit still on her lap like he did with Aunt Nellie. "Oh, and while we're talkin', I want to ask 'bout an old quilt I found in Mamm's blanket chest the other day. I've never seen it before." Maggie went on to describe the Sixteen-Patch pattern done in plain-weave cotton. "The colors are muted, but not just from age, I don't think."

"Most likely that was the style of the era when it was made," Nellie suggested.

"Would ya like to see it sometime?" Maggie asked.

Nellie's face lit up. "How 'bout right now?"

Maggie was pleased and—at least for now—dismissed the idea of discussing a few Scripture verses, as well. "Let's be sure Siggy stays put, *jah*?" She closed the door to Nellie's place before they headed into the interior hallway that led to the front room in the main farmhouse.

In Maggie's room, the two of them carefully removed the quilt in question from the chest at the foot of her bed. They placed it flat on top of the summer quilt already on the bed, and Aunt Nellie began to examine every square and small block, fingering the stitching. Leaning closer and squinting, she murmured to herself. "Well now," she said at last. "It's been many a year since I laid eyes on this special quilt."

"So you recognize it?" Maggie was thrilled.

"It was made for my Mamm back when she was sick for months on end. My father's mother and six of my aunts worked together on it—and with every stitch, they prayed for Mamm's healing."

A genuine family heirloom, Maggie thought, pleased as pie. "How old would it be?"

"Well, Mamm was married in 1864, and I was seven when she fell ill." Aunt Nellie gave her a little grin. "Can you do the arithmetic in your head? Remember, I'm the firstborn."

"Born two years after your parents married?"

"Eighteen months, to be precise."

Maggie closed her eyes and thought hard. "I'm guessin' it's seventy-eight years old."

Aunt Nellie nodded. "That's right, dear. And since it was in your Mamm's lovely blanket chest—however it ended up here—I say you keep it for when you set up housekeeping someday."

Maggie's breath caught in her throat. *But I won't be marrying,* she thought.

"What's a-matter?" Aunt Nellie asked. "Your face just fell like a half-baked cake."

Maggie couldn't resist a smile. "Young men want strong wives, ya know. I doubt I'll be marryin' any time soon. If at all."

"*Puh!* That's up to the Lord, ain't so?" Aunt Nellie touched the quilt lovingly. "It was my Mammi Yoder's idea to make this. Her husband was one of the preachers here in Lancaster County back in her day. Dawdi Yoder believed strongly in praying daily for God's will. And for His healing touch, too." Nellie's eyes glimmered at the corners.

"Your Dawdi was a preacher?"

"Many decades ago." Nellie nodded her head. "Back then prayer for the sick wasn't talked about much in our circles. It still ain't." She looked back at the quilt. "Have ya ever read James, chapter five, verse fourteen, Maggie-bird?"

Do I know the verse in James? Maggie wondered. She must have looked like she was pondering this very thing, because right then Nellie began to recite the Scripture about anyone who was ill going to the church elders to be anointed with oil, followed by prayer for healing.

Maggie was surprised to know this was in the New Testament. And in that moment, she wished again for the opportunity to hear the rest of Glenn Brubaker's story. Had someone prayed for him in this way? She'd never heard of prayers for healing being offered by anyone amongst the People. Even at her mother's bedside, they had just prayed silently for God's will to be done.

Knowing its story, Maggie admired this wonderful old quilt all the more, with its unusual soft gray, cream, yellow, and cherry-colored blocks. She couldn't help thinking that the Lord must have let her stumble upon it. *So I could hear Aunt Nellie's inspiring story.*

That night, when she was ready for bed, Maggie replaced the summer quilt with the heirloom Sixteen-Patch quilt, which she had aired on the clothesline the rest of the day. *A comfort quilt*, Maggie thought as she nestled down to read the verse Aunt Nellie had mentioned in James. She read it several times, and after she had prayed her silent rote prayers, Maggie offered thanks to God for answering the quilters' prayers and healing Nellie's mother all those years ago.

She got up and put out the lantern and hobbled back to bed, wondering why the sovereign God and heavenly Father chose to heal some people and not others.

The mules in the barn must have heard it in the distance before Rachel and her husband ever did—the stark, abrupt smack of thunder. The air was still outside their open bedroom windows, oppressive and damp. The very next moment, a sudden wind kicked up, howling past the eaves and sending dust spitting against the north side of the old stable.

Joseph rose from his chair and hurried to the windows to close them. "Once the rain's over, I'll open them again to let in some cooler air." He mentioned that too much rain might put a damper on the Bird-in-Hand Fire Company Carriage and Antique Auction tomorrow. "Wish I could go, but work comes first," he said.

"I wonder if I shouldn't go down and close the first-floor windows. They're all wide open," Rachel said, moving toward the hallway.

Downstairs, she made her way quietly to the kitchen, then to the middle and front rooms, going through the house to lower all the windows. At last, she slipped by Maggie's little haven and saw her closing her window. She could hear her murmuring, evidently in pain, and once again Rachel felt sorry for her.

Surely something could help her, Rachel thought as she made her way back upstairs to Joseph. "Maggie was closing her window," she told him.

"Still up at this hour?" he said, settled now in his chair.

"The whistlin' wind must've bothered her." Rachel began to pull her hair back into a loose ponytail. "Like father, like daughter."

"Well, she's more like her mother, really." Joseph looked over at Rachel.

"And the boys . . . they're like you, *jah?*" Rachel went to their bed and sat there, aware of how stuffy it was already getting with the windows closed. She left the sheet and quilt folded below her feet.

"I see some of myself in all my children, but Leroy's the most like me, odd as that may seem." Joseph drew a deep breath. "He's hardworking and leaves no stone unturned to get what he's strivin' for."

Rachel leaned against the headboard.

"But I'm more concerned now than before about how he's been acting, even toward me, here lately. I plan to take him fishin' Saturday morning. Something's gnawing at him, and I'm going to get to the bottom of it."

"What if it fans the flame?" Rachel asked, concerned.

"*Ach*, can't get much worse. Can it?"

Rachel wasn't going to say more. Joseph's decisions about his children were up to him. Still, she feared further upheaval from Leroy, whose perpetual scowl was all too obvious.

"I'll make sure he knows how much I love him, too," Joseph said quietly.

"*Jah, des gut*," Rachel was quick to agree.

On Saturday morning after breakfast, Rachel, Grace, and Miriam left for market to sell many of the pint jars of strawberry jam, leaving Maggie home, as was her wish. Since she was feeling more energetic today, she decided to get word to cousins Luke and Lila about going with them to the tent meeting that evening. But because Dat and Leroy had gone fishing, just the two of them, she would have to wait to honor her promise to Dat first, before sending Andy or Stephen over with the pony cart so that Luke and Lila would know to pick her up.

Meanwhile, Maggie baked two strawberry pies for supper—one to share with Aunt Nellie. And as she worked, she read one verse after another, many of them about the healing miracles of Jesus. She could scarcely stay away from the Good Book, so she kept it lying open on the counter as she baked.

Before the noon meal, Aunt Nellie brought over tuna salad sandwiches and a macaroni salad, which made putting together a meal for Dat and her brothers very easy. Rachel and the girls wouldn't be back from market till late afternoon, as was typical.

Like always, Dat sat at the head of the table and bowed his head to ask the silent blessing. Once everyone had food on their plates, Dat began to tell about the four fish he and Leroy had caught and tossed back.

Maggie had been curious about the lack of fresh fish to clean and fry, but there were times when her father just enjoyed fishing for the relaxation of it, and by the look on Leroy's face, this had been one of those times. Leroy's scowl had disappeared, and he looked as pleasant as before Mamm had become so weak and ill.

"The rain of the past couple nights soaked the ground real *gut*," Leroy said, holding the second half of his sandwich near his mouth. "It was still *glodsick* out in the pasture."

Andy nodded and grinned. "Soggy's right!"

Stephen pulled a face. "My feet got stuck deep in a suck hole when we were roundin' up the mules, an' Andy had to pull me out."

"I thought he was sinkin' clear away to China," Andy added.

"Oh now, boys," Dat said, reaching for his coffee cup.

It looked to Maggie as if they'd washed off at the pump before coming inside. Mamm had taught them well. "*Gut* thing ya weren't wearin' work boots," she said.

"That's for sure." Dat grinned at Leroy now, who smiled back.

Maybe the worst is past, thought Maggie, hoping so. *What did Dat say to Leroy while they were out fishing?*

CHAPTER

16

Maggie's brothers hurried back to the stable to continue cleaning out the horse stalls, but before Dat left to join them, she shared her plan to attend the tent meeting again that evening. "I just wanted to tell ya this time."

Dat paused a moment before letting out a sort of groan. "At least we'll know where you are," he said as he stood in the kitchen doorway, his eyes serious.

He's displeased, she thought as he headed out to the stable. Because of this, she decided not to ask to use the pony cart to get word to her Witmer cousins. *I'll see if Leroy will run over there once he's done working,* she thought.

As it turned out, Lillian Beiler, Jimmy's mother, dropped by an hour later to bring some homemade doughnuts. "I made an extra batch," Lillian said, dressed in a bright green dress and matching cape and long black apron.

Lillian surely knew that Rachel and the younger girls were still at market, so it seemed like her way to be able to visit with just Maggie. "Would ya like to sit and have some iced meadow tea?" Maggie asked, feeling as awkward as she had when seeing Jimmy's mother at the fabric store.

"Sounds delicious," Lillian said, her face beaming. "I won't stay long, since I'm headed to see my sister down the road a ways."

"How far's that?" Maggie asked, curious if maybe Lillian might stop in at Witmers' for her.

"Oh, three miles or so."

Nervous about asking, Maggie said, "Would ya mind takin' a note to my Mennonite cousins for me?"

Lillian shook her head. "It's right on the way."

"It would be a big help," Maggie said, reminding herself as she went to the refrigerator for the pitcher of meadow tea that she needed to actually write the note. "Hope ya like your tea sweetened . . . we sure do."

"Honestly, I'm partial to sugar." Lillian laughed and sat down with a great sigh right where Rachel always sat. *Mamm's old spot . . .*

Maggie shuffled to the cupboard and poured the tea into two tumblers, then carried them slowly to the table, where she sat across from Lillian.

They sipped their tea, and Lillian wiped her brow and cheeks with her hankie, then slipped it back under her sleeve. "Our neighbors had a lengthy visit the other day from a man sellin' encyclopedias," Lillian told her. "Can ya imagine?"

"I'm sure there's plenty to learn from those." Maggie smiled. "Did your neighbors purchase a set?"

Lillian laughed and waved it off. "I guess the wife was actually interested, but the husband thought it was against the *Ordnung.* So 'tween the two of them, they started tossin' round the idea of buying a set and sharin' it with all us neighbors."

"Like a lending library?" Maggie thought this was an amusing way to get around the church ordinance, especially if they were providing the learning for *Englischers*. "So what happened?"

"I guess the deacon dropped by for coffee, and the husband sent the door-to-door salesman on his way right quick, much to the poor fella's disappointment. He was that close to sealin' the deal."

Maggie shook her head. She could just imagine the situation. "Guess we oughta be ready in case that salesman drops by here."

Lillian nodded. "'Tis *schmaert* not to even invite him in. My husband says that people end up buyin' just to get the salesman on his way." Now she was laughing, her hand on her chest.

Maggie had never known Lillian to be quite so frank—or so humorous.

Before Lillian rose to leave, Maggie scribbled off a note to Cousin Lila. She thanked Lillian very much for the doughnuts and for stopping by. "I'll let Rachel and my sisters know they missed ya."

"You do that, dear. Have yourself a nice afternoon!" With a smile, Lillian took the note and headed out to her horse and buggy.

By now, Maggie was thankful for the empty house. She went to her room to rest up for her evening at the revival meeting. Opening her Bible on the "comfort quilt," she read all of James again, rereading chapter one, verse four, twice: *But let patience have her perfect work, that ye may be perfect and entire, wanting nothing.*

Sighing, she leaned back on the pillow and wondered if she might ever be perfect and whole. *How much longer must I be patient? For a lifetime?*

When she dozed off, Maggie dreamed she was a young girl again, running lickety-split up the road toward the old mill to meet her father, his strong arms wide open to her as she hurried toward him. *"Dat!"* she called. *"Let's skip home to Mamm and Gracie and Leroy and baby Andy, okay?"*

"All the way home?" Dat said in the dream.

"If ya want to," little Maggie said, laughing.

"Like this?" He skipped all wobbly, just for fun.

In the dream, she giggled. *"Don't forget to whistle, too!"*

A doughy scent caught Rachel's attention as she and the girls walked into the kitchen. There on the counter, she noticed two pies and a big batch of doughnuts. *Ach, how did Maggie manage to do all this?* she thought.

Then, seeing two tumblers near the sink, Rachel realized someone had come by. Perhaps that person had brought the doughnuts, which were in an unfamiliar basket.

But who?

She cautioned Grace and Miriam to keep their voices low, lest they wake Maggie. "She might be resting."

"I'll check," Miriam said, walking out of the kitchen toward Maggie's room.

"We sure sold lots of jam today," Grace said in a near whisper.

"Honestly, if we'd had a few dozen more pints, I think we would've sold them, too," Rachel said, thankful that more berries were coming on in the patch out back. She loved gathering berries, especially in the early morning when the air was cool and fresh.

Miriam hurried back on tiptoe. "Maggie's sound asleep, her Bible next to her."

Rachel, too, had noticed this pattern for several days now—Maggie's interest in reading the Good Book almost night and day. No one Rachel knew had ever spent so much time doing so. "We'll let her rest a while longer" was all she said to Miriam's comment.

"I wonder who made these giant gooey doughnuts," Miriam said, removing the plastic wrap and choosing one, then eyeing Rachel. "It won't spoil my supper, I promise."

Rachel smiled. "We'll just see 'bout that."

Miriam opened her mouth wide and took a bite. "Ooh, is this *wunnerbaar-gut!*" she said, holding the sticky doughnut up to Grace, who was counting the market money at the table. "Here, see for yourself," Miriam insisted.

Evidently Grace didn't have to be asked twice. She reached for Miriam's doughnut and bit right into it, her eyes suddenly wide, and then, just that quick, she took another bite. "They're so good—they must've been fried in lard," Grace said, shaking her head as she chewed. "*Ach*, get these out of my sight!"

Now Miriam was giggling, and they all had to cover their mouths to keep the laughter in.

⁂

The evening had cooled off pleasantly, and Maggie enjoyed the breezes flowing through the tent, where she sat with Cousin Lila in the first row. They'd come extra early because of the swelling crowds, securing enough seats for her and Lila, as well as for Lila's parents and their four younger children. Upon arriving, Luke had immediately disappeared, eager to assist wherever needed.

Maggie had seen others carrying their Bibles, some looking up the verses from Preacher Brubaker's sermon. She'd brought hers again, too, having placed bookmarks in a number of spots where she had been rereading since she was last there. She'd even seen Rachel curiously peering into her room as she did so, but Maggie hadn't attempted to hide her desire for Scripture. Why should she?

After the congregational singing and the offering, it was time for testimonies. A young woman about Rachel's age went to the platform and began to tell of beginning her new life in Christ . . . and of her new outlook. And, since confessing her sins at the altar ten days ago, her chronic migraine had disappeared. "And it's still gone, praise God!" she said, folding her hands and looking heavenward.

The crowd responded with a simultaneous amen, and Maggie glanced at Lila, whose eyes were fixed on the young woman. She wondered if Glenn's healing had transpired like this, too.

Preacher Brubaker took the microphone and explained that this particular testimony was an example of the kind of healing Jesus had described in the Gospel of Mark, chapter two: "'. . . the Son of man hath power on earth to forgive sins, (he saith to the sick of the palsy,) I say unto thee, Arise, and take up thy bed, and go thy way into thine house. And immediately he arose, took up the bed, and went forth before them all.'"

Maggie's skin literally prickled, and she located the verse in her Bible on her lap. *Jesus both forgave the paralyzed man's sins and healed him,* thought Maggie, watching as the young woman left the platform and took her seat.

Later, when the evangelist began to preach, Maggie stared at the large white banner stretched across the back of the platform: *Confess your sins and come to the Savior!*

She'd so longed to be here again, it was like walking into

a familiar dream. Maggie breathed deeply, thankful for every word the minister was saying about having one's sins washed away, to be remembered no more. "'Therefore if any man be in Christ,'" he read from his large black Bible, "'he is a new creature: old things are passed away; behold, all things are become new.'"

Another solid amen rose up from the crowd.

Sitting there, something stirred in Maggie, and she wondered if any of the Witmer cousins also felt it. *Or is it just me?*

Sighing, she considered what it might be like to be healed by the power of God, just as the man in the New Testament had been . . . and the young woman who'd given the testimony tonight. Maggie's eyes filled with tears until the words in her Bible became blurry. She held her breath, not wanting to call attention to herself. *That's what I long for,* she thought.

During the altar call, Preacher Brubaker invited listeners to commit their lives to the Savior of their souls, to cast off their pride and make their way to the front. Maggie had struggled all evening with an urge to turn around in her seat and kneel right there, the way the People prayed together silently at Preaching services. So, while many knelt at the altar along the base of the front platform, Maggie made her seat an altar of sorts and managed to kneel there, just as she'd seen others do. Quietly, she recommitted her life to Christ. As much as she longed for healing, she did not ask for it, yet she could not shut out her awareness of the terrible pain in her legs as the sawdust scratched at her ankles.

A lightness filled her inside—an indescribable sensation—and Maggie lost track of time. She wished she could stay there praying longer, except that her legs were becoming numb, and she worried she might need help to get back onto her seat.

After a while, Lila knelt beside her. "Are you all right, cousin? Mamma's askin', too."

Wiping her wet cheeks, Maggie nodded and smiled. "Help me get up, all right?"

Lila slipped her arm around Maggie's waist and pulled her up, steadying her.

"*Denki.*" Maggie lowered herself back onto the chair while Lila's mother leaned forward in her seat several chairs away, making eye contact. Maggie smiled back and then said to her cousin, "Tell your Mamma I'm so glad I came tonight."

Beaming with joy, Lila reached for Maggie's hand.

"Can we stay a bit longer?" Maggie asked, opening her Bible to one of the bookmarked pages. She scarcely felt tired at all. "Is it all right?"

Lila asked her mother, who agreed.

Maggie reread a couple of the passages from the evening's sermon and closed her eyes, pondering many things. She was thankful she'd heard the young woman's testimony of salvation and healing—such a beautiful combination!

Later on, there was a mention of going out for pie with Luke and a friend of his, but Maggie just wanted to linger there, absorbing this most precious feeling she was experiencing, hoping with everything in her that healing might come next.

"If it's not one child disappearing, it's another," Rachel remarked to Joseph as they sat on the back porch, enjoying the cooler evening.

"Mighty strange, too, 'cause Leroy was his usual happy-go-lucky self when we went fishin' earlier."

"How was he at the noon meal?" Rachel asked, curious.

"Well, he seemed just fine then, too." Joseph shook his head and reached for her hand.

Rachel loved when Joseph took her hand. It still put butterflies in her stomach. Even so, she couldn't dismiss Leroy's disappearance. Perhaps he had gone over to neighbor Sam Zook's for supper, or to one of the many cousins in the area. But the fact that he hadn't returned yet had both Rachel and Joseph scratching their heads, particularly when there was no note. Joseph had suggested going in search of him earlier, but Rachel had wondered aloud if Leroy simply needed time alone. And they figured he hadn't gone far.

"Unless he borrowed someone's pony and cart, he's on foot," Joseph said, scratching his head with his free hand. "Leroy and I had a *gut* long talk on the way over to fish, and I made mighty clear what I expect from him."

Did Joseph provoke Leroy? she worried, feeling tense.

Joseph must have sensed it, because he turned suddenly. "This isn't yours to fret over, love. He has to respect ya, or he's goin' to be in hot water with me."

Rachel noted the frustration in his voice, and it, too, concerned her greatly. Truth be known, she disliked this wedge between father and son. "Leroy wouldn't run away, would he?" Her voice cracked.

Joseph was quiet for much too long, and the crickets near the porch filled up the silence. "He's never been one to rebel," he said at last.

"What 'bout the tent meeting? He did show some interest initially," she asked, wondering if perhaps Maggie had given him the idea. "Would he sneak off to that without askin', do ya think?"

"It's hard to imagine after our *gut* time fishin' together. I assured him of my love . . . and for all of his brothers and sisters. Truth be told, we came to a truce." Joseph yawned and said they should head inside, late as it was getting.

A *truce?* If that was the case, then why would Leroy just up and seemingly vanish?

CHAPTER
17

Still in a joyful daze, Maggie went with Lila and Luke to the parking area. After sitting for so long, the pain and stiffness had increased, but she tried not to notice, and she made it to the car with the aid of her cane and some help from Lila. The spur-of-the-moment plan was to meet Lila's family at a nearby restaurant owned by her father's uncle.

"You don't mind if Glenn Brubaker meets us there, do ya?" Lila asked as the two of them got settled in the back seat.

Luke turned to tell them that Glenn wanted to share the rest of his story with Maggie. "I hope that's okay with you girls."

Maggie had hoped she might have the opportunity to talk with him further, so she was pleased at this turn of events. "Your parents must know Glenn, then," she remarked.

"*Jah*, and his whole family," Luke said as he turned the key in the ignition.

"Are they all comin'?" Lila asked her brother.

Maggie held her breath, wondering.

143

"Just Glenn this time," Luke said, backing out of the parking spot. "A little pie and some fellowship will be nice."

Maggie was relieved that Glenn hadn't come along in the car. Then again, as carefree and happy as she felt tonight, it really wouldn't have mattered.

It was nine-thirty when Rachel heard footsteps on the porch out back, and she sat up in bed to listen. If it was Maggie, Rachel would have expected to see headlights shine on the bedroom window shades, but there had been nothing of the kind as she rested, eyes open as she prayed for both Maggie and Leroy.

Now someone was loudly running up the stairs, and that was definitely not something Maggie could do. Besides, Maggie slept downstairs.

Still keening her ear, Rachel heard a creak from the two floorboards toward the end of the long hallway. Leroy must have returned and was headed to the room he shared with his younger brothers.

Rising from the bed, Rachel pulled on her cotton duster and crept barefoot down the hall. She knocked lightly on the doorjamb, and Leroy cracked the door open, only his face showing. "Just wanted to make sure you're home all right," she whispered.

Without meeting her gaze, he nodded.

"We missed ya at supper, Leroy."

He pressed his lips together. "I had someplace to go," he said, staring at the doorjamb.

"Well, you're safely home now." She gave him a smile.

"*Gut Nacht*," he said and softly closed the door.

Making her way back toward her room, Rachel could hear

Joseph's gentle snoring, and the sound of it calmed her some. Even so, she wondered how he'd managed to give in to sleep before knowing Leroy was home. *He knows his son better than I do.*

How much later will Maggie be? Rachel thought, fretting like a mother hen.

At the restaurant, which was filling up with folks Maggie assumed were other tent goers, Luke asked for a table to accommodate ten.

Once they were seated, Glenn came around and sat next to Maggie, Luke on the other side of him. In a few minutes, Cousin Tom and Sally and their other children arrived and joined them, all dressed in their Sunday clothes, the younger two boys looking very sleepy as they rubbed their eyes. One of the boy's black suspenders had broken and was hanging loose.

After pie and ice cream had been ordered all around and everyone else was talking, Glenn asked Maggie how she had enjoyed the service.

She pondered that. "God's presence is the most powerful thing there is, I think. Sometimes it can shut everything else out, even fear." She wasn't ready yet to share fully about the events of this evening. Her prayer had been so very personal, between herself and the Lord above.

"Well, I can't speak for you, of course, but I remember being *afraid* when I realized how weak and needy I was," Glenn said, his expression vulnerable.

Without thinking, she realized she was nodding in agreement, which encouraged Glenn to go on. "I was afraid of being paralyzed, you see."

She swallowed hard. A similar thought had often lurked at the back of her mind. *How bad will my illness get?* she'd wondered, having heard the whispers about Dat's side of the family. The fears had fed into her worries about marriage. What if her husband ended up having to take care of her?

"I want to hear more," Maggie said quietly.

"Sure," Glenn said. "I was hoping I'd have this chance. It was only a few years ago that I, too, was living with constant pain, and no one seemed to know what was wrong with me—not a single doctor, and none of my family." He paused to draw a breath. "It was my first year in college, and I'd fallen and hit my head while playing basketball with some fellows from church. I had to have stitches, but soon the injury began to affect my legs, and within a few days, I could hardly walk."

Glenn seemed so robust, Maggie could scarcely imagine it.

"I was terrified when I asked my father and the elders of our church to anoint me with oil and pray . . . afraid I wouldn't be healed." He opened his Bible and lightly turned the pages, and when he found the verse he wanted, Glenn glanced at her a moment, as if waiting for permission to place the Bible between them.

She nodded, and he pointed to Second Corinthians, chapter twelve, his finger tracing along the words as he read, beginning with verse nine. "'And he said unto me, My grace is sufficient for thee, for my strength is made perfect in weakness.'" Then, skipping down to the last phrase of verse ten, Glenn read, "'For when I am weak, then am I strong.'" He looked at Maggie, his gaze unfaltering. "Just think of that."

She was moved by the words he'd read and equally touched

146

by the fact that he seemed so interested in encouraging her yet again.

"The men prayed, and God healed me," Glenn said, eyes shining. "And to this day, I couldn't be more thankful." He closed his Bible and set it on the table. "I'm praying you'll be healed, too, Maggie."

"*Denki,*" she said, her gratitude threatening to overcome her.

They talked about the fact that not everyone was healed. "But no matter our circumstances," Glenn said, "God's grace is present to carry us . . . always. We can count on Him."

"For some, it might sound too simple," Maggie said softly. "It doesn't mean I'm not anxious for the suffering to pass, though. And I get impatient waiting . . . waiting for something good to come of it."

"I understand, Maggie." He nodded. "I really do."

The journey through difficulties like chronic illness was overwhelming at times, she knew all too well.

"Remember that God cares—He weeps over us." Glenn sighed, then offered Maggie a small smile. "Remember to seek the Healer and not the healing. Whether you're ever healed or not, Christ Jesus is by far the more important gift."

Maggie nodded. It seemed odd, but Glenn had chosen to befriend her. *He understands,* she thought, amazed.

When the waitress brought their desserts to the table, Cousin Tom offered a blessing on the food, and Maggie silently gave thanks for Glenn's encouragement to her. When the prayer was finished, Maggie picked up her fork and took a small bite of the delicious cherry pie, glad that others, too, had ordered ice cream on the side.

Tom and Sally asked Glenn questions about the next location for the tent crusade, as well as how they might pray for
him and his family as they traveled that summer. Maggie listened closely and learned that the crusade would be moving
to Souderton, Pennsylvania, after July twenty-second.

Only three more weeks here, she thought.

CHAPTER

18

While outside the bishop's house before Preaching service the next morning, Maggie observed Grace's beau, Martin Lantz, and his close-in-age brothers. They had lined up toward the end of the men's line behind the house, and Maggie noticed how reverent Martin was, not engaging in talk like some of the other unbaptized fellows did at times. *Grace has a real fine fella,* she thought, happy for her sister while waiting to go to baptismal instruction with the other candidates.

From where she stood with her cane, Maggie could see Grace inching forward in the women's line, Miriam right behind her. *Someday my sisters will be married and have their own families.* Healthy and lively as both Grace and Miriam were, she knew it was true. *And fun-loving Miriam . . . goodness, she'll be snatched right up once she's old enough to attend youth gatherings.* Maggie smiled at the notion.

Since it was the Lord's Day, Maggie forced her thoughts toward worship, forsaking this self-pity she was sinking into and choosing instead to dwell on Christ's redemption. Then, inexplicably recalling the chapter in Mark's Gospel, she was once more gripped by a profound desire to experience her own miracle of healing. *Like Glenn Brubaker.*

If that happened, she thought, *I might someday be able to become a wife and mother.*

The menfolk began to move around the side of the house, to their entrance into the temporary House of Worship. Once the last of the young men had disappeared around the house, it was the women's turn to head toward their entrance at the back door.

When everyone else had gone inside, the twelve baptismal candidates waited for one of the preachers to come for them. Meanwhile, Maggie noticed Jimmy over with the other young men. He smiled at her, as he sometimes did, and then he began to walk toward her. "How are ya doin', Maggie?" He looked so handsome in his black suit and polished black shoes.

Taken aback, Maggie nodded. "I'm all right. How're you?"

"Just fine," he said; then he surprised her by saying he was glad she was taking the classes, too. "I'm learnin' all sorts of new things," he said, more animated than usual, and she wondered why.

She agreed with a nod of her head. "My Dat says it's important to pay attention in these classes." Maggie felt a little ill at ease about this unexpected conversation and inwardly kicked herself for how bland her reply seemed. If only she could have thought of something else to say to this fellow she so admired.

Jimmy smiled. "Your Dat's right."

And with that, she expected him to return to the other young men, but he stayed with her, and she worried his being there would become too obvious, if not awkward.

Without glancing toward the fellows across the walkway,

she could feel their gaze on them. Frankly, it wasn't considered appropriate for young men to mingle with the young women before or after Preaching.

"I'm afraid we have spectators," she said softly. "They're probably wondering what you're doing over here on the girls' side."

"Let them wonder," Jimmy said, eyes serious. "Will ya be at Singing tonight?"

"Not this time," she said simply, her cheeks warming.

Another uncomfortable moment passed before he nodded. "Well, it was nice talkin' with ya again, Maggie. I've been thinkin' 'bout ya." Another pause, and then he added, "Well, I'd better get back."

"*Jah*," she whispered.

In due time, they all filed into the house in an orderly fashion, just like the church members and children had earlier. They headed upstairs to a spare room, where they sat on wood benches to study two of the articles of the Dordrecht Confession with the minister, as well as to go over their own local church ordinance.

Maggie had no trouble paying attention, but after the class, when they made their way downstairs to join the rest of the People for the two sermons, Maggie wondered why Jimmy had approached her.

"I've been thinkin' 'bout ya," he'd said.

Surely it was just his way of being friendly. Besides, wasn't he interested in Deborah?

※

After Preaching, Rachel helped the bishop's wife, Annie Lantz, and a number of other women prepare to lay out the food for the fellowship meal. Meanwhile, Joseph and several other men were turning the wooden church benches into temporary tables for the three seatings of the light meal that always followed the service.

While working in the kitchen, Rachel noticed Maggie standing by herself on the back porch, looking quite solemn. Other young women of similar age milled about the lawn beneath the shade trees, doubtless seeking a cool breeze.

Where's Grace? wondered Rachel. Typically Maggie and her next younger sister were each other's shadows.

As Rachel placed utensils on the tables, she glanced out the side windows, wondering if Grace was with her sister now. But when she went to look out the back window a minute or so later, she saw that Maggie was still alone. *Should I go out? Will it upset her?*

Unsure of herself or the strength of her delicate connection to Joseph's eldest, Rachel continued her duties, distributing platters of bread with cheese spread or peanut butter, and slices of snitz pie, around on the long tables. Despite Maggie's health troubles, it wasn't usual for her to look so forlorn. Had the tent meetings stirred up something troubling? Rachel caught herself frowning—so much so that Annie asked if she was all right.

"Oh, just deep in thought," Rachel told her.

"Are ya sure?" the seventy-year-old woman asked, apparently unconvinced.

Nodding, Rachel decided she ought to at least attempt to talk to Maggie. Maybe this was her opportunity to reach out to the young woman. Rachel had completed her responsibility indoors, and while the first seating took place, the one meant for the oldest church members, Rachel slipped out the back door and approached her stepdaughter. "Are ya feelin' all right, Maggie?"

"Just a little tired." Maggie wiped her brow with the back of her hand. "I thought of sitting over on the steps, maybe."

"Well, do what's best for ya, all right?"

Maggie nodded.

"Is Grace around?"

"Oh . . . she's takin' a walk," Maggie said, looking a bit sheepish. "And Miriam's over yonder with some cousins."

Rachel looked toward the springhouse and spotted Miriam giggling with some other young girls. Turning back to Maggie, she said, "I'm concerned 'bout you, dear."

Maggie looked at her, eyes watering. "I guess I should've stayed home today," she said.

"We might be able to leave earlier than planned. If not, I can run ya home." Rachel meant it.

Maggie looked surprised, if not moved by the offer. "*Ach*, wouldn't want to cut short your fellowship." Maggie brushed tears away. "Really, I'll just go an' sit on the steps."

"Well, if you're sure."

Maggie nodded. "It's kind of you. *Denki*, Rachel."

Reluctant to leave her there, Rachel turned to head back into the kitchen, but she glanced back once she was inside. *Something's dreadfully wrong,* she thought, never having seen Maggie like this.

Seated now on the porch steps, Maggie could see the field lanes where the bishop's mule team came and went from the barn to the perimeter of the field. Grace was in the near distance, swinging her arms as she walked with Hallie Lantz, Martin's older sister. Before leaving to walk with Hallie earlier,

Grace had asked if Maggie minded, and Maggie had assured her it was fine. Yet Maggie couldn't help feeling lonely, and seeing Grace so carefree and happy only served to punctuate what Maggie had thought earlier. *My sisters and brothers will move away from home someday.*

As she rubbed her painful leg below her knee, Maggie pondered the years her parents had taught her and her siblings about divine sovereignty. "Does God mean for me to always be this way?" she murmured.

"Are ya talkin' to yourself?"

Maggie turned to see Miriam leaning down to look at her. "Well, *jah* . . . guess I am."

Miriam frowned suddenly and sat down next to her. "Are ya cryin'?"

Her little sister was so sweet and caring. "Come here," Maggie said, slipping her arm around her. "You know somethin'? My stomach's growling. Is yours?"

"I'm only hungry for some snitz pie," Miriam said, leaning her head against Maggie. "I could eat sweets all day, I think. Like Mamm . . . remember?"

"She did have herself a sweet tooth, but she was disciplined enough not to eat them *all* day, silly."

Miriam grew quiet for a moment. "Do ya think I'll look like her when I grow up?" she asked at last.

"Well, you have her pretty blue eyes and her tiny nose."

"Tiny noses are a *gut* thing, *jah*?"

That made Maggie laugh. "You're a case, ya know it?"

"That's what Mamm always said."

"You miss her, I know."

"*Jah*, but keep it a secret from Rachel," Miriam whispered.

"Oh, but she understands. Of course she does."

Miriam looked up at Maggie. "Are ya sure?"

"Trust me." She nodded.

"I do." Miriam snuggled closer. "I honestly do."

When the call came for the second seating, Maggie took the liberty of keeping Miriam with her, since Grace would likely be sitting with Hallie. Besides, Miriam brought joy to Maggie today, on a difficult Lord's Day—especially so now that Maggie could see Jimmy at the next table over with Cousin Deborah's two brothers, Chester and Edwin.

Will they be his future in-laws? Maggie thought miserably.

Before supper, Rachel heard Joseph and the boys washing up outdoors after doing barn chores, their voices coming through the side door, which was open wide to let in the fresh air, warm and humid though it was.

Later, once all of them were seated in their regular spots, Joseph folded his callused hands and bowed his head for the table blessing. After a few moments, he raised his head and cleared his throat to signal the end of the prayer.

Rachel wasn't prepared for the conversation that ensued as the sandwiches and chow chow were passed around. Joseph began by saying how glad he was to see Leroy present at the supper table. Why was her husband bringing this up now, singling Leroy out like this? True, Joseph had been displeased that his son was gone during the meal last evening. *And later, when Maggie was off at the tent meeting.*

"We're a family," Joseph said solemnly, "*all* of us." He looked directly at Leroy.

"I shouldn't have skipped out on supper yesterday," Leroy

said. "But I'm not tellin' anyone where I went." He stared at his tumbler of cold water.

"Well, and I'm not pryin'," Joseph said. "I just assumed you'd gone on foot to see one of the cousins." Joseph reached for the salt and pepper.

Rachel felt her stomach knot up and wished they'd saved this discussion for any other time, sparing the rest of them. Maggie, too, looked concerned it might move into something too heated for suppertime talk.

Leroy shifted in his seat, then eyed his father. "Guess I might as well say it—I walked clear up to the cemetery . . . to be with Mamm" came the stark words.

Miriam's mouth turned down. "But Mamm's gone," she said sadly, blinking fast.

Leroy winced, his own gaze still on his father. "*Jah*," he murmured.

"Aw . . . son." Rachel's words tumbled out before she realized it. She held her breath, knowing Leroy could well respond negatively.

After a long moment, Leroy looked across the table at her, yet he said nothing.

"I had no idea," Joseph said, his tone gentle now. "The cemetery?"

Leroy slowly nodded. "No one but the Lord God knew."

Sitting there, Rachel's heart ached for him; the struggle to remain strong was apparent in every feature of his youthful face.

"I miss Mamm, too," Stephen murmured quietly. "Awful much."

Andy was nodding his head, too, his chubby cheeks stuffed with food like a squirrel hoarding nuts.

"It's all right to talk about your Mamm in front of me,"

Rachel said softly. "She'll always be your mother . . . it's only right that yous remember her together like this."

"Rachel's right," Joseph said, smiling at her, then at the children. "It's important to keep your Mamm's memory alive."

Surprised at the scope of emotions just displayed, Rachel decided that it was good this conversation had taken place over supper, all of them together.

A step forward in the right direction, she thought, hoping it was true.

Even so, a small emptiness unlocked in her, a sense that she might never find her own place of belonging in Joseph's family.

But that's all right, she thought, dismissing her discontent. *With God's help, I'll honor their dear Mamm by taking good care of them.*

CHAPTER
19

Rachel, Grace, and Miriam started pinning the first load of washing on the line a half hour after dawn the next morning. Nellie was out doing the same, and she asked Rachel how Maggie was feeling.

Rachel was about to reply when Grace spoke up. "She's still resting . . . had a bad night."

Feeling worse after being up reading so late.

Rachel recalled that Nellie had emphasized how important it was for Maggie to rest.

"I wonder if Siggy's with her again." Miriam giggled.

Nellie replied, "That cat knows better than to leave *mei Haus*."

"Sometimes I wish we had a few *cows*," Miriam said unexpectedly. "Havin' a cow or two might help Maggie feel better. She sure needs somethin'."

"How on earth would havin' a *cow* make anyone feel better?" asked Grace, who seemed as puzzled as Rachel felt.

"I don't know," Miriam said. "Our cousins have 'em, and they're *always* happy!"

Nellie tittered, looking pretty in her dark blue sunbonnet. "Cows are right friendly animals. They seem to listen to ya." She went on to tell how she had two favorite family cows when she was a young woman. "If I ever felt sad, I'd go out to the barn and spend time with them, telling 'em my courting woes."

"Would ya trade your cat for a cow?" Miriam asked, giggling.

Rachel enjoyed seeing them banter like this, something she'd enjoyed with her own family growing up. Something she missed, living so far from home.

Grace reached into the clothespin bag and glanced toward the house. "Should one of us check on Maggie?" she asked.

Miriam took that as her cue to leave her basket of damp clothes behind and run to the house, her skirt tail flying as she ran barefoot across the thick lawn.

Nellie reached to pin her blue Sunday dress on the line. "I hear Joseph plans to have the old stable torn down and the new one built."

"He's been savin' up to rebuild, *jah*."

"Will they start flattening the present one soon?" Nellie asked.

"This Thursday they'll begin. Joseph has a crew of men lined up to get it done quickly," Rachel said. "Shouldn't take more than a week for the demolition and rebuild."

"And Joseph can get off work to help?" asked Nellie.

"He's already talked to the mill owner, and since he hasn't missed a day of work in years, it's not a problem." Rachel smiled at all of Nellie's questions, glad for an older woman to talk to— Nellie seemed genuinely interested in her life. *Mamm would ask the same sort of things if she lived closer,* thought Rachel, wishing she might visit her childhood home soon.

Three days later, a good number of men from Joseph's family arrived to move the contents of the existing stable to the barn prior to the demolition. The horses, ponies, and mules were turned out to graze in the pasture for the duration of the project.

Rachel was more than willing to supply meals for Joseph's brothers, nephews, and two cousins, as well as a few men from *die Youngie.* She, along with some help from Grace and Maggie, decided on various recipes to cook for everyone who had offered free labor. Rachel didn't mind having extra feet under the long kitchen table; this was the way of the People back home in Myerstown, too.

Before the noon meal, Lillian Beiler brought over big bowls of baked beans and potato salad, since her sons, Jimmy and Danny, were two of the young men involved in the demolition. Lillian didn't stay to help serve the food, but Rachel was thankful for the extra dishes. "This is a big help."

Maggie, however, seemed cautious about Lillian's arrival, although Rachel noticed that she was polite by engaging in a brief conversation while chopping lettuce for a garden salad. But the minute Lillian left to return to her horse and buggy, Maggie got real quiet, then excused herself to go out and sit on the porch.

What's troubling her? Rachel wondered with a glance at Grace, who seemed oblivious as she set the table for the menfolk. *Maggie hasn't been herself since the first night she went to that tent crusade.*

Maggie felt bad about leaving Rachel and Grace alone in the kitchen like that, but she needed to step outdoors for a little while before the men came in for dinner. She could see Jimmy Beiler out there working with his brother and the others and realized he must have gotten permission from the smithy to miss work for the day. The farmers, of course, would rotate doing their chores, unless they had sons old enough to cover for them.

She sighed as she observed the teamwork, nearly like a reverse barn raising as the men carefully dismantled any salvageable materials. The teardown was going smoothly, and reconstruction would begin next Monday.

At that instant, a holler went up, and suddenly Jimmy turned from his work and ran toward the pump, one hand clutching his bleeding arm. Right away, he began to pump with his other arm until a powerful stream of cold water splashed over the wounded forearm.

Maggie managed her way inside to the small bathroom around the corner from the kitchen, where they kept mercurochrome, gauze, and tape. Gathering them up in her long black apron, she limped back outside to Jimmy.

"Here, let me help," she said as he knelt in the grass, applying pressure to his wounded arm with the handkerchief he kept in his pocket.

Gently, she applied antiseptic to the cut, touching the wound only with the clean gauze, which she took great care to wind firmly but not too tightly before taping it off, much as she'd seen Mamm do over the years.

"Looks like I've got my own nurse," he said with a grin. "Glad the cut's not too deep. I hate getting stitches."

"Well, it's deep enough, so be careful. You want the bleeding to stop before you start work again," she advised, thankful for his help carrying the items back to the porch, where she put them along the rail and encouraged him to sit and rest until the noon meal. "*Gut* thing you're right-handed," she said, more shy now that she thought about how close she'd been to him. *I only did what any caring person would,* she told herself.

"I'll be fine," he said, but he sat on one of the rocking chairs anyway. "*Denki*, Maggie."

She laughed. "My brothers are tough when they're injured, too, but it's also nice to have someone look out for you."

Jimmy smiled pensively and motioned for her to sit on the rocking chair nearest him. "This is good. I've been wantin' to talk to ya, Maggie, but didn't know how to go about it."

"Well, here we are, talkin', *jah*? Sometimes things just turn out."

They shared a laugh, and she was struck by how comfortable she felt around him, despite the flutters in her stomach. She wondered what he was going to say, though. What if it was something about her cousin Deborah? How awkward!

"I ran across something that's helped one of my aunts . . . my Mamm's younger sister." He dug into his pocket. "In fact, she has far less arthritic pain now as a result."

"Oh?" It took a moment for Maggie to register this. *So Jimmy does pity me. . . .* She wanted to disappear.

"It's a blend of herbs and minerals," he said, unfolding an ad and handing it to her. "You can read it for yourself."

She recognized the name of the health food store in Strasburg and began to read the testimonials on the ad. When she finished, she told him, "To be honest, I've already tried oodles of remedies." She didn't go on to explain that she'd experimented with everything from chiropractic care to herbs to osteopathy when Mamm was still living. Mamm had taken her to other doctors, as well, after Dawdi Reuben had suggested seeing a *Brauchdokder*, a sympathy healer or powwow doctor who used chants and other strange doings to "cleanse" folk of illness. Thankfully, Dat had nixed that dangerous nonsense right off.

"I just thought that since my aunt was helped, maybe it'd be worth a try for you," Jimmy said, still rocking as he talked.

Maggie looked at the ad again and gasped at the price. "*Ach,* it's expensive."

"Maybe the deacon would let some of the alms account be used for it," he suggested quietly. "Don't see why not."

"This is kind of you, Jimmy, but I've lost faith in products and procedures that claim to heal."

He nodded slowly, then shrugged. "Hope I haven't upset ya. I didn't mean to. I just wanted to let ya know 'bout it."

She shook her head. "*Denki.*" His kindness was no surprise. Jimmy had always been very thoughtful.

"Keep the ad," he said, "in case ya change your mind."

He seemed sincere enough. *Was* it pity?

Who cares why he told me, she thought now, slipping the folded ad into her dress pocket as they continued to rock there on the porch. *If it helped his aunt, maybe it'll help me.*

Impulsively, she asked, "Have you ever heard of healings that come from bein' prayed over?" The words just slipped out.

Jimmy's eyes widened. "Why do ya ask?"

"Just been wonderin' about it." Since he hadn't answered right off, she decided not to open up further on this, not when it was something the People rarely talked about. It was enough to be able to discuss that subject with Aunt Nellie. Maggie thought of the old quilt on her bed, and the fervent prayers of the women who had come together to make it.

"Well, Jesus healed the sick when He walked this earth, and so did His followers," Jimmy volunteered now.

Pleased, Maggie nodded and wondered when he, too, had discovered the accounts of healing in the New Testament.

And while she wanted to talk more about that, right then, Grace walked out onto the porch to ring the dinner bell.

"I hope you're hungry," Maggie said to Jimmy, scooting forward on the rocker before trying to stand without her cane.

"Here, I'll help." He rose quickly and offered his good hand, the wounded arm wrapped securely in the bandage.

She accepted. "*Denki.*"

Jimmy flashed a smile. "Ya know, it wasn't too bad hurting my arm today, after all."

Maggie felt her cheeks growing warm as they walked around to the side door together.

When Maggie had done her small part to help Grace and Miriam clean the main level of the house later that afternoon, she hobbled out to the back porch and sat down. There, she watched her uncles and male cousins load the old beams onto the back of a flatbed truck driven by an obliging English neighbor from up the road. The beams would be reused on a different structure elsewhere.

Maggie was aware that Jimmy and the other younger fellows had already left for supper. She was still trying to make heads or tails of the unexpected conversation with him earlier. *What does it mean? Was he just being friendly . . . wanting to help?*

It was some time later, when the remaining work crew had

left after cleanup, that Dat came for some cold lemonade. His sleeves were still rolled up past his elbows, revealing arms that were bright red from the sun.

Maggie followed him indoors, wanting to do as much as possible to help with food preparation. She sometimes sensed that Rachel wished she might do more, though her stepmother was too kind to say. Unfortunately, there were times when Maggie simply wasn't up for as much as Grace or even Miriam, and it was in those instances that the disparity between Maggie and her sisters was most noticeable. *Rachel grew up around energetic, healthy sisters,* Maggie thought as she adjusted her work apron.

Now she carefully carried a bowl of pickled beets to the table, then returned to the counter, where she placed green olives in a dish. She looked at the day clock, and Glenn Brubaker's wise remark came to mind: *"Seek the Healer and not the healing."*

Sighing, she believed she was doing just that, because these days, her time spent reading the Good Book was the thing that brought her the most joy.

The next afternoon, Rachel, Grace, and Miriam had finished hoeing the family vegetable garden and were indoors drinking cold root beer when Aunt Nellie came through the connecting hallway. Maggie saw her before she heard the soft footsteps and her hullo.

At first, it seemed Nellie had come only to visit, bringing a freshly made coconut cream pie. But in a few minutes, she mentioned the same health food store ad that Jimmy had shown to Maggie.

Maggie cringed. *This again,* she thought, not yet having talked to Dat about it due to the expense.

"I'll leave it for Joseph," Aunt Nellie said, placing the ad near the cookie jar with a twinkle in her eye. "He'll be sure to see it here, *jah?*"

Maggie felt she ought to speak up. "Thanks, Aendi. But ya know nothin's ever worked before," she said politely. "Truth be known, a friend of mine showed me the very same ad."

"All right, then." Nellie gave a little shrug. "Just thought ya might want to see it."

Maggie sighed. "If it's God's will for me to be like this, He'll give me the grace to endure it," she said, glad Rachel was present, too. "I trust Him to take care of me. I honestly do."

Aunt Nellie's face broke into a beautiful smile. "And that, my dear, is the very best way to live."

Rachel, too, was smiling, though she also looked rather befuddled.

"So is it too early for a slice of your coconut cream pie, do ya think?" Maggie asked.

"Pie's for eatin'," Nellie said with a shake of her head. "That's why I brought it over."

"*Denki.*" Gingerly, Maggie got up and went over to give Nellie a hug for more than just the surprise treat.

CHAPTER
20

The following Monday morning, while her father and the men began to build the new stable, Maggie felt up to taking the pony and cart to Betsy Lapp's Bakery and Craft Shop. Leroy helped her hitch up, and when he asked where she was headed, she just shrugged, not really wanting anyone to know. She just needed some time alone.

While driving nestled in the heavily padded seat, Maggie's heart lightened, and she found herself talking to God in a new way. She had been praying often lately, and it felt really wonderful.

She had also been finding verses that tugged at her heart— most of them on healing. And, in order to remember them, she had written them down repeatedly.

The sky looked brighter, the landscape sweeter . . . the neighbors' smiles more plentiful, too, as Maggie waved to Ruth Zook and others along the route. Many of them called out a greeting. *Do I look especially happy today?* she wondered.

When Maggie was small, people had often remarked to her

Mamm that she was such a cheerful girl. If not for the near-constant ache of pain she felt today, Maggie would have said she was still as happy as that child. Despite her limitations, the world of her existence seemed somehow far better than before. In all truth, she had grown to know the dear Lord Jesus through His Good Book, something she had never dreamed possible. "*Denki*," she whispered, voicing her prayer of thanks as she lifted her eyes to the heavens.

This ninth day of July, she thought, *I am thankful for every blessing.* She stopped to count them, including her immediate family . . . and Rachel, as well. She even thanked God for Jimmy's and Nellie's recent suggestion about the supplements in the magazine ad. At this thought, she wondered if Dat would think the product was worth a try. Then she laughed. *Nee, Dat is a penny pincher.*

She thanked her heavenly Father for both the difficulties and the blessings related to her illness, recalling the verse in Philippians she'd recently memorized. It was so pertinent to her, she had rejoiced the first time she'd come across it. *That I may know him, and the power of his resurrection, and the fellowship of his sufferings. . . .*

Cousin Lila was another one of her blessings. The fact that Dat was so friendly to his cousin Tom's family, considering their beliefs, showed what an accepting and generous man he really was. "He's not said another word 'bout the tent meetings, either," she murmured. "Prob'ly hopin' I'm done with them."

She watched a cloud of birds flying and creating wavy designs against the bluest of skies. *Thank goodness at least the pony's paying attention to the road!* she thought with a smile as she directed the pony to turn toward Betsy's shop.

She headed straight to the hitching post nearest the door

so that she wouldn't have far to walk, glad she'd remembered to bring her cane.

The interior of the bakery and display area had a small space for tables and benches over near the windows, and another area where handmade crafts and aprons and other items were on display. Walking into the familiar setting, Maggie breathed deeply the delicious mingled smells of dough, sugar, and chocolate.

Glad to be out of the pony cart, she took her time looking over the fresh assortment of doughnuts, half moons, and ginger snaps. She had some birthday money burning a hole in her pocketbook, but everything looked so mouthwatering, it was hard to decide on just one.

"Ah, that's it," she whispered, spying the delicious treat her Mamm used to make. She asked plump Betsy for a couple of walnut kisses.

"How nice to see ya out and about, Maggie," Betsy said, her dimpled face rosy with all the rushing around she was doing. She and Maggie's mother had been close friends since their school days. "You here by yourself?"

"Just me and the pony."

"Well, why don't ya stay an' sit a spell? I'd like to visit with ya." Betsy tilted her head with apparent concern. "Ain't so easy goin' over those bumps in the road, *jah?*"

Maggie acknowledged that..

"Glad ya came durin' the mornin' lull." Betsy handed her two walnut kisses on a small paper plate, motioning toward the table in the corner. "I'll come over and join ya for a bit, all right?"

"Okay." Maggie slowly made her way, making sure she held on to her treats with one hand while clumping over to the table with her cane with the other. When she sat, she realized how pretty the sunny spot was.

"You never get to stay very long when ya drop by," Betsy said, her face dotted with perspiration. "So this is real nice." She dabbed at her forehead with a paper napkin from the dispenser.

"Things have changed some since Dat remarried."

"Oh, 'spect so, but I pray it hasn't been too hard on ya, Maggie. Or your brothers and sisters."

"We're adjusting . . . and thankful to have a kind woman like Rachel for our *Schtiefmudder*."

Betsy's eyes were soft, almost glimmering. "I imagine it's challenging for Rachel, too." She looked away. "I still think of your Mamm nearly every day."

Maggie reached to touch the back of Betsy's hand. "She loved ya dearly."

Betsy nodded and wiped away a tear. "She and I double-dated our fellas when we were courtin' age . . . did ya know?"

Maggie shook her head. "Mamm always said yous were nearly like sisters." She noticed a tour bus pulling in just then. "Looks like you've got a bunch of tourists comin'."

"Never much time to sit for long in the summertime," Betsy said, spotting the bus, too. "Just when I think I'll have a chance to catch up with ya, here come some more customers."

"Oh, I'll be back again—you can count on that." The people were filing out of the bus now, walking briskly toward the popular bakery. The women and girls wore pretty dresses and skirts, or pants rolled up at the ankle. Several teenage girls had ponytails, and others short bobs. The men had on dark blue jeans or pressed black trousers and short-sleeved shirts, and some of the boys sported shorts and T-shirts with designs on the front. It was hard not to take notice of how the English dressed. Fascinating, truth be told.

"We'll talk more another day," Betsy said, going back to scoot behind the counter.

It had been nice to visit briefly, but with the crowd coming in, Maggie couldn't imagine staying there to be squished in with so many tourists. She didn't mind being around fancy folk, but she disliked being stared at, even if in a friendly I'm-just-curious-about-you sort of way.

She glanced outside, noticed the empty tables, and decided to move out there. Exiting by way of the side of the shop, Maggie was surprised to see Glenn Brubaker there eating a half moon. An older woman with a strong family resemblance was with him.

Goodness, she thought, pleased yet shy.

"Maggie . . . come join us," Glenn said, waving her over.

"Hullo," she said, feeling awkward.

"I'd like you to meet my mother, Esther." He motioned to the smiling woman surrounded by sunshine. Her gold hair shimmered and was swept back into a bun partially concealed by a pleated, cup-shaped head covering. Like Cousin Lila's, her floral-print dress hung to her midcalf.

"So *gut* to meet ya." Maggie shook hands with Esther, who smiled warmly in return. "Are yous just out sightseeing?" Maggie asked, taking a seat at their table.

Esther glanced at Glenn and smiled. "My son's never driven the back roads here. And since my husband's studying for his message tonight, we thought we'd experience the peace of Amish farmland for ourselves."

"It's a perty day for it," Maggie said, taking a small bite of her treat.

"And too warm to sit inside," Glenn said.

"The breeze is nice right here," Esther said, making small talk.

Maggie could see that the line of customers snaked clear out the door now. "It's a *gut* thing yous came before the bus did."

"Definitely." Glenn laughed and then asked what she was eating.

"Oh, these? Well, if you've never had a walnut kiss, it's a meringue with egg whites, plenty-a sugar, vanilla, and walnuts. Really delicious."

"I'll have to come back to sample that another day," Glenn said, glancing at his mother.

"Yes, before the crusade ends," Esther said. "I can tell you wouldn't mind a second visit."

"Mom knows me well," Glenn said, chuckling.

Esther gave Maggie a smile, then rose lightly from the table. "Would you excuse me for a moment? I'm curious about some of the crafts inside."

"Sure, Mom. Take your time," Glenn said, and when Esther made her way toward the front entrance, he seemed to relax, his shoulders visibly dropping as he smiled at Maggie. "What a surprise, bumping into you like this."

She asked if the meetings were still growing in attendance every night.

"Are they ever! But more than that, God is using them to advance His kingdom," he said, saying that they'd had to add another tent to the existing one.

She was about to express her surprise about the second tent when she noticed her brother Leroy coming toward them. "Leroy . . . hullo," she said. He was carrying a bag that appeared to have blocks of cheese inside. "Did ya buy some sweets?"

He ducked his head a bit, then saw Glenn and frowned.

"Not yet . . . I had a hankerin' for chocolate chip cookies and thought I'd stop in." He was studying Glenn real hard. "But then I spotted you out here."

Probably because Glenn and I are sitting together alone, she thought, not sure if she should introduce him, or what to say if she did.

But before she could, Glenn reached out his hand, introducing himself and inviting Leroy to the tent meetings. "You certainly resemble your sister." He chuckled amiably. "It's Leroy, then? I heard Maggie say your name just now."

At first it looked like her brother might turn and skedaddle, but then he asked, "I've been curious 'bout that crusade. I hear our cousin Luke's helpin' out with the lights and whatnot."

Glenn nodded. "Luke's become a great friend of mine," he said. "Maybe you could come to a meeting sometime with Maggie?" He smiled appealingly, then changed the subject. "By the way, I guess you know how fortunate you are to live near this pastry shop."

Leroy bobbed his head and gave Maggie the oddest look. "Well, I should get home before Dat wonders what's up." His laugh was a bit forced, and Maggie worried what he might tell Dat about her being there with Glenn. "Nice meetin' ya, Glenn," Leroy said. Then to Maggie, he said, "Well, I'll be seein' ya at home . . . *soon.*"

Maggie agreed, feeling a bit perturbed as Leroy hurried off to the family market wagon he was using for errands.

"Well, he's certainly in a hurry," Glenn remarked. "And forgot to buy his cookies."

"I'll get some and surprise him," Maggie replied, not letting on that she, too, noticed how uncomfortable her brother had been just now.

Leaning back a little to get out of the sun spilling in on one side of the umbrella, Glenn asked if she'd had a chance to read from Mark's Gospel, chapter five. "Not to press you . . . simply curious."

"I've read it a dozen or more times." She was glad he'd asked, because it meant so much to be able to talk with someone who knew his way around the Bible. "I've been readin' so much, I think my family's beginning to worry 'bout me."

Glenn smiled. "Maybe your hunger for Scripture will spill over onto them."

"You could be right." She paused. "Still, it's not like we don't read the Bible. Dat reads it to us as a family twice a day."

Glenn's eyebrows rose, and he nodded approvingly. "You're blessed. Many families don't have devotions together."

At that moment, she thought of Aunt Nellie. *She'd really like Glenn.*

"I've been praying for you, Maggie." Glenn looked serious now. "For your healing."

Once again, his words caught her off guard, but in a good way. But really, why would he do that? They weren't related or even close friends. "That's kind," she managed to say, feeling tenderhearted around him all of a sudden as the tourists milled about, some standing with their pastries, waiting for a table.

She suggested they let someone else have theirs, and Glenn agreed, saying he ought to track down his mother soon, before she used up all her spending money.

"It'd be easy to do here," Maggie replied as they walked slowly toward the parking lot.

"Pastries and crafts . . . sheer heaven for tourists," Glenn said.

"Betsy does have a thrivin' business." Maggie wondered

how Glenn and his mother had stumbled upon this particular shop and not one of the dozens of others around the county. However it had come about, she was happy they had.

"Do ya plan to come to any more of the meetings?" Glenn asked as she untied the pony from the hitching post.

"I'd like to, but I really shouldn't."

A frown flickered across his face. "*Shouldn't?*"

"I was pushing the boundaries by goin' at all."

He nodded thoughtfully. "Well, it was great to see you again." She smiled. "*Da Herr sei mit du,*" she said softly.

His eyes registered his question.

"Our way of saying *The Lord be with you,*" she told him.

Glenn's face beamed. "You too, Maggie. I mean that."

Carefully, she placed her cane inside the pony cart, then got in. She was reaching for the driving lines when she realized Glenn was still standing there.

"*Hatyee,*" she said, smiling. "That's farewell in *Deitsch.*"

"Of course." He nodded thoughtfully and folded his arms as if he wanted to say more. "Say, not to hold you up, but would you happen to know anything about tours around the area? There's an old gristmill a couple of miles up the road that looks particularly interesting."

"I know that place." She smiled. "My father works there."

Glenn was pleasantly surprised, and Maggie offered his family a tour.

"My mother and I would enjoy that, but—"

"It's no trouble, really," she said quickly.

"Well, isn't this providential!" He ran his hand through his wavy blond hair.

"Could you be there a few minutes before twelve tomorrow, when the workers break for the noon hour?"

"We certainly can! Thanks, Maggie."

"I'll let my father know—he's workin' to erect our new stable, so it'll have to be a short tour."

"That's fine, but I'd hate to put him out."

Maggie nodded, wanting to please the Brubakers.

"Okay, we'll look forward to it." Then, glancing toward Betsy's shop, Glenn motioned to his mother, who was emerging from the shop, a large sack in hand. "This will be a huge surprise for my mom . . . she's been real curious to see inside a working mill."

"All right, then, sounds like Dat and I will see ya tomorrow." Maggie signaled the pony to move forward and settled in for the ride home.

CHAPTER
21

Thick gray clouds hovered near the horizon as the pony trotted along, although the sky was bright and blue where Maggie rode. As a child, she'd often reached her arms toward the clouds while sitting in the branches of the mature trees in her father's yard, but today she was thinking back on her conversation with Glenn. *I might've made a mistake in suggesting the tour,* she fretted. *Dat's not keen on the tent meetings . . . he might be suspicious of Glenn and his mother's motives.*

And it hadn't slipped her mind that Leroy had stumbled upon her sitting outside the bakery with the evangelist's son. *Goodness, am I in trouble if Dat hears about that!*

All of this made Maggie feel especially awkward about arriving home with the noon meal in full swing—she hadn't been there to help Rachel and Grace with food preparation as she'd originally planned.

I lost track of time. . . .

"Thought Maggie'd be back by now," Grace told Rachel as they hurried around the kitchen, putting the final touches on the hearty barbeque beef dinner.

"Last I heard, she didn't want to be gone long," Rachel said, thinking that Maggie's disappearing was becoming something of a joke. "She didn't happen to leave a note, did she?"

Miriam giggled over where she was setting the table. The little sweetie had asked if she could put on the paper napkins they used only for special occasions, saying it was a "messy meal" and she didn't like to see her brothers lick their fingers. Also, with the construction of the new stable under way, today they would again host as many menfolk as could fit around the table.

Rachel could see Miriam carefully folding the napkins and placing one under the fork on the left side of each plate. "The table looks real nice," she said with a smile at Miriam when she looked her way.

"It's like for special, Mamma Rachel," Miriam said.

Grace looked suddenly at Rachel, as though she hadn't heard her younger sister talk like this before. "You're fussin' too much over those napkins," Grace said. Her tone wasn't exactly disagreeable, but it was clear that Grace was befuddled. She glanced at the day clock and turned back to the freshly made bread she was slicing on a large cutting board. "I sure hope Maggie didn't get herself in a pickle somewhere."

"Pickles! *Jah*, that's just what we need," Miriam declared, evidently not sensing Grace's anxiety.

Rachel chuckled. "Sure, go down cellar and get some right quick."

And Miriam, rather gleeful, rushed to the door to the cold cellar, running all the way downstairs.

"Are ya concerned 'bout Maggie?" Rachel asked, taking the opportunity to inquire since she and Grace were alone.

"Honestly, I worry over her a lot," Grace said as she carefully placed the bread slices in a rectangular basket. "Guess I feel kinda protective of her."

"Her ailment is so erratic." Rachel glanced at Grace, wanting to be careful what she said.

"She's more frail than most folk realize," Grace replied.

Wondering if that comment was meant for her benefit, Rachel checked the barbeque beef on the cookstove. That Grace adored Maggie was obvious, yet there were also occasions when Rachel sensed a slight discord between the two. Did it have anything to do with Maggie's staying home from Singing lately? Rachel had noticed that Grace hadn't been happy about going alone last time.

Grace looked back at Rachel as if she was about to say something, but she merely reached to untie her work apron and went to the side door to look out, frowning.

Why's she so troubled about Maggie? Rachel wondered.

Partway home, Maggie had abruptly turned around and hurried the pony back to Betsy's to pick up a dozen chocolate chip cookies for Leroy, like she'd planned. The cookies might help to smooth over her tardiness with her father, as well, who also loved a soft, delicious cookie. *Especially one from Betsy's.*

Maggie directed the pony's turn into the narrow lane through the densely wooded area that led up to the house, then into the sunlit front yard. Going clear up to the walkway adjacent to the side door, she halted the pony and got out to tie it to the hitching post. As usual, Dat came to help her, but today his smile and cheery greeting were absent.

"Sorry I'm so late," she said quickly.

"You certainly are," Dat said as he reached for the lines. "I'll take care of this."

"But surely your meal's getting cold," she protested, removing the dozen cookies from the cart.

"Go inside and wash up, daughter." He shooed her toward the house.

Feeling terrible, Maggie tried to apologize again, but her father simply nodded toward the side door.

It was best to mind him, and she hooked her cane over her arm as she reached for the handrail up the steps, the box of cookies dangling from her other hand by the kitchen-twine handle Betsy had fashioned. Maggie noticed a few men sitting out on the lawn to eat. *Must be more than our table can accommodate*, she thought, glancing at the rising structure of the stable.

Inside, she set the cookies on the counter and went to the sink to wash her hands.

"You're home," Miriam said happily, looking up from the table, where she sat with some of the work crew.

"We were wonderin' what happened to ya," said Gracie, a question in her eyes.

Rachel, however, asked the girls to keep their attention on their food. "We're all thankful that Maggie's back safe and sound."

This made Maggie feel all the worse.

Leroy coughed as Maggie sat down at the table filled with neighboring farmers. Since the meal was well under way for everyone else, she bowed alone to ask the silent blessing.

When she lifted her head, Leroy was staring at her, and she didn't have to guess what was on his mind.

"I bought some cookies for ya." She indicated the box on the counter.

He looked over his shoulder. "Chocolate chip?"

"What else?"

Leroy cracked a smile. "*Denki.*"

"Hope ya don't mind sharin'," she added for good measure as Dat came in just then and removed his work boots, his stocking feet light on the linoleum.

"Mamm always taught us to share," Leroy said, looking over at Andy and Stephen.

Maggie held her breath. Every chance he could lately, Leroy was bringing up Mamm. And in that moment, she felt for Rachel. How did she manage to live in Mamm's shadow every hour of every day?

Dat sat down and picked up his fork.

"I'll reheat your food," Rachel offered, reaching for his plate.

"No need." Dat gave her a smile and started eating once again, striking up a conversation with his brothers and one of his cousins—all kind enough to step away from their own farming duties to assist in building the new stable.

Maggie ate, too, considering how best to bring up the mill tour she'd hastily promised her English friends. Now was definitely not the best time.

"I hope you're not still upset with me, Dat. I couldn't bear it," Maggie told her father that evening, after the day's work was done.

They were outside on the back porch, sitting out of earshot of the rest of the family—or so Maggie hoped.

"Upset that ya were late for dinner?" Dat asked with a tug on his beard. "*Jah*, I was. You know better, daughter. 'Specially on a day when Rachel and your sisters had their hands full, feeding extra mouths."

From his remark, it didn't sound as if Leroy had told him about coming upon her sitting and talking with Glenn, and she felt a sense of relief.

"Next time, I'll be more mindful," she assured him, going on to mention that she had run into the tent evangelist's wife and son at Betsy's little shop, of all places.

Dat seemed preoccupied now, staring out at the horse paddock.

"Turned out that Esther and Glenn Brubaker are interested in seein' the inside of the gristmill . . . and I foolishly volunteered a short tour tomorrow at the start of your dinner hour." She cringed as the words fell out of her mouth. "I'm sorry for not askin' ya first, Dat."

"Just how do ya know these folk?"

"They're friends of cousins Tom and Sally."

"Well, how about that," Dat muttered and shook his head. "So Tom and Sally know the minister who's drawing in thousands of curious people every night?"

"*Jah*." She fidgeted in her rocking chair, feeling ever so tense. "Would ya mind terribly showin' the Brubakers around a bit?"

He sighed. "Well, I can't take much time away from the crew here." He sounded displeased. "I hadn't planned to go to the mill tomorrow."

"Maybe the owner could show them around instead?" she suggested.

BEVERLY LEWIS

"*Nee* . . . that's all right. For you, Maggie, I'll make the time," he said, surprising her.

She exhaled, not realizing till then that she'd been holding her breath. "*Denki*, Dat . . . and next time, I won't speak out of turn."

Her father checked the time on his pocket watch, then shifted in his seat. Something else seemed to be on his mind. "By the way, I read that health food store ad Nellie put near the cookie jar."

"*Ach*, so *koschtlich*, ain't?" Maggie shook her head. "I don't expect ya to—"

"If it helps, I'll thank the Good Lord above for havin' the extra pennies to spend." He excused himself to go inside and soon returned with a small sack, which he handed to her.

"I wanted to do this for ya, daughter," he said, sitting down again.

She opened the sack and looked inside. There was the very bottle pictured in the ad. "You already purchased it?"

"I know you've tried near everything your Mamm and I could get our hands on, but one more possibility can't hurt, *jah*? Just follow the instructions, and we'll hope an' pray you get some relief." He talked about his conversation with the health food store owner. "He declared that several local people have experienced significant help."

Maggie remembered what Jimmy had said about his one aunt. "*Denki*, Dat."

After a few more minutes of small talk, her father got up, dug his hands into his pockets, and moseyed around the house to the side door.

Watching him go, Maggie was so touched that he would

take a chance like this and spend so much on her. She loved him all the more for it.

She rose to go inside, too, and noticed Leroy standing at the window, then swiftly backing away.

Why must he eavesdrop?

CHAPTER

22

Maggie stared at the bottle of pills her father had spent his hard-earned money for.

She wished she could will away her uncertainty about starting yet another experiment. If she took the pills and nothing happened, like every other time, wouldn't she become disheartened again? Then again, if she actually got well, might this be God's way of healing her?

She contemplated the latter, really wanting to adopt an optimistic outlook. *Like Aunt Nellie would if she were in my shoes.* But after so many unsuccessful attempts at treatment over the past years, Maggie was skeptical.

Following evening prayers and family Bible reading, she slipped away to the kitchen and turned on the faucet to fill the tumbler half full, then opened the pill bottle, having read the directions on the back: *Take one twice a day, twelve hours apart.*

"I may as well start tonight," she murmured, opening her mouth.

Just then, Grace appeared in her pastel pink cotton duster.

"You're talkin' to yourself again," she said, opening the cupboard door and reaching for a tumbler, too.

"And you must be thirsty." Maggie took a sip of water and swallowed the pill.

"It's so hot upstairs, I thought of comin' downstairs to sleep."

"Want to?"

"Would ya mind?" Grace looked hopeful.

Maggie hesitated, then said, "Not at all." But the damage was done.

"Are ya worried I might bump ya?"

"You'll be careful, I'm sure," Maggie replied, knowing that to say more would hurt her sister's feelings.

But Grace could read her pretty well. "On second thought, I'd rather sweat it out upstairs than risk that."

"*Ach*, Gracie—"

"I mean it," Grace interrupted, carrying her water to the kitchen table and taking a spot on the side near the open windows. "I'm wide-awake," she said. "Want to sit with me a while?"

"Sure, I'll just get my cushion."

"*Nee* . . . I'll go an' get it for ya." Grace scurried off to Maggie's bedroom, then rushed right back. "There, that'll be better."

"*Denki*." Maggie wondered if Grace had heard about these new pills, so she said, "I started takin' somethin' different than aspirin for my pain."

Grace looked surprised. "Something Rachel dreamed up?"

"Why would ya think that?"

"Oh, she sometimes has a way of pushin' her nose into things."

Maggie thought about that but wasn't sure she agreed. "Rachel's comin' along, I think. Don't you?"

"Maybe . . ."

Maggie didn't feel at liberty to reveal that it was Jimmy Beiler who'd first mentioned the pills to her. "Well, I will say that this is probably the last time I'm gonna try a newfangled product. I get my hopes up, and then they come fallin' down."

"It's up to you, isn't it, since you're eighteen now?"

Maggie didn't agree. "As long as I'm livin' under Dat's roof, that really ain't true."

Grace took a long drink of cold water. "S'pose you're right, but you went off to those meetings with Luke and Lila that time, without askin'."

Maggie acknowledged that. "I regret it. And made it right with Dat, too."

Grace nodded. "I should've known ya would." She rose and walked back to the pantry and brought out a box of crackers. "Are ya hungry?"

"I rarely am this time of night." Maggie wondered if there was something more on Grace's mind.

Grace opened the box anyway and took several crackers. "Am I keepin' you up?"

"*Nee*, not if ya have somethin' you wanna talk about."

"But I'm sure you're tired." Grace rose again and asked to see the pill bottle. "If it's all right."

Maggie handed it to her, glad to have this opportunity to talk about it, knowing Grace would keep it to herself.

I wouldn't want my younger siblings asking every few minutes if I'm feeling better yet, Maggie thought. "I'm fairly sure Rachel knows, 'cause Dat bought them, but I'd rather the rest of the family not. Let's just keep it 'tween us. The younger ones might just get their hopes up if they know."

"Like you have before." Grace's words seemed to hang in the air.

"But this time, I'm putting my faith and hope in the Great Physician."

Grace looked solemn there in the flickering lantern light. "I daresay you're a stronger person than I'll ever be."

Maggie thought of the verse Glenn had shared with her. *My grace is sufficient for thee: for my strength is made perfect in weakness.* "When we are weak, we can trust Christ to make us strong," she said softly.

Grace agreed. "I need to remember that." She smiled, then outened the lantern.

They said good-night and returned to their separate bedrooms.

Bees swarmed in the flower garden around the summer phlox Mamm had planted years ago, as Maggie headed outdoors with her cane a little after eleven-thirty the next morning. Leroy had already hitched up for Dat to drive over to the mill with her and was waiting to help her into the family carriage.

Maggie glanced at the sky. "It's sure a nice, clear day for workin' on the new stable," she remarked.

"It's a *gut* day for getting my nose sunburnt, that's what." Leroy chuckled as he pushed down on the crown of his straw hat, then offered a hand so she could climb into the buggy.

"*Denki* for helpin' me."

Leroy bobbed his head. "Thought I'd surprise Dat by hitchin' up, too." He glanced toward the stable, more than halfway built now.

She stuck her neck out. "I take it ya didn't mention to Dat who I was sittin' with at Betsy's yesterday." Maggie hoped she sounded less concerned than she felt.

Leroy smiled then. "That there fella seemed harmless enough."

"Well, I did tell Dat that I ran into Glenn and his mother," Maggie said. "It was just a coincidence—they were out sight-seeing."

"That Glenn's real *freindlich*, ain't so?" Leroy observed.

She nodded. If her brother had seen Glenn greet her after one of the tent meetings, Leroy would know this for certain. But she didn't need to add firewood to his curiosity.

Then, seeing their father head to the pump to wash his arms and hands, she quietly thanked Leroy for not making a mountain out of yesterday's impromptu encounter.

"Just have yourself a nice time at the mill . . . with your *English* friends," Leroy said with a sly smile.

"Well now, I will," she said, laughing.

Three vehicles were parked outside when Dat pulled into the parking area next to the old gristmill. The trees on the south side of the small lot shimmered in the sunlight, and birds flitted back and forth, calling merrily.

"I appreciate this," Maggie told her father as she got out of the buggy. Stepping down, she momentarily winced, though she felt happy at the thought of seeing Glenn and his delightful mother, Esther, again. *Their family has done so much to bring the gospel into our community.*

Taking her father's arm, Maggie walked to the door and entered, immediately aware of the rhythmic rumble and clatter of the moving machinery powered by the waterwheel outside.

It wasn't long before Glenn and his mother arrived. Dat let them in through the mill's Dutch door and shook hands with

Glenn. He introduced himself, then joked that he was "a man who keeps his nose to the grindstone."

Glenn chuckled, and his mother smiled as Maggie welcomed them inside, as well.

"What're ya most interested in seeing?" Dat asked them.

Glenn deferred to his mother, who said she appreciated simply being permitted to look around. "I've seen waterwheels close up, but not the interior of a working mill," Esther said.

"Well, I'll be glad to show ya what I do all day," Dat said.

Maggie was pleased at how cordial he was, even though he likely wasn't keen on encouraging her acquaintance with the son and wife of the man making headlines in the Lancaster papers.

When the last of the already cleaned grain had been sent through the center of the millstones to be sifted, Dat directed the other workers to halt the process.

"It's so fine!" Esther exclaimed, evidently surprised at the quality of the flour as it went through the large sifter before dropping into the bin.

Once the machinery ceased its motion, Dat led them over to the enormous quartz stone and demonstrated the process of dressing, or sharpening it. "It can take up to three days to dress a set of stones," he mentioned.

Next, her father showed how they adjusted the studs and checked the texture of the flour. "Something I do pretty often during the process—all day long, really." He chuckled before adding, "It's the same old grind, ya know!"

It was plain to see that Dat was enjoying himself.

At the end of the tour, Maggie went with the Brubakers to look at the wheat flour and cornmeal packaged for sale in white paper bags, the name of the mill printed on them.

After Esther had looked around and asked several more questions, Dat led them back outdoors. Maggie walked with Glenn, who held the door for them, seemingly pleased about the tour. He thanked Dat for his time, and Esther reached to squeeze Maggie's hand. "Lord bless you," she said, eyes sparkling.

When Maggie glanced up, she saw Jimmy Beiler sitting in the lot in his father's market wagon, looking her way. He waved, and she swallowed hard, wondering what he was thinking at the sight of her and her father talking so animatedly with two *Englischers*.

"The tour was very informative," Esther was saying. "You're so thoughtful, Maggie, to arrange it for us."

"Yes, thank you both again," Glenn said.

Feeling a bit uncomfortable with Jimmy still parked there, Maggie waved to the Brubakers as they got in their car. They backed up slowly, the tires crunching over the pebbles on the dirt lane as they waved again through the windows.

The minute they were gone, Jimmy hopped down from the wagon. "Nice to bump into ya here, Maggie," he said, walking up to her.

"I rarely come over anymore," she admitted, looking down at her cane and feeling self-conscious.

Jimmy's black work trousers were a bit grubby, no doubt from the smithy's shop, and for some reason, his green short-sleeved shirt made his eyes look bluer. Glancing over his shoulder, he looked in the direction where Glenn's car kicked up dust as it exited toward the paved road. "Do ya know those folk?" Jimmy asked, returning his gaze to her.

"*Jah*, for just a short time." She left out who they were, or that she'd gone to the tent meetings. Dat would likely want that kept quiet, so she didn't broadcast it. "They were curious to see a workin' mill," she told him, her heart still thrumming. Oh, if only she could just talk normally to Jimmy!

"And your father showed them around?"

She nodded, wishing Jimmy would just go in and do what he'd come for.

"S'pose you're headed home now," he said, his smile inquisitive. That same remarkable smile had caught her attention so long ago.

"The new stable's comin' along nicely," she said, looking for her father, who must have gone back into the mill for something. "But I'm sure Dat needs to return soon."

In a moment, her father poked his head out the door. "I need to talk to the boss for a while, Maggie," he said. "Say, Jimmy, would ya mind runnin' Maggie home?"

Her stomach did a flip-flop.

"Glad to," Jimmy replied. "Maggie?" He turned to offer her his arm.

What on earth? Her heart pounded as she went with him to the wagon.

"Here, I'll help ya in." He boosted her up like she weighed no more than a feather.

Fortunately, Maggie found her voice quickly enough to say a quiet *Denki* before he went to the other side to get into the wagon.

Jimmy didn't ask how she was feeling; she figured it was apparent. Besides, he saw her every other Sunday during baptismal classes. And of course he was the one who had so thoughtfully mentioned the special supplements to her.

Suddenly eager to tell him about her father's recent purchase, she said, "I started takin' those pills ya told me about."

Jimmy gave her one of his good-natured smiles. "Did ya?"

"They were a surprise from my father."

"Well, I sure hope they help, Maggie."

"*Denki.* I'll gladly accept hope . . . and prayer," she said, conscious of the light in his eyes when he looked her way. Blushing at the memory of his strong hands around her small waist as he'd boosted her into the wagon, Maggie wondered if he might be able to guess what she was thinking right now.

Quickly, she looked over toward the horse paddock on the side of the road nearest her and noticed a section of broken fence, which she pointed out to him.

"I noticed that mess on my way to the mill," Jimmy said. "Do ya know when it happened?"

"There was a windstorm a couple weeks ago."

"Wonder why I didn't see it till just today," he said.

It was such trivial talk, she felt nearly dishonest; there was so much more she wished they might share.

Just then, she glanced down and saw a New Testament on the seat near Jimmy's side of the wagon. She almost reached to pick it up.

Jimmy seemed to notice. "I take it with me on errands," he told her. "There's a lot in the Good Book we don't hear much about," he said, a bounce in his voice now. "I like to read passages when I've got a chance."

"I've been readin' from the Gospels quite a lot," Maggie said.

"Our Lord's compassion reached out to the sick everywhere He went," Jimmy said quietly.

In that moment, she felt a kinship with him, knowing that Jimmy, too, had read the same chapters she'd become so attached to.

"I've been learnin' new things," she admitted.

He looked her way with tender eyes. "I'll keep you in my prayers, Maggie. All right?"

She suddenly felt wistful and wondered why he hadn't spoken of Deborah, then worried she was overstepping her bounds.

"I appreciate it," she said. *More than you know.*

"It's the least I can do." He smiled.

When they turned into her lane, Jimmy halted his horse adjacent to the side door, and Maggie thanked him for bringing her home. "It sure was a quick ride," she said, wishing to say more.

"Just glad I showed up at the mill when I did," he said as he stepped down and went around to offer his hand this time.

She accepted, putting much of her weight into it, but using her cane, as well. The combination of the two set her aright.

Jimmy smiled, but something about the way he looked at her seemed to relay more, though she couldn't decipher just what.

After he left in the wagon, Maggie remained on the back porch, catching her breath not only from the effort it took to get up the steps, but from the happiness of seeing Jimmy again. *So unexpected,* she thought, still savoring every moment, every gesture.

She placed a hand on her face. "*Ach,* I must go in without flushed cheeks," she whispered, wondering if this was how she might feel after riding with wonderful Jimmy Beiler some evening in the future.

Silly me, she thought just as swiftly.

CHAPTER
23

I f asked, Rachel would gladly have owned up to her eagerness for the new pills to make a difference in Maggie's quality of life. Perhaps better health would even make it possible for Rachel to have a closer relationship with her husband's eldest.

Prior to Joseph's purchase, Maggie had been getting worse, or so Rachel thought. Joseph, however, insisted that hot and humid summers had always been the hardest for his daughter since she had come down with the dreaded illness.

"But it's not just the limpin' and the strain on her face," Rachel told her husband when they were alone in their room that evening. "She's also become preoccupied with the Good Book. Every time I turn around, she's sitting in her room reading."

Joseph jerked his head up from where he sat waiting for her in their bed. "Ain't nothin' better, *jah?*"

Brushing her hair more vigorously, Rachel agreed. But she was hesitant to bring up that she had also noticed a page of writing on the floor outside Maggie's room. The paper must have slid out from under her bedroom door.

"Dear?" Joseph said absently when she'd gone silent. "What is it?"

Rachel stopped brushing and shrugged. "I'm not sure."

"Something I should know?"

She felt torn down the middle. If she told Joseph, she would betray Maggie's new zeal. If she kept mum, she'd neglect her duty to be honest with her husband. Which was it to be?

"Rachel?" Joseph wasn't an impatient man, but there was an urgency in his tone.

"It's just that she's writing down verses—the same ones—over and over." Rachel set her hairbrush on the dresser and moved across the room to sit at the foot of the bed.

"She might be tryin' to memorize them." Joseph's voice sounded thoughtful. "How long has she been doin' this?"

Rachel told of finding the paper on the floor just after Maggie had gone to the tent meeting the last time.

"Do you recall which verses?"

"Where Jesus heals the sick," she said.

Joseph nodded. "It wonders me if she hopes to be healed like that."

"By a miracle?"

"Something she might've picked up at the meetings," he said.

Rachel couldn't discern what reasons Maggie might have for writing the verses, but she knew she certainly wanted to be healthy and whole, like her brothers and sisters. *Nellie has said as much.*

"Did I ever share with you that I attended revival services at a Mennonite meetinghouse?" she asked softly.

Joseph's eyebrows rose. "When was this?"

"Oh, I was younger than Maggie and seeking answers. But mostly I needed consolation." She didn't care to delve into all of that just now. "I really don't think ya have to worry that outside teaching will prevent Maggie from going ahead with baptism. I doubt anything she'd hear at such meetings would jeopardize her commitment to the Amish church."

He smiled and reached for his Bible from the bedside table. "It hasn't affected your commitment, to be sure. Guess that's all I need to know."

Rachel was touched by this image of Joseph there, in his nightclothes, holding the Good Book.

Joseph patted his side of the bed. "Come sit with me . . . let's have a look-see at the things Maggie's been reading about healing."

She smiled when she realized that Joseph didn't seem too interested in hearing about her brief venture outside of Amish circles. And that was fine with her. What had happened in the past stayed there. She was where she was supposed to be, next to her husband, whom the Lord had clearly led her to meet.

And as Joseph read aloud to her, she couldn't help thinking that Maggie's passion for Scripture might just help all of them.

⁂

A week later, Rachel's sister Sarah came for a surprise visit. Rachel was delighted to see her arrive in a passenger van early that Tuesday afternoon. It had been one of those rare mid-July days when she had no need to keep a timetable. Caught up with her canning and cleaning for the week, Rachel had been sweeping the front porch, shooing away mosquitos while the girls were next door helping Nellie. Truth be known, Rachel was also trying to push away the homesick feelings that continued to creep up on her from time to time. Sometimes she felt as though she still had a long way to go before she fit in here, a feeling she had been trying to dismiss.

This is my role, she told herself. *And I'm grateful for it. My love for Joseph is enough to carry me through anything.*

"*Willkumm, Schweschder!*" she called now to Sarah, leaning the broom against the house and running out to meet the sister who'd helped Ruth Zook play matchmaker.

"I took the chance you'd be home," Sarah said, looking mighty red in the face from her ride. "I had a couple errands not far from here—delivered some custom orders to *Englischers,* one for an embroidered tablecloth, and the other for several sets of pillowcases. I met both at market last month."

"Aren't you ambitious!" Rachel kissed her cheek. "You can keep me company."

They sat on the porch for a few minutes, catching up; then Rachel slipped inside for some cold homemade root beer. "Here, this'll help cool ya some."

"Our Yankee neighbors down the road just put in air conditioning," Sarah told her.

"Well, then you should go over and visit regularly, ain't?"

That brought a good laugh; then Sarah fanned herself with the hem of her long black apron and turned to smile at Rachel. "You don't know how much I miss ya."

"Aw . . . we'd better not talk like that, or we'll both start crying." Rachel didn't tell her how gloomy she'd felt a little while ago, before the van pulled into the driveway. "We're together now, and maybe you can spend the night?"

Sarah shrugged. "I'd thought of it, but David and the children wouldn't stand for it. They think they can't manage without me."

Rachel snickered. "Maybe you should let them find out." She cupped her hand over her mouth. "Did *I* say that?"

They talked about the circle letters presently making the rounds to the other sisters. "It's one way to keep in touch," Sarah said, "but there's nothin' like sitting here face-to-face, havin' such *gut* fellowship together."

Rachel agreed wholeheartedly. "Can I talk ya into stayin' for supper at least?"

"I told the driver to return for me in two hours."

"All right, well . . . I'll take what time I can get."

Sarah said, "You must come visit us sometime. Dat and Mamm would love it. They said they had such a nice time here for your eldest's birthday supper."

My eldest . . . Rachel wondered why Sarah had said it that way, and quickly changed the subject. "Well, so, how are Dat and Mamm doin'?"

"As busy as the rest of us, what with all the vegetables needin' picking and puttin' up." Sarah also mentioned having new window screens installed, a chore that her husband and two of his brothers were doing together.

"You do have lots of windows in your *Haus.*"

Rachel marveled that Sarah had somehow managed to show up on the least busy day of this particular week. They talked about this and that, and then Sarah mentioned the nearby tent meetings.

"They're comin' to an end soon, yet the crowds continue to grow." Rachel wouldn't reveal that Maggie had gone several times, and that they'd seen Joseph's Witmer cousins more than usual because of it.

Sarah listened, taking it all in. "My David says the crime rate is way down in this area—s'pose all the trouble-makin' folk are goin' to the meetings."

"Well, your husband may be right. But simply going won't

make any difference unless they're fallin' to their knees to repent."

About that time, Nellie and the girls came out onto the front porch of the *Dawdi Haus*. When they saw Rachel there with Sarah, they waved, and Nellie invited Rachel and her sister over. *Always hospitable*, thought Rachel. "*Denki*, but why don't yous come over *here* in a little while, all right?" she said, wanting more time alone with Sarah.

While Sarah was talking about her coming grandbaby, Rachel noticed that Maggie seemed to be moving around better and without the constant limp. Could it be a result of the pills? Yet she'd taken them for little more than a week.

"Before ya go, I'd like you to say hullo to the rest of the family," Rachel told Sarah, still wishing her sister could stay for supper, which was going to be BLT sandwiches and Jell-O, if Rachel had her way. It was much too warm to eat heavily.

"If ya don't think they'd mind spendin' time with your ornery sister."

"Ornery? You're too sweet to be called that." She patted Sarah's arm. "You helped lead me to Joseph, remember?"

"Wasn't the easiest thing I've ever done."

Rachel nodded. "True, I was never much for blind dates."

"Sometimes you just have to trust your big sister, right?"

"I'm so glad I did."

Later, when Maggie and the girls returned from Nellie's, Rachel enjoyed observing them with Sarah. Miriam ran out to get the boys, too, and it warmed Rachel's heart to see young Stephen be the first to put out his hand to greet Sarah, followed by Andy. Even Leroy was more cordial than Rachel expected. *Ever so slowly, he's warming up*, she thought.

Rachel sat on the back porch the next morning, waiting for her peach pies to bake during the coolest time of the day. Being a sister herself, she greatly valued the connection she witnessed now between Maggie and Grace as they worked together in the garden. And sitting there rocking for a moment longer, Rachel noticed something different about Maggie—more stamina, perhaps.

Des gut, Rachel thought. *Is she doing better because of the pills? Or is she gleaning strength from reading the Scripture so often?* Rachel had found this to be true for herself, especially after her teenage beau had ditched her, leaving her dumbfounded and despairing. *So long ago now,* she thought, dismissing the thought as she looked over at the newly built stable, so sturdy and striking with its fresh coat of white paint.

She'd ventured out there yesterday, hoping to somehow break the ice with Leroy, who was busy freshening the stall bedding. She'd taken some ice-cold meadow tea, which he drank in nearly a single gulp, but when she asked if she might help fluff the straw, Leroy declared he could do it himself. When she had persisted, his look turned as blank as a wiped chalkboard. It was as though Leroy spoke a different language. Perhaps he didn't comprehend how willing, even eager, she was to get to know him. Or maybe he simply didn't welcome Rachel's desire to reach out. Despite how polite he'd been to her sister Sarah yesterday, he was still resistant to Rachel's efforts.

Thankfully, she had something pleasant to look forward to tomorrow over at Ruth Zook's house—a Sisters Day picnic. And while Rachel had no sisters locally, Ruth had insisted she come anyway.

I'll hear all the neighborhood news, Rachel thought, looking across the expanse of field to the Zooks' big spread of land. *And have some good fellowship, too.*

She smiled at the prospect of seeing Ruth and her family. It would take her mind off how stubborn Leroy continued to be. *But not rude enough to tell Joseph,* she thought, going inside to check on her pies. *I'll spare my husband that, dear man. He's heard enough from me.*

Hours after Maggie's evening dose of her special supplement, she wandered out to the kitchen, lit the small lantern, and sat at the table with a glass of milk and an apple. To her surprise, her pain *had* subsided a bit here lately, and she sat there thinking that she just might be getting better.

"You're still up?" Miriam whispered in the dim light of the kitchen as she tiptoed in.

"Couldn't sleep," Maggie said, taking a sip of milk. "Why're *you* awake?" she asked her little sister.

Miriam came to sit next to her. "I had a bad dream."

"Aw, sweetie . . ." She slipped an arm around her.

"But I don't wanna talk 'bout it."

"You don't have to." She drew Miriam near. "Will a cookie help?"

Miriam nodded, and Maggie set her free to go to the cookie jar across the room. "Do you ever dream of Mamm?" Miriam asked as she removed the lid.

"*Nee,* but I'd like to."

Miriam returned with her cookie and again took a seat.

"I'd love to see Mamm again . . . even if only to spend another day with her," Maggie admitted.

Miriam took a bite of her snack. "I miss talkin' to her. We used to walk through the meadow together, too." She was quiet for a while, taking her time to nibble. Then suddenly she asked, "Do you remember the last thing Mamm said to you?"

"Not really, but I guess I was still expecting to have more time with her. Nobody expected her to pass over to Glory quite so soon." Maggie sighed as she recalled that terrible day. "Dat was at the mill. Grace and I were in the sewing room, working. . . ."

"I should've stayed put that afternoon," Miriam said, sniffling. "She wanted some water, so I hurried to the kitchen to get it." Miriam leaned closer to Maggie. "When I took the water upstairs to her, Leroy was standing at the foot of the bed, white as the bed quilt. Mamm died that quick. . . . I'd never seen Leroy cry before," Miriam whispered.

"Well, tears are precious to God. It's all right to cry."

"Even for boys?"

"Sure, even them."

Miriam seemed to consider this. "Leroy kept lookin' at Mamm lying there so still, and then shaking his head. He was so awful sad." Miriam trembled. "He kept mutterin' somethin' I couldn't hear."

Maggie's heart broke anew for her little sister.

"I couldn't believe she was gone," Miriam whispered. "I stood there and cried with Leroy."

"I'm so glad he was with ya."

"Mamm had a little smile on her face, I remember."

The Lord Jesus came for her, thought Maggie, caressing Miriam's long, straight hair as she rocked her and whispered how much she loved her.

CHAPTER
24

Five days later, Maggie had to admit, if only to herself, that something *was* different. She had awakened that Monday feeling still better, strong enough to help Rachel and Grace with all the washing. She had even helped run the whites through the wringer while Rachel divided Dat's and the boys' trousers from their shirts. It felt wonderful to be more useful.

The following morning, Maggie left the cane in her bedroom, wondering if any of the family might notice. For once, she helped set the table without stumbling around the benches on either side. She was also the first one up to clear the table and start heating water on the cookstove to wash the dishes.

Leroy left the table and came over. "What's happenin'? You're not hobblin' today."

She smiled. "It's *wunnerbaar-gut*, that's what."

He grinned, looking the happiest he had since Mamm died. "I really hope you're better, sister."

"*Denki*," Maggie replied as she watched him head out the side door, the screen door slapping behind him. Oh, she wished she might talk to him soon. She'd noticed tiny hints lately that he might be coming around. *Ever so slowly.*

Grace got the dish detergent out of the cupboard below the sink and poured cold water into the deep sink, filling it partway. She glanced at Maggie. "Should I ask how you're feelin'?" she said quietly.

"I'm a bit stronger, *jah*," Maggie volunteered.

"I see you're not usin' your cane." Grace smiled sweetly.

"So far, I don't need it today." It felt so good to be free of it, and Maggie breathed a prayer of thanks as she added a stick of wood to the cookstove.

When the mail was delivered that afternoon, there was a letter from Cousin Lila. Maggie sat right down on the front steps and opened the envelope, finding a note from Lila, as well as a sealed letter. *Glenn asked me to send the enclosed letter,* she had written. *I hope it's all right.*

Maggie opened the sealed letter and began to read.

Dear Maggie,

How are you? Hopefully you're not surprised to receive this letter!

Thank you again for setting up that mill tour with your father. It was very kind of him to take time out of his busy day; my mother is still talking about it!

I had wondered if we might have a chance to talk again and to say good-bye. But I understand from your cousins that the fact that you came to any of the meetings was quite remarkable. My family's so glad you did.

And thanks for allowing me to share my testimony,

Maggie. In some small way, I hope it helps. Know that I will continue to pray for your healing . . . and for God's highest and best for your life.

> *Your friend and brother*
> *in Christ,*
> *Glenn Brubaker*

Maggie closed the letter and placed it back in Lila's envelope, truly surprised. She looked across the road at the cornstalks swaying gently in the breeze, glad to have met Glenn. *He helped to plant a yearning for God's Word in my heart.*

Barefoot, Maggie wandered down the porch steps and around the side of the house, where Mamm's roses were still in bloom. Walking in the sun-warmed soil, Maggie heard the sounds of summer all around her—birdsong and insects buzzing in the bushes. The air was heavy with the sweetness of roses and all manner of other flowers that Rachel had planted near the house.

She pondered Glenn's kindness and the bond they'd shared. His thoughtfully written farewell reminded her of his promise to pray for her.

To think that this letter arrived on my healthiest day of the summer! she thought, knowing she must return to help Grace with the mending inside. *Is it a sign that I'm on the way to being healed?*

With a joyful sigh, she decided to walk to the mill later that afternoon to meet her father, once chores were done. *Like old times,* she thought, making her way to the side door, grateful to feel better.

"Your face is all rosy," Grace remarked as Maggie worked with her in the sewing room off the side of the kitchen nearest the small bathroom.

Maggie nodded and smiled at her sister. "I'm thankful for this reprieve."

Tilting her head, Grace frowned. "A reprieve?"

"Remember, I've felt nearly this well before. The last time was in the early spring."

Grace nodded, seemingly lost in thought. Something else was on her mind. She mentioned having read in *The Budget* about an Arthur, Illinois, Amish girl who'd put a note in a bottle while on vacation and tossed it into the Mississippi River. "She wanted to see how far it would travel, and if anyone would find the note and contact her."

Maggie perked up at this. "Did anyone?"

"*Jah*, and I guess the fella who found it is from Memphis, Tennessee. Evidently they've become pen pals."

"Such a sweet story!"

"Makes me wonder if they'll remain friends," Grace added.

"It's fascinating how God brings people together," Maggie said, switching out the thread in her needle from white to blue to stitch up a small tear in Leroy's shirt. "But it wonders me how a bottle could travel so far and not break along the way."

Grace appeared to consider this. "I guess it was just s'posed to."

"God took care of it. That's what I think." These past few days, Maggie had often considered divine Providence. Could it be that Jimmy Beiler and Aunt Nellie were supposed to have shown her the ad for the pills from the health food store? Was that part of God's plan?

In the past, certain products had occasionally helped Maggie for a short while. But for whatever reason, a time came when they no longer had any effect.

I'll keep trusting God day by day, Maggie thought. *And be thankful for the blessings I already have.*

Maggie finished with her mending a mere twenty minutes before Dat would finish up at the mill. So she told Grace where she was going and took her time walking down the narrow lane, through the trees and out to Olde Mill Road. The sun was so hot, she removed her blue bandanna and let the wind ripple against her tightly wound hair bun.

When she reached the near side of the mill, Maggie sat down to wait for her father, the grass cool beneath her feet. And while she waited, she prayed, thankful for God's goodness to her and to her family. She also prayed for the Brubaker family, and for the many people who would be attending the tent meetings in Souderton. And she prayed for Jimmy and his future, as well. That was harder than other prayers, but it was the *right* thing to do.

In a few minutes, she noticed her father coming this way and waved to him.

"*Hullo* there, Maggie!"

She rose to greet him. "Thought I'd surprise ya, Dat."

He was grinning now. "Surprise me, ya did!"

She shared then how she'd missed her childhood days of coming to meet him. "*Ach*, how could I be so fit those first eleven years, and then become so sickly?" she asked. "And now, look at me: I'm havin' a real *gut* day."

"You do seem to be getting stronger," Dat agreed.

"I'd really like to earn some money to help with the expensive supplements," she said, mentioning that she'd thought of working for Betsy Lapp at her bakery. "Ain't far, and maybe Leroy could drop me off and pick me up."

"Have ya already talked to Betsy 'bout this?"

"*Nee*, wanted to know what you thought," Maggie said,

walking in step with him on the roadside to avoid the occasional buggy traffic.

"Why don't we wait to see how you're feeling when the pills are close to running out before decidin'?"

She had wondered if he might suggest this, wise as he was.

"Say, this is beside the point, but I've been thinkin' about making a Scripture wall plaque," he said. "And I thought you could help me with it." He suggested she could put the stain on it when the etching was finished.

"Sure, I'll help." Maggie wondered which verse he would choose but didn't ask.

They were about a third of the way home when Maggie noticed Jimmy Beiler riding this way, driving his father's market wagon. As he drew closer, Jimmy waved to them and called a hullo, his expression delighted and quite surprised.

"Now, there's a *wunnerbaar* young man," Dat said after he passed by.

"You sound like Gracie . . . *and* Cousin Lila," Maggie told him, remembering how Dat had asked Jimmy to take her home after the mill tour.

"S'pose that makes three of us." Dat chuckled.

"Jimmy's gonna be our next blacksmith, from what I'm hearin'," she offered now.

"And a mighty fine one, I'm sure."

Maggie smiled, enjoying her walk with her father and looking forward to doing this again another day, Lord willing.

CHAPTER

25

"When can we go for a walk together?" Maggie asked Leroy, catching him near the hand pump the next day before the noon meal.

He removed his straw hat, and she held it for him as he worked the pump handle hard. "Too busy," he said.

"You seem upset."

"Just makin' plans to leave here."

Oh dear. She refused to react, though she certainly wanted to. Where could a boy of fourteen possibly go? Quietly, she asked, "Where to, *Bruder?*"

"Our cousins in Mount Joy offered me three weeks of work on their farm. I'll be stayin' with them."

Maggie sighed. This wasn't what she'd expected to hear. More than ever, she wanted to talk further with her troubled brother, like they'd always done before Mamm died. Heart to heart.

Leroy gave her a glance. "You don't think I'll do it," he said. "Do ya?"

"So it's all set, then?" Maggie asked.

"Not accordin' to Dat, it ain't."

She was baffled. "Are you tellin' me you're goin' to go against his will?"

Leroy eyed the house. "I'd be out of the way of the lovebirds."

"Oh, for pity's sake . . . I'm not sure you know your own mind."

"An' that's where you're wrong!" He drank from the old cup they kept by the pump, then hurried toward the little *Dawdi Haus*, opened the screen door, and walked right inside.

What on earth? Maggie couldn't believe her brother would talk so. And why was he going to Nellie's for the noon meal?

Maggie was so beside herself, she pumped up some water, splashed it all over her face and neck, and stood there, letting it drip down onto her dress and apron.

"Why not just let him, dear?" Rachel asked her husband, upstairs in the privacy of their bedroom. "Three weeks might make Leroy miss home . . . and miss *you*."

"He's defyin' me, that's why," Joseph said.

Rachel touched Joseph's shoulder as they stood beside the window overlooking the meadow. "I know you don't have long before goin' back to the mill, but just think 'bout this—what if ya give him some time to cool off? Maybe some time away will—"

"Time away from the very family he needs to be with?" Joseph's voice rose; then he shook his head.

"I'm only tryin' to help."

"I know you are, love. I know." He slipped his arm around her and kissed her cheek. "I'll be late for work if I don't head back now."

"All right," she said. "But remember—he's just a boy."

"That's exactly it. Leroy's too young to make this kind of decision. You and I both know his reasons for wantin' to help my cousins."

Slowly, she let out a breath as Joseph headed for the doorway. His feet were quick on the stairs. Truly, she had no idea how this was going to play out. Leroy clearly needed a break, and Joseph was determined for his son to behave the way he always had before Joseph's remarriage.

That's the problem in a nutshell, Rachel thought, wishing she could have a nap. Here lately, she felt ever so tired.

***

Two days later, Cousin Lila borrowed Luke's car after supper and came to visit Maggie. While she and Maggie sat out on the front porch, she confessed to being curious about Glenn's letter. "If it's not too nosy of me," Lila said, eyes alight.

"You came over just to ask *that?*" Maggie smiled.

"Well, you know me; I'm as curious as a cat."

Just then, they heard a *meow.* "Look, it's Siggy!" Maggie was laughing. "Right on cue."

Aunt Nellie's cat came strolling across the adjoining porch and squeezed through the balusters, coming right up to Maggie.

Lila giggled as Maggie reached down to pet him. "He's fond of being rubbed under his neck, but not on his head. Never that," she said. "Most cats prefer beneath the neck and tummy."

"I wonder if he'll let me pet him this time," Lila said, leaning down to softly coax him over to her. "Here, Siggy, Siggy."

Arching and purring, Siggy circled Maggie's leg. Soon, he opened his mouth and yawned widely, then flopped down onto Maggie's bare foot.

"Well, lookee there—he clearly prefers you," Lila said. "So . . . you were goin' to tell me 'bout Glenn's letter."

"Oh, that's right!" Maggie began to share everything Glenn had written. "It was nice of him. He sure didn't have to do that."

Lila nodded. "He's a very caring person . . . should make a good minister someday." She sighed. "It was bittersweet to say good-bye to the Brubakers following the final tent meeting."

She looked sad, and Maggie wondered if Lila and her family would stay in touch with the evangelist and his family.

"Wouldn't it be interesting to hear him give a sermon?" Lila said just then, eyes sparkling. "You know, years from now, if he has his own church?"

"It would. Seems to me that sharing the testimony of his healing with everyone, like he did with me, would be a fine place to start."

Lila leaned back in the wooden rocker and rested her long arms on those of the chair. She was quiet for a while, just sitting there and watching the buggies go by. Then she said, "Are you glad you went to the meetings?"

"Oh *jah*! They made a big difference for me in many ways." Maggie mentioned how she was reading her Bible at every opportunity and trying to memorize certain verses, too.

Lila reached over and squeezed her hand. "Sounds like you're growing in the Lord."

Maggie was touched by this. "I'm so pleased you came over. I've missed seein' ya."

"You seem really well today," Lila observed now. "No limp."

"*Nee*, not for several days now." She told Lila about the new supplements. "And I'm makin' an effort to be thankful for each day, like it's a fresh page."

"Will ya keep taking them?"

"Dat and I've discussed that. I'm waiting a little longer to decide."

"Does this mean you'll be goin' back to Singings, then?" The twinkle in Lila's eyes was more mischievous now.

"Ya know, I just might." Despite her recent prayer for Jimmy's future happiness, her thoughts kept straying to him. She hoped Lila wouldn't come right out and ask about Jimmy this visit, not when he wasn't really Maggie's to care about. "I'll decide before Sunday, but I'm sure Gracie will want me to go, since I'm feelin' better."

They sat and talked leisurely until Rachel tapped on the inside of the screen door and peeked her head out. "Would yous like some cold lemonade? Miriam and I made a fresh batch."

"Sure, we'll come in for it," Maggie said, rising and disturbing Siggy, who let out a loud meow. "Aw, I'm so sorry, cat." She reached down to pet him.

She and Lila headed into the warm, stuffy house, glad to get their lemonade and return to the breezy porch.

"How many times did ya go to the tent for meetings?" Maggie asked Lila as they drank their lemonade.

"I lost count, but it's safe to say maybe three times a week. Sometimes more. Luke, of course, was there nearly every night for all six weeks. He even talked of wantin' to go along to help with the next crusade." Lila shifted in the chair, careful not to spill the glass in her hand. "I wouldn't be surprised if my parents decide to drive over to Souderton one of these evenings. They've become close friends with Lloyd and Esther."

Maggie nodded and wondered what Glenn's parents were like in their normal, run-of-the-mill daily life. She sipped some more of her lemonade, then said, "If you do go and happen to see Glenn, please tell him I appreciated his letter."

"I will," Lila said, nodding. "He is one amazing fella."

"*Jah.*" It crossed Maggie's mind then that maybe, just maybe, her pretty cousin was secretly interested in the evangelist's friendly son. *Can it be?*

CHAPTER

26

"Thought I'd come over and check on ya," Rachel told Ruth Zook as she entered the back door of the Zooks' home. Rachel found her neighbor busy with some tatting over in a cozy kitchen corner where an upholstered chair backed up to the sunny window.

"How *gut* to see ya, dear. It's always nice to have company," Ruth said, waving her toward the nearby rocker. "Sam's been so busy with the third cutting of hay, and now the trim on the house is needing paintin'. Sam and our son-in-law have been sanding it, gettin' it ready."

Rachel had sat with Ruth in this very spot more than a few times, discussing relationships and what it might mean for Rachel to be courted by a widower with children. Oh, the frank talks they'd had!

"Are ya doin' all right?" Ruth asked, interrupting Rachel's musing.

"Oh, just remembering how helpful you were when I stayed here with you and Sam, before Joseph and I tied the knot."

Ruth nodded her head slowly. "It was a sweet time for me," she said. "Felt like I had yet another daughter in the house."

"I don't see how Joseph and I would've gotten together otherwise."

Ruth pushed her *Kapp* string over her shoulder. "Where there's a will, there's certainly a way . . . at least when it comes to love and things of the heart."

"S'pose you're right, but it would've been difficult for Joseph to make the trip to Myerstown on weekends, considering his family and all."

Ruth stopped tatting and placed her needle and the pillow case in her lap. "You know, I don't recall ever hearin' how it was that you weren't yet married when your sister Sarah and I conspired for you and Joseph to meet."

Laughing, Rachel said, "Well, that's because I've never said why. Haven't talked much 'bout it, really." She paused and glanced out the sparkling clean window, out to a small garden with a white wrought-iron bench. "Not even Joseph knows."

"So it's a secret, then?"

"Not really . . . just complicated."

Ruth leaned forward, an air of expectation about her. "Now you've got me real curious."

Rachel shook her head. "It's not painful anymore, so I s'pose I can talk about it."

A faint flutter of surprise appeared on Ruth's face as Rachel began to share what had kept her single into her thirties.

The August that Rachel Glick was turning sixteen had been quite memorable. She'd been itching to attend the Sunday evening Singings with her next older sister, Kate, who at eighteen already had a beau. That beau had a younger cousin, Eli Fisher, and while Eli had been known to date more than one girl at a time—against the rules of their church district—the deacon hadn't talked to him yet about it, since everyone just assumed he'd settle down right quick once he joined church the following year, as per his intention.

One night after Rachel's second Singing, Jonathan Fisher, Kate's beau, arranged for Eli to double up with Rachel. Shy and not sure this was a good idea, Rachel reluctantly agreed, heartened by the fact her big sister was along, too. After all, it wasn't as if she'd be alone with Eli.

The moonlit ride along the back roads was lovely, the summer air fragrant with honeysuckle, and the familiar sounds of insects mingling with the tinkle of the tack and traces on Jonathan's road horse. Rachel decided to quit fretting and enjoy herself. The conversation with Eli turned out to be fun and made her laugh and kept her engaged during the long ride.

By the time Jonathan dropped off Rachel and her sister at home, Rachel secretly hoped Eli might seek her out the next time the youth gathered for activities. And when one date led to one more, and then to another, until it was time for Rachel to celebrate her seventeenth birthday, she was sure Eli Fisher was the fellow for her. Thankfully, Eli was talking about moving toward a serious courtship. With all of her heart, Rachel believed he was earnest. She was falling in love.

"I'm real nervous, sittin' here," Ruth said, frowning and leaning forward just then.

"Well, there's more to the story. But that's how I found my way to the Mennonite revival meetings not far away, seeking solace after another girl caught Eli's attention. The meeting-house was filled with singing and sermons that helped soothe my heart, let me tell ya. I'm not sure how I would've managed to survive the pain of it all without those," Rachel said. "And I promised myself I'd never let another fella care for me like that."

"I certainly understand why you'd think thataway." Ruth gave her a comforting look. "You were so young, too."

"But stupidly, I broke my own promise," Rachel revealed qui-etly, still feeling ever so frustrated with herself when remem-bering what had later transpired. "After several months, I let Eli talk me into goin' back to him. It was wintertime by then, and he managed to convince me how sincerely sorry he was . . . said he'd been a *Dummkopp* to let me go."

"Oh, my dear." Ruth's hand flew to her chest. "So what happened?"

"Well, the same thing: Just two months after we got back together, another girl caught his fancy . . . and this time, he was gone for good."

There was a long silence between them, and Rachel felt surprised at how caught up she'd been in this account—she'd experienced something of a release, sharing all of this. "Perhaps now you understand why I was still unmarried in my thirties."

"Hard as this was for ya, my dear, your heartache brought you to Joseph Esh," Ruth said, her eyes searching Rachel's. "Never forget."

"*Jah*, out of all of that rubbish came my present happiness."

Ruth added, "I've learned from my own experience that hope often springs from despair."

The woman's words resonated with Rachel. "You're quite right," she whispered, ever so thankful for the passing of years.

CHAPTER

27

Maggie waited outdoors after Preaching service with a group of young women her age, including Cousin Deborah, who mentioned in passing that she was thinking of accepting Elijah Zook's invitation to go out riding after Singing that evening.

It took a moment for this to register, and then astonishment swept through Maggie.

"Aren't ya goin' with Jimmy Beiler?" Maggie asked, trying to sound only mildly interested.

Judging from Deborah's expression, it was her turn to be surprised. "We're not dating," she said, "if that's what you think."

"No, it's just that—"

"You mean because he took me home that one time?"

Maggie shrugged, feeling silly now.

"I just needed a ride," Deborah said as she glanced over at the fellows hanging around the stable. Elijah Zook smiled real big just then, returning Deborah's glance. "Jimmy's nothin' more than a friend."

223

Hoping she hadn't let on how bewildered she felt, Maggie did not reply. To think she assumed the two of them were a couple! How had she been so clueless?

The thought of Jimmy's being free to spend time with *her*, perhaps, made Maggie wonder if he actually *did* like her as more than a friend. Oh, she wanted him to notice that she was doing fairly well now—no cane, no limp—and could even go with him after Singing if he chose to invite her. And now, the more she was around him, the more she wished their relationship could lead to something more. *Dear Lord, what do I do?*

"Maggie?" Deborah was poking her. "They're calling *die Youngie* in for the fellowship meal. You comin'?"

"*Ach,* sorry."

Deborah giggled, and Maggie didn't know if she was laughing at her or whether she had caught Elijah Zook's smile again.

Jimmy never was seeing my cousin, she thought, trying to comprehend this fact. It was the only thing on Maggie's mind as the youth filed in for the light meal.

"I'm planning on goin' to Singing tonight," Maggie told Grace that afternoon as they sat on the grass beneath the backyard's biggest shade tree, a tree Maggie and Grace had climbed many times during their childhood to sit and share secrets where no one could see or find them.

This was one of the few Sunday afternoons they hadn't gone as a family to visit Dawdi Reuben, because Dat said it was too hot for even their best road horse. Although Maggie missed seeing Dawdi, she was thankful, wanting to be well rested enough to stay out should Jimmy ask her. Of course, she dared not let on her hopes to Grace.

"Glad to hear it," Grace said, flicking an ant off her dress.

Stretching her legs out on the grass, Maggie truly felt wonderful. How good it was to be with her close sister on this summer day, the pretty landscape all around them. "It'll be nice to spend time with the other young folk."

"Other than just me, ya mean?"

"Oh, you!" Maggie poked her playfully.

They smiled, enjoying being together, teasing and laughing.

"It's *gut* to see you out of your room . . . and the house," Grace said. "Are ya still readin' the Good Book a lot?"

Maggie said she was. "I must be hungry for spiritual food. That's what the tent evangelist called it during his sermons."

Grace listened, seemingly thoughtful.

"Preacher Brubaker says all of us have a great yearnin', whether we admit it or not—a longing to fill the void in our hearts. We either fill it with things that bring no contentment, or we fill it with the Lord."

Grace was nodding her head now. "Martin talks like this sometimes. He reads the Bible quite a bit, too."

"Well, it's a comfort," Maggie said, hoping that might interest Grace in reading it, as well. "It's changed my life."

"You sure it's not those tent meetings?"

"The meetings were wonderful, but reading the Bible is something I can do on my own. In fact, just reading a single chapter in the book of Proverbs each day for a month would fill you up with oodles of wisdom."

"*Jah*, I could do that, starting in August," said Grace.

Maggie smiled, glad her sister was open to the idea.

At that moment, Miriam came around the house, bouncing her ball down the back walkway.

"I wonder where Andy and Stephen are," Maggie said, feeling sorry for their little sister, over there by herself. "They usually play with Miriam on Sunday afternoons."

"Dat and the boys all ran down to the fishing hole. Maybe they'll jump in and swim in their trousers, it's so hot."

"Hope they changed out of their for-*gut* clothes first," Maggie said. She'd only known Dat and the boys to do this occasionally, and only when it was this warm out. A trip to the swimming hole wasn't a typical Lord's Day afternoon, to be sure.

"Oh, they changed." Grace laughed softly. "Dat saw to that."

"Well then, we'd better go an' play catch with Miriam," Maggie said.

Grace rose to go over and join Miriam, who was counting how many times she bounced her ball without stopping.

Maggie was getting up when she heard someone behind her. She turned, and there was Leroy, wet to the skin, running toward her. "Leroy!" she called. "*Hoch dich naah!*"

Surprisingly, he came and sat right down exactly as she asked, smelling like pond water, his black pants sopping and stuck to his legs. His short-sleeved white shirt was dry, however, so he'd evidently stripped down to the waist. "Looks like ya had a nice dip."

He gave a quick bob of his head. "Cooled me off some."

She figured Dat and the younger boys hadn't returned yet, because they were nowhere to be seen. "Is now a *gut* time for us to talk?" she asked gently.

"Guess so. Just till I dry off, though."

She could tell he wasn't too keen on it, but she was relieved he didn't go into the house to change clothes simply to avoid her. "It hurts me to see ya upset so much of the time, *Bruder*," she began. "If there's any way I can help, please tell me."

Leroy seemed to take that in, though he didn't offer any ideas. He listened as she continued to talk, keeping her voice low so as not to let her sisters hear what was on her heart. Grace appeared to have taken Miriam around toward the front of the house. "I was readin' a psalm this past week—somethin' I've memorized, I've read it so often."

He glanced her way, not scowling now. Yet she sensed his walls were up.

"'The righteous cry, and the LORD heareth, and delivereth them out of all their troubles. The LORD is nigh unto them that are of a broken heart; and saveth such as be of a contrite spirit.'"

Leroy's expression was blank, like he'd heard the words but didn't embrace their meaning.

"None of us can know how long our troubles will last," she told him, "but deliverance is bound to come eventually. I really think that's what this verse is sayin'." She noted Leroy's suddenly sad face and sighed. "I try to remind myself that God is near when we're heartbroken. Like you are right now."

He looked at her, his hazel eyes ever so big. "You don't understand, Maggie. I may be brokenhearted, but I'm not at all righteous . . . so how can that verse be for me?"

She pondered that. "None of us is righteous, but I happen to know that you do seek to follow God's path." She wasn't inclined to preach at him, so she was careful how she said it.

"*Jah*, before the day Mamm died, I did." His voice was taut.

She gently touched his shoulder. "What happened that day? Can ya tell me?"

Bowing his head, Leroy stared at the grass between his feet. He was silent for so long, it was painful for Maggie to witness. She looked away, praying silently for wisdom . . . for a way to help her dear brother.

Then, when she thought he would never speak, he lifted his head and sighed audibly. "Just before Mamm passed, I made a promise to her."

A promise? Was this what had been eating away at Leroy all these months?

"But then Rachel came along and kept me from followin' through with it." He stopped talking suddenly, his face flushed and perspiring.

A wave of sorrow passed over Maggie, and she wished she knew how to comfort him.

"I failed Mamm, don't ya see?" Leroy said, pressing his lips together in a grimace. "Dat took his eyes off all of us kids the moment he met Rachel. And then he married her."

Maggie was startled; while she had been taken aback by the speed of her father's remarriage, in her view, Rachel was a gift to their father, not a distraction. But she knew it might make things worse if she pointed out how mistaken Leroy was.

"I promised Mamm I'd never forget her . . . that I wouldn't let any of us forget her, either." Leroy was weeping now into his hands. "And look what happened."

Maggie was thankful that neither Aunt Nellie nor Rachel was out sitting on the back porch like usual on such a hot Sunday afternoon. In the distance, she could hear Grace and Miriam's muted laughter.

"It was right after I made my promise that Mamm closed her eyes. She took one last breath, and that was it." His face was streaked with tears. "I couldn't believe she was gone, Maggie."

"You loved her dearly," Maggie said quietly, moved by Leroy's account. "I hope ya won't forget that."

"But I let Mamm down, and now there's nothin' I can do about it."

Maggie would not argue that their father was a grown man who had every right to remarry. *Mamm would want him to be happy again,* she thought.

"God knows everything 'bout ya, Leroy. He knows that you made Mamm a beautiful promise. Better yet, He knows why ya made it. And you know what else? The deeper our heart aches, the more we need to ask God to fill that ache."

Leroy seemed to take this in. He got up and stood there, looking down at her, the sun on his face now. "You're the only one who cares what I think, Maggie," he said, shielding his eyes with one hand.

And before she could reply, he rushed off to the house and disappeared inside.

"O Lord in heaven, please help my poor, confused brother," Maggie whispered to the sky. "Send Thy love and surround him with it, every minute of every day. In Jesus' name, I pray."

CHAPTER
28

Not only was Maggie pleased to be back at Singing that Sunday evening, but she was delighted when Jimmy walked across the freshly swept haymow to her during the refreshments of cold root beer and peanut butter cookies. As was their way, he was still wearing his Sunday clothes, looking more handsome than Maggie had ever seen him.

There they talked, with the earthy smell of farm animals below and the sweet scent of the neatly stacked hay above. Never once did he mention Maggie's missing cane, or that she typically just sat with other girls during this halfway point in the gathering. Rather, Jimmy asked about her week and what she had been doing. He also seemed eager to mention that he'd seen her walking back from the mill with her father. "It made me smile to see the two of you together, out for a walk." That was the closest he came to mentioning her renewed vitality.

The thought crossed her mind that the fact she looked as strong as the other young women present likely played no small part in how they were standing there, talking so animatedly.

And so, while she hadn't planned to bring it up today, she felt now might be a good time. "I really appreciate you telling me about those pills, Jimmy."

His eyes lit up. "You're still taking them, then. Have they been helpful?"

"So far, yes," she said shyly. "And I have you to thank."

He waved it off. "Any *gut* friend would've done the same thing."

Jimmy's smile warmed her heart. And later, when everyone resumed singing, she couldn't recall ever seeing him smile at her quite like that—with his eyes, too. It gave her such joy, she found herself singing all the more energetically. So much so that Grace glanced at her several times, grinning as if she sensed what Maggie was feeling.

Afterward, quite a few of the youth milled about for more than an hour, fellowshipping with the cordial couple who'd hosted the barn gathering. And, perhaps because it had gotten quite late, Jimmy headed for his courting buggy without asking Maggie or anyone else out riding. She wondered at that when he'd been so attentive to her during refreshments, but it could be he had an early start tomorrow morning at the smithy's. *It's all right,* she told herself. *Another time, maybe.*

Though a little disappointed by the evening's end, she was grateful for a ride home with Grace and her well-mannered beau. Still, the truth remained: Jimmy's endearing smile surely meant something. How could it not?

At the end of the walkway to the side door, she thanked Grace and Martin for the lift, then walked to the porch and stood there, thinking she might just stroll around the backyard a bit, since she was still feeling good and the moonlight was so bright. Oh, the simple joy of walking without pain!

There had been moments since Rachel's marriage to Joseph when she had to stop and pinch herself. One of those had taken place on this first day of August, a very busy Wednesday. She'd turned around from beating the rag rugs on the clothesline, and there was Leroy, carrying the kitchen scraps in a trash bag, heading for the compost pile. He didn't say a word, just whistled a tune she didn't recognize. *Like Joseph does,* she thought. If she hadn't witnessed it herself, she might have thought she was dreaming. And when he returned, she thanked him whole-heartedly, though Leroy simply nodded and tapped his straw hat in return.

Then later, without being told, he hooked up the hose to the outside spigot and began watering the flower beds along the house. Again, Leroy said nothing.

Did Joseph encourage him to do this? Rachel wondered.

She stood there, observing Leroy from afar as he moved toward the other side of the house. *What's come over him?*

At the dinner table that noon, Rachel casually mentioned that she wanted to deliver a dried beef and noodle casserole to Joseph's elderly great-uncle Paul, who lived several miles away.

Right then, Joseph volunteered Leroy to drive her.

Goodness. Rachel nearly dropped her fork. *This won't go over well.*

Andy and Stephen exchanged glances, eyebrows raised.

With a delayed nod, Leroy agreed.

Scarcely knowing how to respond, Rachel just sat there eating, wondering how she and Leroy would manage such a journey. She was actually on the verge of tears, something that seemed to be the case much too often here lately.

It was after a dessert of sliced peaches and vanilla ice cream that Joseph caught her eye and gave her a reassuring wink.

My husband's up to something. . . .

Following the meal, while the girls cleaned up the kitchen, Rachel got in the family carriage, Leroy in the driver's seat.

He mentioned how smoothly everything had gone in erecting the new stable. "With so many pitchin' in to help."

Glad that he was making an effort to be friendly, she enthusiastically agreed. "Plenty-a teamwork."

A few seconds passed, followed by more silence, and then Leroy spoke once more. "I'd like to be on a crew to raise a barn sometime."

Even though it was a small admission, she felt pleased that he felt up to sharing it with her. "I think you'd be *gut* at it," she replied.

And then it was as if he remembered where he was and who he was riding with, and the conversation turned awkward, more like usual. Rachel asked him a few questions, but the answers were shorter and less candid now, and nothing seemed to really interest him.

All the same, the fact that Leroy had actually talked to her—and with more than the usual one-word responses and assorted grunts and mumbles—was curious. He wasn't overly friendly, but he wasn't rude, either.

Eventually, Rachel simply stopped pressing him and appreciated the progress they'd made. *Inch by inch,* she reminded herself.

After Rachel and Leroy made the delivery to Great-uncle Paul, Leroy unexpectedly pulled into the parking area for

Betsy's shop. A number of cars were parked there, as well as a motorbike. He got out and tied Buster to the hitching post, then walked around to Rachel like a young gentleman before accompanying her inside, where customers sat at tables along the open windows.

"Dat gave me some money for a treat," Leroy said quietly as they waited in line to place their order.

"He did?" Her Joseph was a man of surprises!

Rachel chose a cinnamon twist and encouraged Leroy to select something, too, but he said he was only thirsty, and Betsy gave him some cold water in a cup. Rachel, however, persisted, and finally he agreed to order a giant chocolate chip cookie, as large as three regular-sized cookies combined.

They talked with Betsy at the counter for a while, and then an Amishwoman with five children in tow came into the shop. Suddenly, Leroy stood taller, even ran his hand through his hair, glancing now and then at the family.

Curious, Rachel looked their way again and noticed the oldest of the children, a slender blond girl about Leroy's age, who smiled discreetly at him. When Rachel glanced back at Leroy, his face was all lit up. *They must know each other,* she decided.

Leroy's mood seemed to improve considerably as a result of the brief encounter; he even hummed a bit as he and Rachel rode toward home, and she had to cover a smile. Compared to the previous months, it was as if a shadow had lifted from Leroy—just the fact that he'd spoken to her respectfully was a step forward.

Rachel hardly knew what to make of it and looked forward to sharing all this with Joseph. *Tonight,* she thought, *when we're alone. And I want to tell him something else, too. . . .*

Later that afternoon, Maggie and Miriam spent some time weeding and hoeing the large family vegetable garden while Rachel took a nap. There on the high ridge overlooking the wooded area near the road, Maggie felt at peace. Expending her energy like this had always given her a sense of satisfaction, and today it meant so much more to her, because she'd missed working the soil like this, doing her part for the family.

When the work in the vegetable garden was done, and while Grace and Miriam were indoors planning supper, Maggie took on the rose bushes, paying close attention to mixing the right amount of fertilizer with water. Mamm had always doted on her roses. *Nearly like they were her children,* Maggie thought, smiling at the memory.

Despite the heat of the afternoon, Maggie felt renewed. And as she worked, she prayed silently, not wanting anyone to think she was talking to herself, like Great-aunt Lettie did sometimes.

It had been an effort not to think too often of Jimmy. She still found him more appealing than any other young man she'd met, but she just wanted to be thankful for his friendliness toward her. *His seeking me out in conversation at the last Singing doesn't need to mean anything more than that.*

Tonight, she and Grace planned to go for a walk after the supper dishes were done, and tomorrow, Rachel wanted all of them to pick white peaches at a nearby orchard. Maggie would definitely go and help. For once in the longest time, she could pull her weight and do many of the chores expected of a young woman her age.

My life has returned to near normal, she thought, breathing a thanks to her heavenly Father.

CHAPTER

29

Olde Mill Road seemed to buckle in the heat that evening as Maggie and Grace walked together, their arms swinging in unison. The main topic of conversation was Martin Lantz—he was all Grace wanted to talk about. And who could blame her? She was so happy.

"Dat would think I'm too young to be getting serious," Grace said, her skirt flowing about her legs as she walked. "Ain't so?"

"And what's the hurry?" Maggie replied, savoring this time alone with her sister. "Martin's only a few months older than you. Just enjoy your courtship, if it's moved to that already."

"Martin's goin' to be helpin' with the apple harvest at his Onkel's orchard down in Quarryville, where he'll stay even over the weekends. Sounds like we won't be seein' much of each other this month or next."

"Then it'll be that much more special when ya *do.*"

"Oh, it will." Grace grinned, her bandanna slipping back on her head. "But let's not just talk 'bout me. I saw you and Jimmy together at the last Singing." Grace looked at her expectantly.

Maggie smiled. "*Jah.*"

"That's all you're gonna say?"

"*Jah.*"

They laughed.

"So you're really not gonna tell me anything?" Grace asked, nearly pleading.

"What's to tell?"

"Well, he looked so pleased to see you and was talkin' nearly nonstop the whole refreshment time."

Maggie smiled. "Hmm. I'd have thought you'd be too busy with Martin to notice."

"Oh, I was keepin' my eye on you, believe me," Grace said, pausing a moment to wipe her face with the handkerchief she pulled out from under her sleeve. "Honestly, it was so nice to see yous together."

They had moved to the grassy slope along the roadside to cool their bare feet, the road was so hot. "Sure wish we had some water," Maggie said. "My mouth is parched."

"Mine too."

"So let's head back," Maggie suggested as they waited for two carriages to go by. "We've already walked at least a half mile."

"We could stop in at Aunt Nellie's and say hullo."

Maggie agreed. Even this close to sundown, it was still nearly too hot to be out walking.

Their great-aunt was sitting on the wooden bench that encircled the hickory tree just to the side of the *Dawdi Haus*, not far from the porch where the sun shone hard this time of year. The tree was a favorite of Aunt Nellie's, whose grandfather had planted it many years ago.

Maggie noticed her great-aunt's lips moving as the girls

approached her, and Maggie wondered if she was talking to herself.

"Hullo, Aendi," Grace said right away.

Nellie turned to look their way, and a big smile lit up her wrinkled face. She opened her hands to them.

"Hope we didn't interrupt you," Grace said as she went over to sit on one side of Nellie.

Maggie sat on the other. "This is one of those days it's so easy to be thankful, ain't so?"

Nellie chuckled softly. "*Jah*, and I was thankin' the dear Lord for every blessing I could name. This here lovely shade, for one. And for your father's kindness to me in my old age . . . and you girls an' your brothers, for bein' so attentive to this ol' lady."

"Now, Aendi, we love ya," Grace said. "Of course we want to spend time with you."

"Have ya always prayed out loud?" Maggie had to know.

"Just since I lost my Matthew to Glory." Here Nellie glanced toward the sky. "I sometimes ask God to let Matthew know that I still think of him every day. I'll always love him."

"That's so dear," Maggie whispered against the lump rising in her throat.

"I don't see anything wrong with prayin' aloud like that," Grace said just then. "Sometimes my beau does, too."

This surprised Maggie.

"He told me he even slipped away to the tent meetings. In fact, he went twice." Grace was fanning her face with her hankie. "I wonder how many other Amish youth did that."

Maggie didn't reveal that she'd seen a few Amish young people there, standing outside mostly, though none she recognized from this church district.

After a while, Grace said, "Would ya mind if I got some cold water for us?"

"Oh, let me go an' get a pitcherful," Maggie offered, rising and going to the main house. *Grace will benefit from talking alone with Aunt Nellie,* thought Maggie, glad for the many times she'd shared with the faith-filled woman.

Inside, she found Miriam pouring cold root beer for herself, Dat, and Rachel. "They're out on the back porch, tryin' to cool off. It's the hottest day of the summer so far, Dat says." Miriam picked up the tray with three tumblers full of the homemade treat.

Maggie was too thirsty to bother with root beer, so she filled a pitcher with cold water and stacked three tumblers to carry outside.

When she returned to Aunt Nellie and Grace, Nellie was holding Grace's hand, leaning near her to talk more privately. Hanging back, Maggie thought it was the dearest sight ever. It reminded her of Mamm's tenderness with all of them.

In a few moments, Grace looked up, and Nellie released her hand.

"C'mon over, Maggie-bird . . . we're all right, ain't so, Gracie?" Aunt Nellie said, a twinkle in her eyes.

"Don't want to disturb yous." Maggie came over, gave a tumbler to each of them, and poured the cold water clear to the top. "This'll wet your whistle."

Nellie took a long drink, then sighed. "Ah, this is the life . . . sittin' here after the day's chores are done, just soakin' up the beauty of God's creation." She looked into their faces. "And with such *wunnerbaar-gut* company, too."

Grace nodded and smiled over at Maggie.

"Do ya ever think of each new day as fresh soil spread out

before us? What we choose to do, think 'bout, and yearn for are like seeds falling from our hearts into the earth," said Aunt Nellie. "I once heard a minister say that we're constantly sowing seeds, whether we know it or not."

"Preacher Brubaker's sermons sounded a little like that," Maggie said, recalling his impassioned words. "They really made me ponder things."

"I should think so," Aunt Nellie said, smoothing her apron. "Before I take my last breath, I hope to be sure I've sown seeds of obedience, kindness, and grace . . . and have pulled out the weeds of selfishness, impatience, and wickedness."

Grace was squinting. "It's awful hard to imagine the word *wicked* and you belonging in the same sentence, Aendi Nellie."

Nellie nodded her snow-white head. "All of us are born with a wicked streak, ya know. Born into sin, as the Good Book says. We're all the children of Adam and Eve."

"Still, you're the kindest Aendi ever," Grace said, making Maggie smile and tear up at the same time.

"Only one holy person has ever walked this earth," Nellie said. "And you both know Who I mean."

Maggie and Grace nodded.

"Without the Lord's Spirit in us," Nellie continued, "we're as wicked as any person who chooses to live for themselves . . . not heeding God's ways."

"You must be a preacher like your Dawdi," Maggie observed softly.

"Oh, I just say what's in my heart." Nellie reached over and patted Maggie's hand. "What we fill our minds and souls with counts. If God's Spirit lives in us, we'll sow *gut* seeds."

Maggie mentally stored away all these things, thankful that God had given her so many healthy years.

After family prayers, Rachel and Joseph leisurely prepared for bed, then went around and opened the windows in their bedroom as high as possible. Rachel even said she wished they had a downstairs room on a hot night like this.

"Leroy was a little different today," Rachel mentioned.

"I noticed, too." Joseph sat near the window in only his pajama bottoms, fanning himself with the afternoon newspaper. "And he didn't protest when I volunteered him to drive ya to Paul's."

"He was certainly polite," Rachel said, telling of their conversation in the buggy and then the stop at Betsy's shop.

"Well, an' he apologized to me for sayin' he wanted to leave to work in Mount Joy," Joseph said, still fanning himself.

"That's a relief. I was scared he might disobey ya on that." Rachel pulled her brushed hair up off her neck into a loose bun to cool herself off. "Thank the Lord he had a change of heart."

Joseph nodded in agreement. "One of God's gifts to us . . . a bit like those pills seem to be to Maggie."

A blessing . . . and a relief, she thought, going to stand near the window on the other side of the small table. There, Joseph kept *The Budget* and other periodicals, including *Farmer's Almanac* and the old German *Biewel* that he used for his early morning reading. Thinking about blessings, she asked, "By the way, Joseph, can you afford to keep buying those pills?"

He looked over at her. "Maggie mentioned that, too—even offered to work in Betsy's bakery, if she's hiring."

"Ain't too far away, really."

"*Nee*, but Maggie hasn't joined church just yet, and even

though I believe she will, come fall, I'd hate to think of her rubbin' shoulders with all those tourists."

Rachel nodded. She understood where Joseph was coming from.

"Of course, if she really wants to, it would be hard to deny her workin' alongside Betsy." He rose to go across the room to lie down. "*Ach*, I'm afraid if there's no breeze tonight, we won't be getting much sleep," he said, kicking off the bedcovers.

She could see that Joseph wasn't interested in talking further about Maggie on this miserably warm night. Not when he was tired and understandably out of sorts.

"I have some very happy news that might make ya feel better," she said, going over to sit on his side of the bed and stroking his arm. "I'm expectin' a baby."

Joseph rolled onto his back and smiled up at her now. "Is that right?" He reached for her gently, kissing her. "The best kind of news, *jah?*"

She agreed, smoothing his beard gently. "I love ya so."

He sighed and clasped her hands. "We'll have us a little Rachel, maybe," he suggested.

"Or a wee Joseph." Her heart was so full, Rachel wanted to hold him and never let go.

CHAPTER
30

Maggie was doing surprisingly well picking peaches the next morning with her sisters and Rachel. She stood on the ladder amidst the leafy branches, the sun warm on her face. Even the bees nearby didn't bother her. This was a task she'd missed for years, now that she thought of it.

Below her, amongst the lowest peach tree branches, Miriam hummed happily as she worked, talking now and then to Maggie while Grace and Rachel worked together the next tree over.

"Can't remember when I last saw ya on a ladder," Miriam said, pressing a ripe peach to her nose and smelling it.

"I've been takin' some new pills—special supplements," Maggie said, reaching for the ripest peaches and giving them a gentle twist, then tug. "Hopefully they'll keep workin'."

"Aunt Nellie says she prays no one else gets what you had."

Maggie looked at her little sister, so energetic and healthy. "Me too."

"We're pickin' extra for Aunt Nellie, *jah?*"

"With four of us pickin', we should have plenty."

"We all know how much Dat and the boys love peaches." Miriam's eyes shone. "Peach pie, peach cobbler . . ."

"Don't leave yourself out, silly," Maggie said, smiling down at her.

"I'm just tryin' to think of others first, like Mamm always said." Miriam worked for a while without talking.

Maggie nodded her head. "We can talk more later, if you want," she said gently. These past months had been a tough time of transition for all of them, not just for Leroy and Rachel.

Miriam looked up. "I'm glad you're my big sister."

"Well, fortunately for you, I always will be," she told her with a grin as Miriam steadied the ladder.

When they arrived home, Maggie carried a quarter bushel of plump peaches over to Aunt Nellie's.

At the sight of the beautiful fruit, Nellie clapped her hands. "My mouth's waterin'." She eyed Maggie. "You carried these over on your own?"

"*Jah*, I'm doin' fine," Maggie said, tickled to bring her such happiness. "I'll help ya bake up some cobbler, if you'd like."

Nellie smiled but shook her head at the suggestion. "I know you've got plenty to do next door, but it's nice of you to offer."

"Well, if you're sure."

Maggie gave Nellie a gentle hug and headed for the back door. "I'd best get back to help Rachel with the noon meal."

"All right, then," Nellie called to her. "So *gut* seein' ya so perky, Maggie-bird."

"You too, Aendi!" She laughed as she opened the screen door and went around to the main house.

That afternoon, Maggie helped Leroy sharpen the blades of the push mower. Her brother had been pitching manure onto the spreader with Andy while Stephen and Grace tended Sam Zook's roadside vegetable stand for a few hours. Sam was running an errand, and Ruth was busy canning peaches with her married daughters.

"You sure you're up to this?" Leroy asked Maggie as they worked together.

"It's time I did my share round here."

"You surprise me, sister . . . peppy as ya are."

"I think everyone's surprised, me most of all," she replied. "But just now I feel *wunnerbaar* . . . and I'm ever so thankful."

Leroy nodded his head and cast a smile her way. "Even Danny Beiler's talking 'bout it—the whole Beiler family is."

Maggie stared at him. "What on earth?"

Leroy grinned. "And it's not just Danny and his family . . . some of my other friends are talkin' about it, too."

"Well, what're they sayin'?"

"That those pills must be heaven-sent," Leroy said, squatting down to get under the lowest blades of the push mower. "I wonder if the health food store's gonna sell out of them."

"God does use herbs and medicines to heal," she said, "but I doubt that many folk would need this particular pill."

Leroy just kept working to rotate the mower's blades, not replying now.

She caught herself smiling at the notion of Jimmy's brother talking about her health. But Maggie wouldn't let her imagination take over, running away with hopes and dreams about being more than friends with Jimmy. Since he hadn't asked her out yet, Jimmy might just have his eye on another girl. *After all, he's had plenty of chances in the past couple of weeks,* she thought.

Fatigued and hot though she was, Maggie kept pushing the newly sharpened mower over the grass on the south side of the house, past Mamm's pretty roses and around the front to Aunt Nellie's little front porch and back. She leaned hard into the mower, thanking God for everything in sight—the old hickory tree, the fertile soil for the flower beds and the family vegetable garden beyond, the little potting shed where Mamm and now Rachel worked with cuttings and whatnot. She was also thankful for the flock of birds high in the sky to the east just now, her brother Leroy working so diligently and so pleasantly, and for her own renewed health.

"If I live as long as Aunt Nellie, Lord, please help me remember to be as grateful as she is," Maggie said. In the backyard, she stopped to pick up twigs near the base of a tree. As she leaned down, she heard Miriam talking to Rachel through the kitchen window.

"You oughta rest," Miriam said, her small voice insistent. "Should I go an' get Maggie?"

Hearing this, Maggie stopped what she was doing and went around to the side door. There, she discovered Rachel sitting on the bench, her back to the table and her head between her knees.

Quickly, Maggie went to the sink and drew water, then opened the drawer and grabbed a clean washrag. She ran the cool water over it and wrung it out loosely before going to Rachel and placing it on the back of her neck. Mamm had done this many times for Maggie and the other children when they were overheated in the summertime or had a queasy spell.

Without speaking, Maggie sat next to her stepmother and pressed the cloth against her neck, then after a minute or so, turned it over to the cooler side to do the same.

"I thought she might faint," Miriam said, wide-eyed as she crept near. "Will she be all right?"

Maggie nodded. She offered her free hand to Miriam, who came to sit quietly next to her. "Dear Lord God," Maggie began to pray softly, "be with Rachel and take care of her. I trust Thee to help her, in Jesus' name."

For what seemed like a long time, Maggie kept turning the cloth and resting it against Rachel's slender neck, keeping quiet, since she knew how little she herself liked to be questioned when nauseated. And as she soothed Rachel, Maggie began to feel closer to this woman who'd so swiftly come into their lives.

At last, Rachel slowly raised her head and sat up, taking a long, deep breath. "Didn't mean to worry yous," she said in a near whisper.

"Let's get ya to my room. You can lie down there," Maggie said. With Miriam's help, they guided Rachel through the sitting room and into Maggie's bedroom.

"Don't fret about a thing, Rachel. Miriam and I will finish makin' supper," Maggie told her as she helped lift her legs up onto the bed. "Just rest for as long as you need to."

She left the door open in case Rachel called for them. Then she and Miriam went quietly to the kitchen.

"Rachel got too hot or somethin' when she was cookin' supper," Miriam said.

"Maybe so." But Maggie remembered how their mother had

suffered with nausea before Stephen and Miriam were born and wondered now if Rachel might be in the family way. After all, she had also been real tired here lately, which wasn't like her at all.

"I'll check on the turkey and rice casserole, an' you set the table," Maggie told Miriam, opening the oven.

Miriam did what she was told, then said, "I've never heard ya pray like that before, Maggie."

"For Rachel, ya mean?"

"*Jah*, out loud and whatnot. I liked it."

Maggie smiled. "Well, Aunt Nellie prays like that, too, at least privately."

"I like to pray the Lord's Prayer sometimes when I'm alone," Miriam said, coming to open the utensil drawer for more forks. "But I just say it to myself."

"Sometimes I say it softly before I fall asleep," Maggie admitted.

Miriam looked at her, eyebrows raised. "Ya think it's all right with God?"

"That's the very prayer He taught His disciples to pray."

"Are *we* His disciples, too?"

Maggie smiled and walked to the table. "Disciples just means followers, so *jah*, we certainly are."

Miriam came over and hugged her waist. "How'd ya get to be so *schmaert*?"

"Oh, I have lots to learn yet."

"But you know more'n me, that's for sure."

Maggie paused a second. "That's because I've been readin' the Good Book."

A light seemed to go on in Miriam's eyes. "Then I'll try an' listen better when Dat reads to us tonight."

"That's a *gut* place to start," Maggie said, listening for Rachel.

She slipped away to the bedroom and saw that Rachel was sound asleep.

Dear woman, she thought, wondering again if Rachel was indeed expecting a baby.

Maggie's bedroom was not as spacious as those upstairs, but as she stood in the doorway just now and peeked in at Rachel, who was up from her nap, she realized how much of a haven this room really was. She raised her hand to knock softly. "Rachel?"

"Come in," Rachel said, yawning. "*Denki* for lookin' after me, Maggie." Even sitting there on the bed after a long nap, she still looked spent.

"I hope you're feelin' better now," Maggie said, going to sit in the only chair in the room, near the window.

"Oh, I'm just fine. And it was nice of you to let me rest for a while in here."

Maggie waved her hand. "Anytime, really." She looked at her, this woman who had been in charge of Dat's house since they married. She looked so vulnerable, even a bit forlorn.

Rachel glanced at the wind-up alarm clock on the bedside table. "Goodness, it's nearly suppertime. The hours got away from me."

"I was worried 'bout ya," Maggie said. "At times like this, you must sorely miss your family clear up in Myerstown."

Rachel looked surprised. "I do, my Mamm especially."

Maggie nodded, hoping she was saying the right thing. "I just wanted to tell you that I understand."

"Well, of course ya do, Maggie. How rude of me!"

"*Nee*, not at all," Maggie protested and shook her head. "We *both* miss our mothers terribly, ain't so?" She skimmed her gaze across the bed quilt to Rachel. And it was as though a bond was forming—a common cord, maybe—and Maggie felt it all the more as Rachel rose to come to her, smiling through her tears as she sat down on the near side of the bed.

Rachel reached for Maggie's hand, gently holding it. "I can't begin to imagine what you must feel every day, wakin' up to your great loss," Rachel said sweetly. "Missin' your Mamm as I know ya do."

"Well, and yours isn't just up the road, a stone's throw away." Maggie looked down at Rachel's pretty hand around her own and pressed her lips together, lest they both end up weeping.

CHAPTER
31

Maggie knew something was very different the next morning when she awoke. At first, she wondered if she'd overdone it by picking so many peaches while awkwardly balanced against the ladder. Or was it because she'd thrown herself so vigorously into mowing when she really should have taken time to rest? Whatever the reason, she felt feverish and was having a terrible flare-up of pain.

She moaned as she stiffly sat up in bed. Reaching for her pillows, she placed them under her right arm and horizontally across the bed, leaning on them for support. Eventually, she managed to lift her legs over the side. Then she just sat there and thought, *Now what?*

For the longest time, she did not stand, afraid she might fall and hurt herself. All the same, she resisted the urge to call out, not wanting to alarm anyone. Besides, no one was up yet—not a sound came from the kitchen or overhead. Instead, she bowed her head and folded her hands to pray. "Lord, please help me get up and dressed for the day. I'm ever so thankful for all the blessings in my life. . . ." She stopped, sighing now. Yes, she was thankful, but she felt dishonest praying that way when here she was practically crippled again.

Ach, to think I've been so diligent about taking the expensive pills, staying right on schedule. Why, Miriam had even helped to remind her last night. Maggie thought fondly of her little sister's caring nature and hoped that she might soon come bounding down the stairs. *Otherwise, I might be sitting here all day,* Maggie fretted.

Minutes passed, then a quarter of an hour crawled by.

Exasperated in spite of her desire to keep calm, Maggie hoped she hadn't taken the past days of well-being for granted. *I was almost normal,* she thought sadly. *I hoped and prayed it might last. . . .*

Gingerly, she reached for her Bible on the nightstand and opened to the passages she so loved. The verses of encouragement had kept her going before when she'd felt so pain ridden, though never as bad as now. She spotted Aunt Nellie's gift for her eighteenth birthday—the white hankie edged with pink tatting—and sighed.

Eventually, there were footsteps on the stairs and the clatter of a pan being removed from the bottom drawer, and Maggie knew that either Grace or Rachel was preparing to cook breakfast.

Maggie tried to inch forward to stand on her own, slowly, cautiously putting her weight on her feet. She was almost up when she abruptly dropped back into a sitting position on the bed, jolting herself.

Am I crippled, Lord?

Feeling nauseous once again—a regular occurrence now for hours each morning—Rachel realized her heart was racing.

And oh, this annoying fatigue! It was as if she hadn't slept a wink!

Joseph kissed her on the temple as she sat on the edge of the bed and loosened her nightgown around her middle. "You must rest more, love," he said. "Please do what you need to and take care of yourself."

She nodded, and Joseph pulled her close. "The girls can handle most everything in the house, if need be. And I'll help out more, too." Joseph kissed her square on the lips. "May the Lord God bless our little one."

"Amen to that," she replied, her hand on her stomach. "But let's not tell the children quite yet. Not till it's obvious, *jah?*"

Joseph agreed. "Though I expect Maggie and Grace will put two and two together soon enough, if they haven't already." He offered to bring a breakfast tray up to her.

But Rachel couldn't think of eating. "I'll just move over to your favorite chair and try to get my mind off myself."

"Isn't there somethin' you can take to calm things down?"

"Mint tea and toast have helped," she said, but just now the thought of anything at all in her mouth made her nearly heave.

"I'll make some toast, then, and Maggie or Grace can brew some tea." With that, Joseph left the room and headed downstairs.

"Bless his heart," Rachel whispered, rocking back and forth and wondering how many more weeks she'd have to put up with this.

———

Maggie was so relieved when Grace came to check on her.

"What's a-matter?" Grace's eyes were solemn as she quickly moved across the room to feel Maggie's forehead. Then, shaking her head, she said, "You have a fever again."

"And the pain's back, too. I doubt I can walk to the kitchen."

Grace seemed to hesitate, but only a few seconds, and she didn't raise any alarming questions. "Don't worry," she said. "I'll bring your food in on a tray. Whatever ya need, I'll help ya, sister."

Maggie touched her long hair, feeling the snarls. "At some point, someone might help me brush my hair," she said. "I must've slept awful fitfully."

Again, Grace assured her that she'd assist in whatever way necessary. "I can help you dress and brush your hair after breakfast," she promised. "Miriam will want to help, too."

"Oh," Maggie groaned. "I hate for the family to have to hear 'bout this."

Grace gave her a compassionate look. "Well, we love you, sister. We want to share your burdens."

"Take your time to make breakfast for everyone else first, though, ya hear? I'll be fine here." Then Maggie remembered that Rachel hadn't been feeling well in the mornings lately. "Best be lookin' after Rachel, too, in case she needs something to eat."

"Dat's already been down to get her some toast, and I've got some peppermint tea brewin'. That seems to be the drink she prefers here lately."

Maggie exchanged a knowing glance with Grace. "Are ya thinkin' what I am?" Maggie whispered, offering a smile.

"*Jah.* I've suspected something for a week or so." Grace gave her a little smile, then wiggled her fingers and said she'd be back in a little while with a nice, hot breakfast.

"Bless your heart," Maggie said.

When the mail arrived later, Miriam came running into Maggie's room, excited to present to her a letter from Leola. "I looked at the return address—I think it's from cousins Nancy and Linda."

"How nice . . . they remembered to write," Maggie said, using the letter opener. She'd been resting in her room since the noon meal, which she'd managed to eat with the rest of the family in the kitchen, thanks to Dat and Leroy, who carried her out in a seat they made with their hands and arms.

The pain was so bad, moving at all made her feel nauseous. *Worse than I've ever felt*, she thought.

She sat propped up in bed to begin to read the letter from her cousins, recalling how much fun it had been to visit with them on her eighteenth birthday at Dawdi Reuben's. *Seems like ages ago now.*

As she finished the letter, Maggie heard meowing; Aunt Nellie stood in the doorway, holding Siggy.

"We came to bring cheer," Nellie said, smiling as she tiptoed into Maggie's bedroom and sat on the chair. "Gracie said you had a setback."

"I'm really not sure what's goin' on." Maggie was so glad to see her. "I wish Siggy could snuggle with me on the bed."

"I'll just sit with him there, so you can pet him." Nellie moved over to the edge of the bed. "Pets tend to soothe."

Maggie had to smile and reached to touch Siggy's neck, feeling the vibrations of his purrs. "He's a lesson in contentment, *jah?*"

Nellie nodded and watched Maggie stroke the cat.

"I'm tryin' to be brave through this," Maggie confided.

"You don't have to, an' you don't have to be strong, either," Nellie said, then quoted Second Corinthians, chapter twelve, verse nine, a verse Glenn also had once shared.

"That promise sure helps on a day like today," Maggie said as she watched Siggy's eyes slowly close. She mentioned that she'd taken her morning pill in the hope it might help, but it hadn't at all. "Never wanted to put my faith in them, ya know. But I'm afraid I did."

"I daresay all of us were hopin' they might be what ya needed." Nellie reached over and touched Maggie's long hair. "Did ya want your hair put up?"

"Grace offered, but I feel more comfortable havin' it down loose."

"Well, you do what ya have to," Nellie said, picking up Siggy and heading to the doorway. "I'll keep prayin' for you. Right now, though, I'm gonna check in on Rachel, too. She's been havin' quite a bout."

Maggie nodded, not letting on that she felt sure she knew why. That was Rachel's news to share. "*Denki* for comin' over, Aendi."

"I love ya, Maggie-bird. And so does the Lord." Nellie blew her a kiss and left.

Maggie watched her go, touched by Nellie's sweet spirit and her promise to pray. And reached for her comfort quilt and drew it near.

CHAPTER

32

Come that first Sunday in August, Maggie was relieved there was no Preaching service to attend, even though she'd always looked forward to them. It also meant there would be no baptismal class, and she still wasn't feeling up to either one.

Rachel, too, seemed to be in a bad way, although she came downstairs and sipped her mint tea first thing that morning, just as she had been doing lately. Maggie, on the other hand, had to have help walking from her bed just to the kitchen, despite the fact that she was still faithfully taking the pills as directed.

Before the rest of her siblings sat down for breakfast that sunny Lord's Day, Maggie found herself at the table with her father. "It doesn't make sense to order any more of that special supplement," she told him. "Not since the pain came back."

Dat's frown was evident. "Are ya sure?"

"I'm sure." Truth be known, her pain was increasing each

day, she told him. "But more than anything, I dislike not bein' able to help round the house."

Rachel carried her teacup and saucer over to the table and stood there. "You mustn't worry 'bout that, Maggie."

Dat said, "Rachel's right. Put your energies to better use."

"I'm hopin' the high humidity is to blame for this setback," Maggie said, thinking that in the past some of her worst days had been on hot, muggy, or rainy days. Yet it was hard to understand why she had consistently done so well recently, only to experience such a drastic turnaround. *Did I push myself too hard with all those chores?*

"Well, I suggest ya keep takin' the pills till they run out." Dat gave her a smile. "Let's see what happens."

Later, when all the family sat down for breakfast, Maggie enjoyed the scrambled eggs and bacon her sisters had made. Poor Rachel, however, made do with a few saltine crackers and a second cup of mint tea.

While Maggie was drinking her orange juice, it popped into her mind that both Nellie and Glenn Brubaker had promised to pray for her, and she smiled, heartened by it.

After they'd all finished eating, Maggie added a thank-you to God during the closing silent prayer, this one for everything she'd learned just this summer about His power to change lives . . . and to heal. While this sudden reversal made it easy to give in to discouragement, she refused to give up hope.

Jimmy dropped by unexpectedly later that morning with a walker he'd picked up from Betsy Lapp. When he brought it into the house from the market wagon, Maggie thanked him profusely for the very practical surprise. "Betsy's Dat said to use it as long as you need it," he told her, concern evident on his handsome face as he placed his straw hat on the kitchen bench.

"That's so nice . . . but how will *he* manage?" Maggie asked, quickly discovering how much easier it was to balance herself with the walker than with the cane. The extra support meant she could get around on her own.

"Betsy says he's doin' fine without it. His gout's easing up." Jimmy sat next to his hat as Maggie slowly shuffled along behind the walker, going around the kitchen. "You'll get used to it," he said.

"It's a big help, *jah*." She turned at the far end of the kitchen and inched back. "How can I ever thank ya?" she said, feeling more fond of Jimmy than ever, if that was possible.

"*Ach*, no need for that, Maggie." He smiled and sat there, looking at her so tenderly it startled her.

The side door opened, and Rachel and the girls came in from a morning walk. Miriam noticed the walker first and went to look at it but didn't make a fuss like she might have even a year ago. *Thank goodness*, Maggie thought, smiling at how much her youngest sister had grown up.

Miriam's expression held oh so many questions, but she didn't voice them and instead turned to go into the front room with the rest of them. *They're giving me some time with Jimmy*, she thought appreciatively.

Maggie hobbled to the side door, hoping Jimmy might come over, which he promptly did. He held the door and helped her out to the porch, where they stood for a short time, talking more privately as birds flew back and forth to the purple martin birdhouse her brothers had made recently.

"I'm sorry to see ya sufferin' again," he said. His hair shone in the sunlight, and she realized he'd left his straw hat inside.

"It's hardest when I want to leave the house," she told him, still hoping she could think of a way to properly thank him for being so kind as to get the walker. How had he known she needed it?

"Still hopin' those pills might help again," he said.

She told him what her father had said about taking them till they ran out.

"And what then?" Jimmy asked.

She sighed, unsure how to answer. "I don't know, other than to take it a day at a time and to praise God for whatever happens."

Jimmy seemed surprised at that. "Well, He must be giving you the grace to bear it, Maggie."

She gave a small shrug, feeling oddly close to him.

"I think most people would be tempted to give up, after all you've been through," he said.

She pondered his words and realized that, in a sense, giving up was exactly what she *was* doing. Only it didn't feel like quitting.

"Honestly, my life, and my health, is in God's hands. If He wants me well, then I will be." She paused and looked down at the walker, thankful for the stability it brought. "I just want to rest in what Jesus did for me—for all of us—when He took the stripes on His back for our healing."

"Your faith is strong." Jimmy nodded his head, studying her. "I really believe that."

Wanting to move the conversation to something else, Maggie asked, "By the way, which do ya like better—pie or cake?"

"Oh, you don't have to bake anything for me, Maggie."

"Well, I'd like to."

Jimmy pushed his hands into his pockets and shook his head. "Just knowin' you can get around more easily is enough for me." He looked out toward the meadow. "I mean that."

They talked a while longer, mostly about the farm sale Jimmy was interested in attending this Thursday. Then, for a few moments, they were somewhat awkwardly silent, there in the still of the morning. The heat of the August day was tempered by an occasional breeze.

And just when Maggie thought for sure that Jimmy wanted to say something more, something personal, he offered to help her back into the house. "Before I head home."

She agreed, and when they were inside again, Jimmy waited for her to take a seat in the kitchen before picking up his straw hat. Then, saying good-bye, he made his way to the door.

Aware of how quiet the kitchen was in that moment, Maggie swallowed the lump in her throat. Part of her wished she hadn't turned him down the one and only time he'd asked her out, so many months ago now. She had been so convinced that he only pitied her.

She sat there, hands folded in her lap, the walker within arm's reach, and recalled how he'd talked with her all during refreshments at Singing more recently but left at the end of the gathering without inviting her out. He must have assumed she only wanted friendship. *Jah, surely that's why Jimmy didn't ask me again,* she thought. *What fellow wants to be refused twice?*

But in the end, it was for the best. *We might've starting dating,* she thought, *and here I am, dreadfully sick again. Poor Jimmy might have been saddled with a cripple for the rest of his life.* She shivered at the thought.

I won't do that to him!

Besides, Jimmy had undoubtedly come to the same decision. He'd refused her offer of a cake or a pie as a thank-you. It seemed he did not want to be beholden to her even in that small way.

Yet the realization didn't ease Maggie's broken heart. Not at all.

The following Saturday afternoon, once their chores were done, Joseph suggested to Rachel a trip to Myerstown to visit her parents. It was something Rachel had been hoping for, though she hadn't whispered a word to Joseph, who must have guessed that it would cheer her up. She had been feeling much better yesterday and today, so Rachel happily agreed to go, just the two of them.

As they approached the familiar countryside of her childhood, with all the landmarks of home, Rachel recalled the first time Joseph came with her to meet Dat and Mamm. They had been so polite and welcoming, as with any guest in their home, but there was a twinkle of anticipation, especially in Mamm's eyes. Mamm had also gone out of her way to ask Rachel in advance what meals Joseph most enjoyed so she could surprise him with pork chops with rice and gravy.

Rachel let her musing take her back to how Joseph had asked Dat for his blessing on their marriage. *Dat actually chuckled,* Rachel recalled. *"She's old enough to make up her own mind . . . but jah, I'm glad to give my blessing,"* her father had said.

"What're ya thinking 'bout, dear?" her husband asked, interrupting her thoughts.

She told him.

And, winking at her, Joseph discreetly reached for her hand on the seat between them, and they rode that way until the van pulled into Dat's long dirt driveway.

Rachel felt like a child at Christmas, she was so overjoyed to see her parents again. She hugged her mother while Dat greeted Joseph with a warm handshake and the typical hullos, and then her parents accompanied them into the old farmhouse where Rachel had grown up. The spacious kitchen was sunny and cheerful, and Dat invited them to sit and relax at one end of the room, where a multicolored braided rug filled the space encircled by three cane-back chairs and one rocking chair. Nearby, a long brown sofa hugged the wall.

Dat inquired about their trip, and soon he and Joseph were talking about farm auctions and tool sales while Rachel chatted contentedly with Mamm, who asked how she'd been since last seeing her at Maggie's birthday celebration.

After a time, Mamm mentioned that she had been washing all the windows inside and out for the past couple of days, since they'd had a number of hard rains lately—"streakin' the panes, ya know."

Rachel nodded. This was the mother she knew and loved, always finding something to do. Mamm couldn't imagine sitting still and just twiddling her thumbs, or whatever it was folks did when they weren't occupied.

Rachel's father spoke up just then. "You womenfolk put us to shame."

"Well, maybe in an' around the house, *jah*," Mamm replied, laughing and rolling her eyes at him. "Remember all the hard work you did for years and years outdoors, Gid? From sunrise to sunset." She grinned at him. "And all the beef cattle you raised and sold for slaughter. Surely you haven't forgotten."

Rachel's father shook his head right quick. "Now that I'm livin' the easy life . . . out to pasture . . ." A mischievous smile crossed his face.

"*Ach*, there's a season for everything," Mamm was ready to say. "And a time for every purpose under heaven. You've paid your dues an' then some."

"Now, Mary Mae," Dat said, his long, graying beard bumping against his chest as he moved back and forth in his rocking chair.

Rachel took note of the way her parents talked to each other, so warm and familiar. *Will Joseph and I have such a comfortable manner one day?* They were still getting acquainted, really, following their whirlwind courtship—if she could even call it that. But each day brought them closer as husband and wife.

How she wanted to whisper the happy news to Mamm about being in the family way, and she hoped to have that opportunity yet before they left for home.

Rachel's father swatted a fly with his hand. "Yous should come up for the big pie auction over at the schoolhouse next week. Bring the youngsters . . . all of 'em."

Joseph nodded. "We'll see. I'm sure they'd like that."

"Your little Miriam is quite the talker, ain't so?" Mamm said to Rachel as they resumed their conversation.

"Oh, she is." And remembering what her mother had asked when they'd gone walking, she quietly mentioned that the older girls seemed more accepting of her here lately.

"Warmin' up to my precious daughter, are they?" Mamm said, her eyes shining.

Hearing her say it that way brought a smile to Rachel's face. She thought just then of Leroy driving her on that errand—and to the bake shop, too—and was reminded that everything was going to work out fine in the end. And she told her mother so.

Rachel soaked in every single minute before, during, and after suppertime with her dear parents, and while she wished with all of her heart they lived closer, she knew that as long as they were alive, she would eagerly look forward to coming to see them.

Maggie was thankful for Aunt Nellie that day, glad she and Grace were over next door making supper together. The three youngest children were in the stable grooming the horses, staying out of trouble, like Dat had told them before leaving with Rachel for Myerstown.

Maggie had been enjoying the solitude there in the front room on the sofa, where long afternoon sunbeams filtered in through the window. Having dosed up on two aspirin after the noon meal, she was able to read her Bible without being too distracted by the now-muted pain.

It wasn't long and she heard footsteps overhead, then a door closing upstairs. Evidently, Leroy had gone to the attic like Rachel had earlier requested.

Soon, Maggie had her answer. Leroy came into the room holding a white half apron. "S'pose this is the one she wanted?" he asked, lifting it up with his thumb and pointer finger, like it was contaminated or something.

Maggie tried not to smile. "Why're ya holdin' it like that?"

"Well, smell it." He came over and held it near her face.

"*Puh!* Mothballs!"

Leroy nodded and dropped it to the floor, his hands on his hips. "It was in that big, dusty hope chest with a bunch of other housewares and whatnot."

Maggie had known about the oak chest that Dat had stored in the attic when Rachel moved into the house—Rachel's idea.

"Wonder why she ain't usin' her own things." Leroy picked up the white apron and laid it across the back of the nearby chair.

"Just think 'bout it," Maggie said softly. "Because she's using Mamm's, 'specially in the kitchen."

Leroy's face went blank.

"It's also probably why she hasn't moved a single piece of furniture."

Leroy frowned and looked toward the window as if he'd never realized this before. "Brides are s'posed to have new things, though. . . ."

"Do ya know why Rachel kept the house—and the kitchen—exactly the way it was?" She held her breath.

Scrunching up his face, Leroy said, "I guess she didn't want us to forget Mamm." He looked downright miserable.

Maggie nodded slowly. "*Jah.*"

Turning, Leroy picked up the white apron and carried it out to the kitchen. She could hear the door to the cold cellar open, and Leroy running downstairs, where the wringer washer was kept. Undoubtedly, he was putting the apron in the laundry basket for Rachel.

When Leroy returned to the front room, he just stood there. "Why didn't ya tell me sooner?" he asked.

Maggie shifted in the sofa. "Would it have made a difference?"

"I'd like to think so." He paused and sat down on the chair across from her, leaning forward with his hands on either side of his head. He sighed heavily, as if bearing the weight of his past behavior. "*Ach*, Maggie . . ."

"It's not too late to make a change in the right direction," she said, echoing one of Mamm's favorite pieces of advice.

He lifted his head and looked over at her. "Mamm would want me to, ain't?"

"For your sake, *Bruder*."

Leroy offered to get her some cold water, then rose quickly to go to the kitchen.

Maggie waited till her brother left before she let her tears come. Tears of joy and gratitude.

All will surely be well. . . .

CHAPTER

33

Days passed, then weeks, and soon it was the final baptismal class with the ministerial brethren, on the second Sunday in September. It was a pleasant sort of day, with hints of autumn touching the landscape, and the green meadow grasses showing glints of gold.

Maggie used her walker to get around, thankful this last class was held in the summer kitchen on the main level, instead of upstairs. She had a feeling the ministers had planned it that way for her sake. *So helpful and kind,* she thought of them.

The older of the two preachers moved methodically around the room, giving each candidate the opportunity to choose to consent to joining church the twenty-third of September, or to change his or her mind. It was an age-old tradition Maggie's mother had shared with her several years ago, when they'd discussed the importance of baptism.

Every one of the candidates ahead of Maggie was quick to agree to follow the Lord in holy baptism in two weeks, and Maggie wholeheartedly agreed as well, but the girl next to her said she wasn't ready to make the lifelong vow. Maggie's heart went out to her as she looked down at her lap, where she was clenching her hands.

"'Tis better not to make the lifelong vow than to do so and go back on it," the preacher said. "I pray you'll choose to be baptized at a later time."

All of the fellows, however, agreed, which was hardly surprising when nearly all of them had a serious girlfriend. After their baptism, most of the fellows would marry during the wedding season that started in November and ran into December.

Later, when all of them lined up to go into the Preaching service, Maggie realized that Jimmy had seemed especially serious during the instruction today, not even cracking a smile, though he had nodded his head in greeting to her before the class. Maggie appreciated his sincerity and studious nature, for certain. At times, he reminded her of Dat.

In the weeks since her health setback, Maggie had ceased going to Singings and other youth activities, including the evening volleyball games, not because she didn't treasure the fellowship, but because it was too much effort. She felt safer at home, and while Grace missed her, of course, she seemed to understand.

Meanwhile, Maggie continued to read the Good Book, writing down the verses that gave her inspiration and hope for healing. Aunt Nellie came over more often, too, and her visits lifted Maggie's spirits. Dear Aunt Nellie had a wonderful knack for doing just that, as everyone who knew her agreed.

Three days later, when Maggie was feeling particularly low, Aunt Nellie wandered over to sit with her on the back porch.

Siggy was with her, which Maggie enjoyed even though she couldn't attempt to hold him on her lap due to her pain. "You must've known I needed company," Maggie said, pleased by the visit.

"Now and then I have my own days of misery. But nothin' like yours, my dear." Nellie smiled lovingly.

They talked about how pretty the fields were this time of year, and how it was becoming much cooler most days. The corn and soybeans were flourishing, and it wouldn't be long before the Jonathan apples were ready to pick and can. And there'd be applesauce to make, too, and sweet apple cider.

"When I long for peace in my most trying moments," Maggie said, "I remember how it felt to stand on the ladder, the peach tree branches tickling my head. There's something calming 'bout the memory of pickin' peaches with Rachel and my sisters."

"Well now, I believe I understand." Nellie mentioned again how nice it was to have had so many peaches to put up. "Thanks to all of yous."

"We look after each other, ain't so?"

Nellie petted Siggy. "I've seen ya sufferin' and have been wantin' to share something with you. Something I've learned over the years."

"I'm all ears, Aendi."

"Well, here 'tis. The Lord calls us to come to Him with all of our weaknesses—body, mind, and spirit. I'm talking 'bout myself, too."

Maggie listened carefully, trusting what Nellie had to say.

"Honestly, I have to remind myself that physical limitations can actually be helpful—even liberatin'—when my deepest longing is to follow close after Christ. It sure teaches me to pray without ceasing."

Maggie let the words sink in; she hoped she'd remember them for always.

"I pray ya never disdain prayer. It's the simplest way you can serve our Lord, and sufferin' won't hold you from it," Aunt Nellie said.

As it often did, the verse Maggie had reread earlier this morning came to mind. "'My grace is sufficient for thee: for my strength is made perfect in weakness. . . .'" Maggie paused as she said it, tears springing to her eyes. She couldn't finish.

"'Most gladly therefore will I rather glory in my infirmities, that the power of Christ may rest upon me,'" Nellie finished, quoting the remainder of the verse.

Maggie gave her a tender look. "That's become one of my favorites. I know it by heart now."

Nellie tittered a little. "When a body's my age, you find you've memorized some passages without tryin', you've read them so many times."

Smiling, Maggie understood. "What would I do without ya, Aendi?"

"Aw . . . you're a love." Nellie's lower lip quivered. She paused a moment, picking at the waistband of her black apron. "The real question is, what would any of us do without our Lord?" she said. "After all, there'll come a time when we must cross over Jordan River."

Maggie reached for Nellie's hand, letting the precious words find their way into her heart.

For old times' sake, Maggie asked Leroy the very next afternoon to take her to the mill while he ran an errand for Dat. Since Leroy needed the market wagon, though, she would need help getting in and out. She had decided to bring the cane instead of her walker today, since her brother, and later her father, when he was finished with work, could steady her if need be.

"I'll come back and pick you and Dat up," Leroy commented as they rode the short distance together. "Can't have ya tryin' to walk home."

"*Denki, Bruder.* I just want to see the mill again, since I rarely go out anymore."

"It's a perty spot," he agreed.

"I have happy memories of sitting in the meadow there, pickin' dandelions and blowin' the puffs when they'd gone to seed. . . ." She sighed and considered her deteriorating health.

Leroy glanced at her. "Thinkin' about the past?"

"*Nee* . . . not really."

"Looking ahead is better." He said it softly. "And I know that from you, Maggie."

"No need to credit me."

"Well, it's due ya." Leroy went on to say how he'd finally told Dat what she'd said to him the day he'd gone to the attic. "I let Dat know how much I appreciated Rachel's sacrifice for all of us."

Maggie nodded, surprised at his sincerity. "Sometimes we just need someone to open our hearts to."

Leroy said, "I'm hopin' Joanne's that sort of girl. I really think she is."

Maggie smiled. "You'll have plenty-a years to find out once you're dating age."

"Only two more till I can get my courting buggy an' start goin' to Singings." He sounded so confident. "I'm crossin' off the months on my wall calendar."

"Well, Aunt Nellie was real young when she was courted by Onkel Matthew. Not that I'm encouraging you, mind ya."

When they arrived at the spot where Maggie had always liked to wait for Dat, Leroy jumped down and came around to help her out of the wagon, letting her lean on his arm as they walked slowly toward the familiar green area. He helped her lower herself into the soft grass. "I won't be gone long."

"*Denki*, take your time." She put her cane down and sighed. *Leroy must think I'm foolish.* But she didn't care as she looked at the sky and then let her gaze drift over the familiar creek and old stone mill out yonder. The birds entertained her as they flew in flocks and called to one another. Did birds greet each other of a morning, announce their new hatchlings, tend to a wounded member of the flock? They were questions she had pondered since childhood but had no answers for . . . and she was okay with that.

I don't need answers for everything. The Lord God knows.

She embraced the sounds of late afternoon—the burr of a baler across the field to the south, a farmer's watchdog barking, and, now and then, carriages clattering by. *Folk are heading home as suppertime nears.*

She remembered a song she'd heard on Cousin Luke's car radio—"No One Ever Cared for Me Like Jesus"—and fought back the lump in her throat. The sermons and the testimonies she'd witnessed at the tent meetings had triggered a similar tenderness in her heart.

Thinking again of Aunt Nellie's wise words, she knew that the hand of the Lord had been at work in her attendance at those services. She was glad, too, for the opportunity to meet Glenn Brubaker and his mother.

She sighed and thanked God again for all the things that were working together for good in her life, as the Scriptures declared. *And even if I'm never healed,* she thought, *I will continue to do Thy will, O Lord.*

It was a promise Maggie was ready to make . . . and keep.

CHAPTER

34

M aggie went *where?*" Rachel asked Miriam as they worked together in the kitchen with Grace.

"Over to meet Dat," Miriam told her, getting the plates down from the cupboard.

"For goodness' sake! Why? And how will she get home?" Grace asked over where she chopped onions, eyes watering.

Miriam shrugged. "I guess Leroy'll come back for both of them."

"Where does Leroy go to get cheese, anyway?" Grace asked, pausing in her chopping and staring at Miriam. "Does anyone know?"

Rachel had to laugh. "If Leroy wanted ya to know, he'd tell ya, *jah?*"

Grace looked at her. "Do *you* know?"

Shaking her head, Rachel kept busy slicing potatoes. They were having scalloped potatoes and baked ham for supper, another one of Leroy's favorite meals. Actually, the whole family seemed to enjoy her cooking.

"Maybe he's in puppy love," Miriam said, smirking.

Grace laughed out loud. "My *lappich* little sister . . ."

"I'm not *that* silly," Miriam protested good-naturedly, and both girls began to giggle.

Indeed, as Rachel delighted in the teasing between the two, she wondered where Miriam had gotten this notion. Yet she remained concerned about Maggie being outdoors without her walker. What was she thinking?

Still sitting in the meadow, not far from the lovely old mill, Maggie closed her eyes and thought of her caring Mamm. So much had changed since her passing. *But God provided a loving wife for Dat.* Rachel had become such a joyful and significant part of their lives. Who would have dreamed it?

Pensive, Maggie tried to embrace hope for the future, come what may. *God holds my tomorrows,* she thought. *I will be content with whatever comes my way.*

Her back toward the road, Maggie became aware of an approaching horse and carriage, but due to her stiffness, she was unable to twist around to watch this particular horse slow and the carriage roll to a stop. More than likely, one of the People had noticed her sitting there and wanted to kindly offer a ride. In their community, such thoughtfulness was rather commonplace.

Now, someone was swishing through the tall grass, coming closer.

"Hullo, Maggie . . . I hope I didn't startle ya."

She knew that voice, and her heart beat faster. *Jimmy Beiler!*

Without thinking, she attempted to turn to see him but experienced a sudden stab of pain and grimaced. Still, not wanting to appear aloof, she worked harder to face him, fighting the discomfort.

By now, Jimmy had made his way around to her, leaning down to ask if she was all right. "I spotted you over here and wanted to check on ya."

"Oh, I'm just waitin' for Dat." She shielded her eyes from the sun as she looked up at Jimmy. "He's prob'ly running late, but I'm enjoying bein' outside."

"Ain't too warm today," he said, sitting cross-legged next to her. "Hope ya don't mind."

Jimmy's casual manner put her at ease, and she thanked him again for the walker. Shrugging it off, he pulled a blade of grass and fooled with it. With Jimmy so near, her heart was melting in a strange mingling of sadness and joy.

Maggie wondered if he wanted to talk about their upcoming church baptism, or that she'd stopped going to Singings.

"I'm sorry I didn't accept your offer of a pie or cake that day I brought you the walker," he said unexpectedly.

She smiled. "It's all right."

Jimmy looked down at his bare feet, clearly hesitant about something. Then at last, he said, "You've been on my mind, Maggie."

She bit her lower lip.

He looked at the sky and seemed to be formulating his words. When he spoke, he turned again to look at her. "You know, it seems like we've been friends forever."

She nodded. "True."

"And then, more recently, it seemed like we were becoming . . . *more* than friends."

Nee, she thought, tensing up.

"But when I asked ya to ride home after Singing that time,

and you didn't want to go . . . well, I figured I was wrong. So I didn't push ya."

She felt embarrassed and terrible for him and at a complete loss for words.

Unexpectedly, Jimmy reached to lightly touch her face. "Maggie?"

She looked into the eyes of the kindest young man she'd ever known.

"Maggie, if I'm right, won't ya say so? Tell me you don't feel the way I do, and I won't bother ya."

She swallowed hard. Now would be the time to let him go, to tell him she didn't want to be his girl.

But that wouldn't be true.

Trying to catch her breath, she felt like she was riding one of the roller coasters she'd heard about over at Hershey Park. Quietly, she asked, "With all the healthy and strong young women in our district, why would ya want *me*?"

He looked mystified. Then, glancing down at her hand, Jimmy reached for it, and the feel of his hand on hers was more wonderful than anything she'd ever known. "Is your illness what's holding you back?"

"You have no idea . . . it would ruin your life."

He frowned and shook his head. "I love ya, Maggie, and I have for a *gut* long while now. I don't care how sick you are. My life would be empty without ya."

She didn't want to spoil this beautiful moment by tearing up. And looking down at their hands entwined there in the grass, she held her breath. This was so unforeseen; her mind was whirling. "I scarcely know what to say," she whispered.

He smiled and said that, while he wanted her to be whole,

he also knew that she was the young woman God had put on his heart.

Without a doubt, Maggie knew she loved him, too.

Jimmy moved closer, and she leaned her head against his shoulder, wondering, *Is this really happening?*

"Will ya be my sweetheart-girl, Maggie?"

She lifted her head and sighed with great happiness. *"Jah."*

By the time her father was out of the mill and walking up the grassy hillock, Maggie was already settled into Jimmy's courting carriage. He waved to her father, inviting him to join them. "Want a ride home?" he called. "There's plenty-a room."

"You two go on," Dat said when he saw Maggie there. He waved with his straw hat, seemingly trying not to grin.

"I'll look after her," Jimmy said as he picked up the driving lines.

But they were heading in the opposite direction of home, and when they ended up at Betsy Lapp's Bakery, there was Leroy, carrying a box of cookies out to the market wagon. Fortunately, he didn't see Maggie there with Jimmy—or if he did, he wasn't letting on.

"I'll go in an' get you a treat," Jimmy said, leaping out of the open buggy and going to tie the horse to the nearby hitching post.

"It's nearly suppertime," she said.

"Save it for dessert, then," he insisted, grinning at her.

She couldn't argue with that or his contagious smile. "In that case, I'll have something small."

"*Ach,* let's celebrate!" He winked at her. "How 'bout I surprise ya?"

She agreed; his enthusiasm was so infectious. *"Denki."*

"I'll be right back!" He hurried toward the entrance of the bakery, and she could see Betsy waving to him through the front picture window.

And hearing the chirrup of birdsong all around, Maggie's spirit rose. *Jimmy loves me. How can this be, dear Lord?*

CHAPTER
35

Maggie set the small kitchen table, savoring the smell of the hearty meatloaf baking. She was boiling a few new potatoes and was beginning to cook up some string beans in another small pot. There would be enough leftovers for several meals, and she was pleased with herself for going to the trouble of preparing a special little supper for her milestone birthday.

Making her way to the back door, Maggie stood there, looking out at the sky, admiring the shifting cloud shapes as she'd always loved to do. "I praise Thee, Lord, for bein' a very present help in trouble," she whispered. All these many years, she'd never ceased saying her prayers aloud. For her, it made praying seem so real, like a conversation with her closest friend.

The day had been pleasant and not too warm or humid yet for June twenty-sixth. She was looking forward to quietly marking the day. *No need to make a fuss about it,* she decided

with a glance at the purple martin birdhouse, an exact rep-
lica of the one her brothers had given her, presenting it after
church baptism that long-ago September. *The precious end of
the most unforgettable season of my life,* she thought, going over
to the stove to check the potatoes for tenderness.

It surprised Maggie that she still remembered how excep-
tionally fragrant her Mamm's roses had been that summer—
how sweet the strawberries tasted, and, oh goodness, all the
applesauce she'd made with her sisters and her great-aunt
Nellie. And the peaches . . .

Thinking of dear Nellie, Maggie recalled the handkerchief
her aunt had tatted in the prettiest pink color. Not meant
for using, rather more of a keepsake, Maggie had kept it in
her Bible to mark Second Corinthians, chapter twelve, verse
nine. *My life verse.*

She was quite content to reside in the comfortable *Dawdi
Haus* where Great-aunt Nellie had lived well into her late
nineties, next door to industrious Stephen and his easygoing
wife, Rebekah. They and their eventual brood of seven had
taken over the small farm after Dat's passing, leaving Rachel
a rather young widow at the time. Maggie had grown even
closer to her *Schtiefmudder* when Rachel agreed to move into
a smaller addition right next door, one Maggie's brothers
had built. *Rachel was always so attentive to all of us,* Maggie
thought, *even though she also doted on her own twin daughters
with Dat.*

The memories continued, and Maggie smiled, remembering
when Rachel had taken time to sort through all of Mamm's
kitchen utensils and whatnot, passing them on to Mamm's
girls. Miriam had ended up with the well-worn flour sifter—
"old as the hills," Mamm had frequently said of it. *Miriam loves*

to bake bread, thought Maggie, *so it was only right for her to have it.*

She, on the other hand, had chosen the everyday set of dishes, while Grace chose the for-*gut* set for her hope chest.

Just then, Maggie heard voices and footsteps outdoors, interrupting her fond reverie. She turned to see her brothers and sisters and their spouses coming up the back walkway, toward the back porch. And as they came, they were singing the birthday song.

Plump and beaming, Grace was carrying a large sheet cake with her tall, graying husband, Martin Lantz. Behind them walked Leroy with his wife, still pretty Joanne, who had brought what looked like hot dishes wrapped in quilted carriers.

"It's a birthday potluck!" Miriam declared when she arrived in her best blue dress and matching cape and apron, coming in behind all of them with her husband, Ike Stoltzfus.

Maggie's sisters and sisters-in-law insisted on taking charge of the small kitchen, arranging all the food, including the meatloaf in Maggie's oven, the beans on the stove, and the potatoes, which Grace set to buttering.

Miriam hugged Maggie and led her to sit at the small table. "For the birthday *girl!*" she announced comically.

"*Puh!* I'm hardly that," Maggie said, shaking her head. "Never thought I'd see all of yous here today."

At that moment, Rachel arrived from next door, trying not to smile too broadly, since it seemed she had been in on the whole thing. She made a beeline for Maggie and placed a card in front of her. "Happiest birthday!"

"Sweet of you," Maggie said, delighted to see everyone and feeling nearly like royalty.

When Andy and Stephen arrived with their wives, all the

men went to the cellar to bring up folding tables and chairs, setting them up around the kitchen. "A few more folk are comin'," Grace said with a grin at Maggie.

Maggie was almost embarrassed; so many loved ones honoring her. It made her heart swell with joy.

Miriam was already telling one story after another about growing up together in the big house next door, which kept everyone in stitches till a car pulled up and parked.

"Can ya guess who this is?" Grace asked, her round face glowing.

Maggie honestly didn't know. "More kinfolk?"

Miriam offered a little hint. "We'll have us a fine preacher at the table tonight."

"Oh, *wunnerbaar*! Must be Cousin Lila and her husband."

Miriam pretended to zip her lips closed, her blue eyes dancing. Her amusing ways were still evident even at fifty-five. "A *child at heart*," she described herself.

Eagerly, Maggie looked toward the back door, and soon her cousin, smiling sweetly, stepped inside with Glenn, his wavy gray hair still showing traces of blond.

"You're here!" Leroy rose quickly and went to greet them, bringing them over to Maggie, who was seated quite snugly between the table and the wall behind her, unable to get out.

"So nice to see you again!" Cousin Lila leaned in to hug her neck. "It's been much too long."

Glenn shook her hand, saying, "Happy birthday, Maggie," and then they were all trying to remember if it had been two years or three since Glenn and Lila had last visited.

"However long, it's great to be back," Lila said, and Leroy escorted them to two saved spots at the main table. "Our children and grandchildren all wanted to come, too," Lila added, "but we figured you'd have a full house as it is."

"Oh, bring them next time," Maggie spoke up. "You really must."

Grace and others began to pass their birthday cards over to Maggie. "Go ahead an' open them now," her sister said, glancing at the wall clock.

What's going on? Maggie wondered, doing as she was told. There were homemade cards and store-bought, and each handwritten greeting meant so much to her. Some, like Grace's, brought tears to her eyes. *For all the years we told our secrets to each other, here's to many more birthdays and sister-times together, Lord willing. Lots of love, Gracie.*

After Maggie read them, the cards were passed around so everyone could share in the words of celebration.

"*Denki,*" Maggie said, glancing at the kitchen counter, where all the food was lined up. "I 'spect the meal's getting cold," she said, wondering why they were waiting.

Not a second later, she heard whistling outside and looked to see dearest Jim coming in the back door, home early from a trip to do some emergency repairs for his elderly uncle and aunt in Somerset. "Happy birthday, love," he said, coming over to greet her with a squeeze of her hand.

"What a surprise!" She beamed up at him. "Thought you were stayin' a few more days."

"You didn't think I'd let ya celebrate your birthday alone, did ya?" Jim winked at her as he sat down at the head of the table, then said hullo to everyone.

The women, all but Maggie, rose nearly in unison to uncover the food and bring it to the main table. And when it was time to ask the blessing, Jim motioned for Preacher Brubaker to do so.

Glenn stood and folded his hands, and they all bowed their heads. "Father in heaven, we come to Thee in the name of our Savior, the Lord Jesus. We give thanks for Thy loving care and the blessings, too numerous to mention, evidenced in each life present here this evening. We ask, most gracious Father, that Thy will be accomplished in our lives as we live to serve and worship Thee. Thank Thee for our dear Maggie's life, for her dedication to Thy will, and for all who are gathered here to celebrate her birthday. In the name of Jesus I pray. Amen."

Maggie noticed she wasn't the only one brushing back tears as the food was dished up and passed to the person on the right. Miriam and Joanne then carried the hot dishes and the meatloaf over to the two smaller tables.

The conversations were interesting, with several going at once, all of them scattered about the kitchen. Never as a teenager was Maggie's sixty-fifth birthday one she had imagined. Back then, she might have wondered if anyone would come to celebrate with her, should she live so long, but so much had changed since those distressing days. Best of all, she'd married the young man who'd accepted her as she was, and who embraced her first Love as his own, their Lord and Savior . . . and closest Friend.

She and Jim had married in the very house where Dat and Mamm had brought up their children, the home where Rachel had stepped in and helped finish what Mamm began, as well as added to the family with her girls. Maggie and Jimmy had said their marriage vows to God and the bishop while Maggie leaned on her trusty walker.

Maggie and Jim had never had children, but they loved to spend time with their many nephews and nieces, encouraging each of them to read the Good Book and to talk to God daily.

Prior to Maggie's cutting the birthday cake, Rachel's twins, Lizzy and Lucy, arrived, another delightful surprise. Jim welcomed them to what had become an out-and-out party.

Extra chairs were brought in from the sitting room around the corner, and Lizzy apologized for being late. "We left our husbands over at the Bird-in-Hand Fire Company Auction."

Jim nodded. "Maybe they'll drop by and join us later?"

Lucy glanced at Lizzy. "They know they're welcome to. *Denki*, Jim."

Having her half sisters present brought Maggie even more joy. Each member of her close-knit family was present now, except Dat and Mamm, who were surely looking down from above.

Because it was such cramped quarters with all of her dear ones there, eating and chatting and having a *wunnerbaar-gut* time, Maggie wondered why someone hadn't thought to have this supper next door at the main house. But then, how would they have managed to surprise her so?

It's all right. We're together, and that's what counts, she thought, looking with admiration at her husband, the kindest and most understanding man—the greatest gift of her life, apart from the Lord Jesus Christ.

When Jim caught her looking his way, he whispered, "*Ich liebe dich,* Maggie." Everyone around them was so busy talking, she doubted anyone noticed as she reached beneath the table to pat his knee, thankful beyond words.

Epilogue

I can't say exactly when it happened—not the very hour, anyway. But a few weeks after Jimmy and I were wed, while we were still staying at my father's house in my old bedroom, Jimmy asked my father to join him in praying for me. Leroy wanted to, as well, and I remember being seated in Mamm's hickory chair there in the front room, where the sunshine tumbled in that early December afternoon.

I felt the weight of their caring hands on my head and shoulders, my cane propped against the chair. Jimmy's voice began to rise, filling the room as he dared to pray for my healing.

Honestly, I didn't feel any particular sensation roll over me, like some folk experience, but I trusted that what the Lord had placed in my young husband's heart was divinely ordained.

Come to think of it, two full days passed before I realized that I was fully without pain. This time, I didn't let myself fall into my old way of thinking of past patterns of good days followed by bad. *Nee*, not when Jimmy had prayed so earnestly, believing in faith for my healing.

After a week and then a month, followed by a year, Jimmy

and I were convinced I was healed. We didn't tell it around like some might, but we daily acknowledged in prayer that God had graciously given me a miracle in the privacy of Dat's front room.

Aunt Nellie was one of the first to declare it a divine healing, and she continued to encourage me. We read the Bible together at every opportunity while Jimmy and I prepared for our move to a rented house and small farm after the relatives had finished dropping by with wedding gifts that first month at Dat's. In the meantime, there had been Christmas cookie exchanges and suppers with the whole family together under one roof to celebrate. Then came Second Christmas, with even more visiting and meals to make and serve.

Recalling that remarkable first year of marriage now, when Jimmy not only got the girl he loved so truly, but also a strong and robust wife, after all, makes me miss the people who were so involved in our lives at that time. Dear ones like Dat, as well as Great-aunt Nellie, and Jimmy's parents, too. It was a tender time, really, and even now, it's the little things that still bring back the smells, the sounds, and the happiness of those months. To this day, I still use Nellie's mother's old comfort quilt as a reminder to pray for everyone I know, especially for those who are in need of the Savior's touch.

Thanks to our heavenly Father, Jimmy and I have built our life together on those former struggles and every lesson we learned along the way. Lord willing, we still have some years ahead, and we pray that we honor Him in every choice we make.

When I find myself alone with the Good Book or in prayer, I realize afresh that God brought something beautiful and good out of what had been so devastating. And when He planted a seed of desire for healing in my heart, it was not a passing whim or a mere dream. It was an absolute gift.

Author's Note

At the time of this writing, I have just completed the first draft for this book, and word of Rev. Billy Graham's passing is being reported on every news outlet around the world. His first tent crusade in 1949 was the inspiration for the Lancaster County tent revival meetings of 1951 featured in this book. Billy Graham was, of course, the most famous tent evangelist of all, a man who influenced many ministers to travel the country and spread the Good News to any who would listen. My own father pitched a large tent not far from the location of the crusade Maggie Esh attends. There, for two consecutive summers, he conducted six-week evangelistic meetings where various evangelists preached the gospel and the sick were healed by God's miraculous power.

My sincere appreciation goes to the Plain friends I interviewed who remembered specific aspects about the actual Mennonite tent crusades in Lancaster County during those summers of 1951 and 1952. It was a privilege and a blessing to hear their accounts of salvation and great encouragement in the faith. I am also thankful to Hank and Ruth Hershberger for help with the Pennsylvania Dutch words and phrases in this book.

Dave Lewis, my dear husband, was my greatest encourager during the writing and revisions of this particular book, so near to my heart. How very blessed I am to have had his insight into this story!

Our children, Julie, Janie, and Jonathan, and our granddaughter, Ariel, also cheered me on, as did my sister, Barbara, who as a young girl also rejoiced in the spiritual victories of Dad's tent revivals in Lancaster County, where we learned firsthand about the power of prayer!

I appreciate the editorial guidance of David Horton, Rochelle Glöege, and Ann Parrish, as well as the faithful prayers of my publicist, Amy Green, and the devoted prayer group at Bethany House Publishers and among my thousands of reader-friends. May God abundantly bless each of you!

Soli Deo Gloria—to the glory of God alone!

Beverly Lewis, born in the heart of Pennsylvania Dutch country, is the *New York Times* bestselling author of more than one hundred books. Her stories have been published in twelve languages worldwide. A keen interest in her mother's Plain heritage has inspired Beverly to write many Amish-related novels, beginning with *The Shunning,* which has sold more than one million copies and is an Original Hallmark Channel movie. In 2007 *The Brethren* was honored with a Christy Award.

Beverly has been interviewed by both national and international media, including *Time* magazine, the Associated Press, and the BBC. She lives with her husband, David, in Colorado.

Visit her website at www.beverlylewis.com or www.facebook .com/officialbeverlylewis for more information.

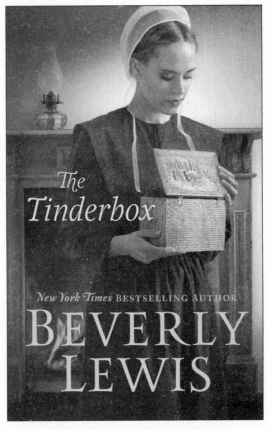

The Tinderbox

The Next Novel From Beverly Lewis

AVAILABLE SPRING 2019

Sign Up for Beverly's Newsletter!

Keep up to date with Beverly's news on book releases and events by signing up for her email list at beverlylewis.com.

More from Beverly Lewis!

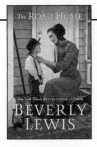

Sent from Michigan to Pennsylvania, Lena Rose Schwartz grieves the death of her Amish parents and the separation from her siblings as well as her beau, Hans Bontrager. She longs to return home to those she loves most. However, she soon discovers that Lancaster County holds charms of its own. Is she willing to open her heart to new possibilities?

The Road Home

You May Also Like . . .

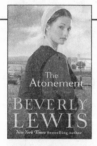

Troubled by past transgressions, a young Amish woman rejects courtship by her longtime friend. Is it too late to embrace redemption . . . and the power of love?

The Atonement

Old Order Amish woman Eva Esch feels powerfully drawn to the charming stranger from Ohio. Will the forbidden photograph he carries lead to love or heartache?

The Photograph

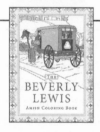

Experience the tranquil, homespun world of the Amish of Lancaster County, the setting of Beverly Lewis's many bestselling novels. This inspiring coloring book is filled with artful depictions of Amish life, including quilting bees, buggy rides, farm scenes, and more. As you color the charming images, you'll be blessed by gems of Amish wisdom and Scripture.

The Beverly Lewis Amish Coloring Book

BETHANYHOUSE

Also from Beverly Lewis

Visit beverlylewis.com for a full list of her books.

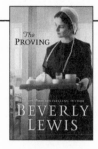

Having left the Amish life for the English world, Mandy Dienner is shocked when she learns she has inherited Lancaster County's most popular Amish bed-and-breakfast. The catch is she has to run it herself for one year. Reluctantly, Mandy accepts the challenge, no matter that it means facing the family she left behind— or that the inn's clientele expect an *Amish* hostess.

The Proving

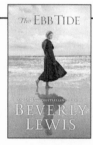

A summer job as a nanny in beautiful Cape May leads a young Amish woman to form an unexpected bond with a handsome Mennonite. Has she been too hasty with her promises, or will she only find what her heart is longing for back home?

The Ebb Tide

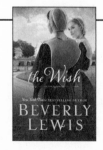

When a young Amish woman sets out on a mission to persuade a friend to return to the Amish church, will her dearest wish lead to her own undoing?

The Wish

⬥ BETHANYHOUSE